QUOTA

Jock Serong lives and works on the far southwest coast of Victoria. He is a lawyer and features writer, and is the editor of *Great Ocean Quarterly*. He is married with four children, who in turn are raising a black dog, a rabbit and an unknown number of guinea pigs. *Quota* is his first novel.

JOCK SERONG

QUOTA

TEXT PUBLISHING MELBOURNE AUSTRALIA

textpublishing.com.au

The Text Publishing Company
Swann House
22 William Street
Melbourne Victoria 3000
Australia

First published in 2014 by The Text Publishing Company

Cover design by W. H. Chong
Page design by Imogen Stubbs
Typeset by J&M Typesetting

Printed and bound in Australia by Griffin Press, an Accredited ISO AS/NZS 14001:2004 Environmental Management System printer

National Library of Australia Cataloguing-in-Publication entry:
Author: Serong, Jock, author.
Title: Quota / by Jock Serong.
ISBN: 9781922147936 (paperback)
ISBN: 9781922148933 (ebook)
Subjects: Suspense fiction.
Dewey Number: A823.4

This book is printed on paper certified against the Forest Stewardship Council® Standards. Griffin Press holds FSC chain-of-custody certification SGS-COC-005088. FSC promotes environmentally responsible, socially beneficial and economically viable management of the world's forests.

This project has been assisted by the Commonwealth Government through the Australia Council, its arts funding and advisory body.

For Lilly,
who makes everything possible and all of it fun.

MELBOURNE

UPON RESUMING AT 2:15 PM:

MR JARDIM: Thank you for the opportunity to speak with my client over the lunch adjournment, Your Honour.

HIS HONOUR: Yes. Have you made any progress? I note your client is not with you, Mr Jardim.

MR JARDIM: She's not, Your Honour. She was quite affected by this morning's cross-examination, and despite my advice to her about the need to continue, she's been unable to come back to court, sir.

HIS HONOUR: Do you mean she's physically unwell, Mr Jardim? Do you have a doctor's certificate, or perhaps a doctor with you?

MR JARDIM: No, I don't have either of those things. Ms Woollacott indicated prior to lunch that she was substantially finished with her cross-examination. Your Honour has now had the benefit of testimony from my client as to her stable accommodation, her reha—

HIS HONOUR: No doctor, then? Your client's abandoned her application has she?

MR JARDIM: —her rehabilitation, her loyalty to her children, the support of he—

HIS HONOUR: No, no. Hold on a moment. Maybe you're not hearing me, Mr Jardim. Your client is not here to complete cross-examination. There's not much point in you making submissions to me about your client's case if she's not here. 'Not here' says to me 'don't care'. Now Ms Woollacott, you did indicate prior to lunch that you were, I think you said, 'nearly complete' with your cross-examination. Would you have more questions you wanted to ask Mr Jardim's client?

MS WOOLLACOTT: I did have, Your Honour.

HIS HONOUR: And Mr Jardim, I would have thought that you need to re-examine in respect of your client's admissions about drug use and about having, well my provisional conclusion is, prostituted herself in the house while the two children were in her care. Are you suggesting to me you don't need to re-examine regarding those matters which arose in Ms Woollacott's cross-examination?

MR JARDIM: In an ideal world I would have, Your Honour, but she's no—

HIS HONOUR: She's not here, is she. Fine for me to be here, not like I've got much else to do. I'm sure you're not busy, Mr Jardim. Ms Woollacott's just passing the time. Mr Tipstaff, are you busy? No, he doesn't look busy. So we can all sort of wander in and out as we please, can we Mr Jardim? Is that how it works?

MR JARDIM: I'm not suggesting that, Your Honour.

HIS HONOUR: It's called 'submitting', Mr Jardim. You don't suggest in my court, you make a submission or you don't talk at all. Now, what is your submission? Is your client's case closed? Because I don't think you have much choice at the moment.

MR JARDIM: No, I don't submit that it's closed. I'm applying to adjourn the matter, or at the very least have it stood down until I can check on my client's welfare and bring her back before the court.

HIS HONOUR: So it's an adjournment application. Ms Woollacott, without wanting to pre-empt the position of the Department of Human Services, you'd be making a costs application, wouldn't you?

MS WOOLLACOTT: Well, Your Honour I'd have to—

4

HIS HONOUR: Right. So Mr Jardim, how would your client satisfy a costs order if I was to adjourn this matter?

MR JARDIM: She can't, Your Honour. She has no money, she has no assets. She's legally aided. It's not an appropriate matter for a costs order anyway. She's not here, and there might be very good reasons why she isn't here. We just don't know. The important thing is that this court has to decide on the permanent placement of two small children, and that needs to be done in a me– measured way. She comes back to court when she's composed and completes her evidence if that's what's required, although I'm fairly sure that she's—

HIS HONOUR: You submit.

MR JARDIM: I submit that she's covered all the areas Your Honour needs to hear about.

HIS HONOUR: Well Mr Jardim, you give me little choice. Your client's not here, and you can't explain why. You seek an adjournment but you say she won't be able to pay the costs thrown away by that adjournment. You say her evidence is complete but you appear to argue that I shouldn't decide the case in her absence now. Your submissions are inherently contradictory. I mean—do you have anything coherent to say about the matter?

MR JARDIM: I suppose I have to say give her a chance, Your Honour. There is abundant evidence in front of you that she's tried. You are aware through the evidence from the clinic that she's attended on numerous occasions and she's—

HIS HONOUR: No, no, thank you. I don't want to hear your case rehashed yet again, Mr Jardim. I want you to tell me why I shouldn't decide the matter in her absence. Now I'll ask you again. Why shouldn't I?

MR JARDIM: Well what do you want me to say? Seriously— I've tried to tell you it wouldn't be fair. You're doing her a major injustice and you're treating this as a procedural chore. It's not, it's the—

HIS HONOUR: Watch your tone, Mr Jardim. I've listened to a lot of your petulance during this hearing, and I've watched you rolling your eyes and huffing and puffing about the things that haven't gone your way. That much has passed without comment. But now you can consider yourself warned: you are being rude and disrespectful.

MR JARDIM: (*laughter*) Did you ever read F. E. Smith? We're both being pigs, Your Honour, but I'm doing it deliberately.

HIS HONOUR: Oh, be original. You're not bringing your snide humour into my court, Mr Jardim. Withdraw that comment immediately.

MR JARDIM: No. I'm not withdrawing it because it should be apparent to you that it's got nothing to do with the merits of this case, just as your small-minded treatment of my client has got nothing to do with the merits of the case. What do you want me to say? What do you want me to say? Could you have cocked this thing up any worse? Bloody helpless kid and you know she's back out on the street now. You know it, don't you? You're known throughout the state as a heartless old prick and a drunk and seeing I've gone this far, your daughter-in-law's appointment to the court is widely viewed as a grubby political payoff. She's got about as much ability as you have. Today's pretty much the lowest I've seen you stoop, but it's been a rich field of excrem—

HIS HONOUR: Senior, will you have Mr Jardim removed immediately, please, and see to it that he's not brought back before me on contempt until Friday. Mr Jardim, you can take a couple of nights in the police cells to think about your conduct here today. I'm reserving my judgment in respect of this matter, and for the sake of completeness your misconceived adjournment application is refused. Yes, have him taken out, please.

MR JARDIM: Fuck you.

CLERK: *THIS MATTER STANDS ADJOURNED TO A DATE TO BE FIXED. GOD SAVE THE QUEEN.*

BARRY EGAN KNEW his way around a steamed dim sim. Warm white paper bag heavy between his thighs, cold can of Pasito wedged by the handbrake. The dusk had been still on the drive out to Antonias Beach, the ocean lying exhausted after days of southerly gales. The night falling wide around him on the way up the gravel track to the cliff top. He knew from long experience he would feel the view from the cliffs more than see it.

He pulled the ute to a halt in the carpark, the bullbar nudging at the pine railing. Rolled the radio dial between heavy fingers around to 3PF, Hits on the West Coast, and killed the motor.

Tuesday nights at Antonias. The quiz at eight and before that the secret sound. Tonight's sound was an odd hollow thump that had him perplexed until some old codger rang from down the coast to pick it correctly as someone banging out a cappuccino handle on a bin.

Not being a drinker of fancy coffee, Barry took this as one for the wankers. No reflection on him. He was a simple man and he liked very much to tell people he was a simple man. But there were things he knew well, things that snapped taut in his head like a reflex. Cars and trivia. Trivia and cars. Trivia about cars.

For most of his fifty-six years Barry had traded auto parts and hoarded information, the factual rubbish others would discard to keep their house-proud minds prim like a brick veneer. His was more of a two-bedroom hardiplank surrounded by rusty wreckage, and Lou Mantello's quiz on PF was pitched right where he liked it. Natural disasters, goal-kicking records, dodgy politicians, Bee Gees lyrics.

He had no interest in ringing in, God no. He'd tried that the first night he listened, had a rush of blood about a footy question and called in as Keith from Newport. 'Wayne C-C-Carey, Lou.' Everyone on the coast knew Barry Egan stammered under pressure. The sniggering followed him around town for days afterwards.

He slotted home a dimmy and sucked the soy from his fingertips while Lou asked for the capital of Peru. 'Looma...' Flecks of cabbage and pork landed on the dash. Barry's eyes roved the void beyond the cliff railing as some idiot came on air, fumbled around and finally had a swing. 'Er, San Pedro?'

'*Lima*, dickhead.' Enjoying the little rush of authority that accompanied his annoyance.

'Sorry mate. Nice try, I can see where you're going with San Pedro.' Lou cut the hapless caller and lined up a very precise-sounding woman from Geelong who nailed it.

'In what sort of craft', pressed Lou, 'did the Japanese invade Sydney Harbour?' Anne of Belmont hesitated. Barry didn't. *Minisub minisub minisub.* He could make out the lights of the salt works now, and the faint white pulse of the lighthouse across the bay. Anne had it, it was some sort of submarine wasn't it Lou? And Lou, whose abiding flaw in Barry's opinion was his laxity, gave her the nod.

Christ. Barry took a swig of Pasito as the last dimmy performed a brief encore in the back of his throat. Anne was perking up. 'Love your show, Lou,' she said. 'I listen every week.'

Barry knew from long memory the low headland invisible on his right, capped with straggly ti-tree, a nav marker and a couple of Norfolk pines. Straight off the point was a channel where the boats came and went, rocking on the swell, their booms swinging through a giddy arc. As they took the corner at the point they'd settle in the water, the bow wave fading. In daylight you could see the deckies hosing off the work area from where Barry was. Sluicing scraps of the kill through the vents in the sides of the vessel.

In a straight line in front of him and maybe a k out to sea there were reefs, low tracts of black boulders arranged in a devilish maze. They were invisible at high tide, sometimes even low tide, seen from shore only when the tide pulled right away from the town. Then they would lie there, sullen and treacherous, the dark clusters threaded by winding passages of deeper water. The sea pulled endlessly from right to left across the reef. West to east. It had something to do with the longshore drift, as Barry understood it.

How many Kardashian sisters are there? Lou's voice was all sniggering guile. *Three and a brother* yawned Barry as he knocked off the last of the Pasito.

The reefs were called Gawleys Kitchen, though Barry had never met anyone who could tell him why. When the swell rolled silently up from the southwest, the surfers would head out there. Some of them paddled the whole stretch from the foot of Antonias cliffs. Mostly they used tinnies or jetskis. On flat days the reef and its creatures belonged to the divers. Hefty crays and glassy-eyed trumpeter, shot through the gill rakers.

To the north and east of Gawleys, to Barry's left, the bay opened up again. A wide, docile bowl stretched out towards the cape, thirty or more k's away. As it curved away from town the land came round parallel to the prevailing swell and the waves turned to long, straight lines sweeping right to left below Barry's cliff-top perch. They ended their run at the eastern end of the bay, finally unburdening the last of the Southern Ocean's mythic fury on the sand. No one went there. Hardly anyone would walk a dog that far. The trail riders wouldn't take their horses down there; the swell dumped deep piles of kelp that clogged the beach. Dirt bikers and the odd fox shooter, that was about it. Barry had been there. But then he had a natural curiosity about things.

'Okay then Darlene.' Lou had someone new on the line. 'Which poison is said to have killed Socrates?'

Bugger. Hemlock? Or nightshade? The callers were going down like they'd been strafed. Arsenic, strychnine, cyanide; some stoner reckoned iocane powder.

Something about Gawleys.

Something out there in the dark wasn't quite dark. Barry made the mistake of looking at the lighthouse again, then had to blink away the purple spot in his vision, violet-violet-pink-white-gone. The water surface had the look of a grubby mirror, streaked with a blacker grey where the reef peered through.

Hemlock. It just sounded...ancient. Laurel wreaths and hemlock. Togas. He glanced down. Soy on his shirt, the sort of thing Deb used to tease him about. 'Did you get any of it in your mouth, dear?'

Lovely Deb, tired and warm. Gone last spring, and with her all of the order and domesticity in Barry's life. The alcohol interlock device now clipped to the dashboard represented the loss and the pain that still echoed. He'd taken very hard to the stout in the weeks after the funeral, one schooner chasing another as he reassured the sympathetic. Yes, doing very well, thank you for asking. Eyes creasing, close enough to a smile.

He'd been warned about driving home from the pub. Taken aside, told it had to stop. He'd just accepted the warning like he accepted the condolences and concern. In the end he'd left the local cop no choice but to book him; the great irony being that once he'd lost his licence he completely lost interest in the grog. Like it had served its purpose, putting him off the road, then gone on to tap some other poor bugger on the shoulder.

The time without his licence didn't worry him all that much, aside from missing his drives out to Antonias. The interlock, though, that was an assault on his way of life. It seemed to choose exactly those times when he was most comfortable to start up its furious screeching for a sample of his breath—horn blaring, lights flashing—until he pulled over to satisfy it, feed it like some mewling infant. Minutes would pass before he could gather his frightened thoughts and restart the car.

He fumbled around under the drivers seat for the binoculars. Took a moment to focus and find his target in the blackness. He could just make out low lines of whitewater on the outer edge of Gawleys, when he found the thing that had caught his attention.

Orange.

There was no fixed light on the reefs—couldn't be, they were too exposed. The fishing boats had a red port light, green starboard, and white all round.

But this was orange, and it was moving. Larger, smaller. Moving or flickering? It was irregular somehow, getting bigger then fading again, then pulsing brightly. It was still a long way off, well over the back edge of Gawleys. The beam of the lighthouse, a cold white shaft through the air, caught it once, then again. Barry knew he was looking at the gunwale of a boat, the side of the cabin. And the idea came to him quietly like another answer. The boat was not where it was supposed to be.

He snapped the radio off. Tried the high beams but they bleached out somewhere in the middle distance. A sheet of newspaper whipped past the front of the ute as though it had taken fright. Barry noted its path—the wind had arrived from the southwest again, punching a violent gust into the stillness, followed by a long stream of colder air. The heavy calm of the evening was done, and a change would reassert the order of things.

He turned the lights off and waited patiently for his eyes to figure it all out. Leaning forward now. Squinting until he felt a little ache under his eyebrows where the binoculars were pressing. He scrunched the greasy paper bag into a ball and fired it backhand at the dark space where the dog lay curled. A moment or two later, light and dark resolved themselves into shapes, and the shapes made sense.

He picked up the phone from the passenger seat and started dialling.

CHARLIE TRIED TO imagine her. Making her way towards him, just a tram ride from one end of Collins Street to the other, running from the revolving doors of the lobby to catch the 109. She hated being late.

He picked up a newspaper from the rack by the door as the waiter approached. 'I booked a table for two. Jardim.'

At the table he scanned the state politics and couldn't settle, his mind flicking back to Anna. She would be intent, calming herself and rehearsing as the tram rumbled westward. Telling herself about the longer view, the good sense of what she was about to do. Good sense being a core virtue in her world, he thought, and the point where their worlds deviated. Him with his contempt for good sense and her with her respect for forethought, for logical outcomes.

He imagined that few women of twenty-eight with a shared address and a rock on the finger would let go without long introspection. Anna had tolerated the outbursts and silences, tried to insinuate change where she could; commented, sometimes, on his lack of insight, his remoteness. He acknowledged these things to himself and from sheer obduracy said nothing. Which had led them to tonight.

The newspaper, trite, repetitive, was irritating him now. He was staring at the print rather than reading. He watched the boyfriends, the husbands, at tables around him. Compared their gestures, some of them made for display, others subconscious: the reaching hand on a shoulder, the turn of the body to convey full and undivided attention. These things were lacking between him and Anna, he knew. The decision had been made gradually through the cumulative weight of failed gestures. She was simply coming to deliver it.

He folded the paper and tossed it. At the end of the street the last glow of the day would be fading over the apartments of the Docklands. Outside, the lights of Renfrey's spilled yellow onto the laneway cobbles.

The door swung inwards with its little bell and she appeared in front of him, slightly flustered as he'd expected. She smiled briefly before her eyes fell to his wine glass. The way he held it, cupped with the stem between his second and third fingers, was one of the first things that had ever annoyed her about him. Back when the glow of lust still hummed over everything, there was already this small discord. She'd make a point of it at dinner parties; half-mocking asides.

As he stood and leaned towards her she turned slightly, enough to ensure his kiss landed on her cheek. This was her way, the aggregation of tiny cues that obviated the need to spell things out, and so it unfolded. He took up the menu and slumped behind it, correctly anticipating that she'd pull down the top edge to look him in the eyes. He'd never liked making direct eye contact with anyone and he remembered being surprised during their first weeks together that he could stare deeply at her, without self-consciousness. She'd always taken it as obvious that people could do this; that if they could have sex they could surely cope with other small intimacies. She'd once said that she felt she was looking straight at the lost child inside him.

Sentimental crap. Ever since she'd found out about his little brother, it felt to Charlie as though she had resolved to open him up about it. She would raise it at the strangest times—out of a long silence in the car, in bed in the darkness. Did he ever miss him? Did he cry a lot back then? Did he ever go to the grave? And while there were times when he wanted to revisit all of that, those times never coincided with her questions.

Her hands were pressed flat on the table before him.

'So...' She was looking for an opening. 'So this is the talk we needed to have.'

'You mean the break-up talk?' Far too quick. He'd slipped it out casually like saying he'd have the salmon. 'Is it Alex Reimers?' he asked, mock-serious.

'No, it's not Alex Reimers, Charlie. It's you.' There was hurt in her voice and maybe a tiny edge of guilt, just needling away in there. It had been a close thing with Alex Reimers at her office Christmas party, the arrogant little prick. As far as he could tell, she hadn't crossed the line.

'You're going red.'

'I'm going red because I'm angry, and you know I hate being cross-examined. It's you, Charlie. *You*. I'm not going to give you that crap about it being me, because it isn't. I've tried and tried. I've listened to your rants about how everybody disappoints you...'

She looked around furtively, conscious that she'd raised her voice, then started again at a lower pitch. 'No one can live up to the expectations you set for them. They always let you down. I'm sure you think I've let you down Charlie, but I haven't. I've stuck by you and I've encouraged you and I, I...'

'Fuck it Charlie. I can't do it anymore.'

He traced lines on the tablecloth with his index finger. *This show is not going to survive to entree*, he thought. As for her thing about expectations, she was of course dead right.

'That's not true,' he said anyway. 'It's a whole lot of horseshit you've thought up to give yourself a reason. If you weren't working six days a bloody week, if we had a life, it mightn't seem like such a slog. What the hell are you trying to do with your life?'

'What do you mean?'

'What do I mean? You want to make partner so you can work

14

seven days? You want to make eight hundred grand a year so you can have a family and never have to put up with their company?'

'Don't exaggerate. It's called building a future, Charlie. You don't seem to have the patience to do it.'

'What's the future in that?' Charlie was almost yelling in his indignation, completely unaware of his own volume. She glanced around the room to measure the attention of nearby diners. 'It's you and me! There's no kids, there's barely any parents, there isn't even a fucking cat. If you can't be selfish now, Annie baby, when are you ever going to be? You're obsessed with squirrelling your life away for a rainy day. Jesus.' He buried his forehead in both hands and felt the fingers spear upwards through his fringe.

She would now know he was grappling with it, with what he was about to lose. The only blow he'd landed, and it was a cowardly one, was calling her *Annie*.

He settled back in his chair, the finger wandering over the table again.

'I really blew it with that Lefcovics thing, didn't I? Bit awkward being attached to a barrister who's facing disciplinary proceedings, hmm? Bet the wires are just *singing* with that one round the big firms...'

'You're overstating your own importance, Charlie. I don't think anyone's even mentioned it to me at work.' This they both knew to be untrue. The email had done the rounds very quickly, before people who knew her connection to 'the barrister who had the brain snap' could intervene.

'If you ask me, it might be a symptom of the wider problem here, but it's not *the* problem. If you can't hang onto your self-discipline in front of that old coot, then you're not in good shape. You're not, Charlie. I mean it.'

'Fucker had it coming.' He sighed loudly and looked over his shoulder for the waiter. 'What about the lease?'

'I've checked it and they'll let us out, but I thought you might want to stay there. It's up to you. I can go stay with Dad for a while if that's easiest.'

'The furniture? You bought the furniture.'

'It's on interest-free. I can't believe you don't know that. I'm paying it off out of the joint account. You can keep it with the apartment if you can make the payments. But don't leave it till the two-year mark or you know they'll go mad on the interest.' Charlie felt humiliated all of a sudden, her telling him how to conduct himself.

'What about the ring?' He was sick with disgust.

She held out her left hand and rolled the damn thing around the finger until the emerald sat in its rightful place. She didn't answer at first, and he could see the tears forming in her eyes. He pressed blindly on.

'There's one thing I've learned,' he said, and it was the first time he'd sounded sincere. 'You can't get hurt if you don't commit, Annie. It's not personal, it's just the truth. I worshipped Harry. I worshipped the air around him. I worshipped the things on the fucking table next to his bed, because they were *his*. The parents idolised him too. So did everyone. And when he went, it just turned off the sun.'

There was silence between them for a long time.

'And then they bared their fangs on each other, dear ol' Mum and Dad. Ripped away at each other until they hated to be in the same room. At the bottom of every tragedy, there's someone who committed. Parent, lover, child, doesn't matter. Love's the root of all misery, wobbly bloody highwire act, and the more of it you've got, the harder you're going to come down.'

She pressed her lips white against each other as the tears welled in her eyes. 'I'll talk to the jewellers about the ring.' She gave him a thin smile. 'I don't know if there's a cooling-off period.'

The tears broke free and ran down her cheeks.

BY THE TIME Barry Egan reached the commercial wharf, a small crowd had gathered. The sou'west change thrashed at everything, lifting a low moan from the pine trees. The crowd stood in beanies and heavy jackets as the rain soaked their shoulders. Most of them had come from the pub, muttering and pointing. *The Lanegans' boat's on fire and one of them Lanegan kids's been burnt to death.*

The onlookers had nosed their vehicles into the carpark, forming haphazard angles in their rush to get to the scene. Some had even left their drivers door open. Headlights shone through the rain onto the crowd.

Barry ambled among them, nodding and grunting, hands buried in his pockets. Deep puddles had formed on the concrete wharf. At the lip of the concrete, a young police constable rested his foot on a bollard with a rope looped over it. At the other end was the Lanegans' shark boat, the *Caravel*. The cop was on the phone, ignoring the push of the crowd. He didn't share their interest in how an experienced fisherman could have burnt himself to death within sight of the harbour, or why he would be out there without a decky. It wasn't a bad night, thought Barry. Just not a night to go off fishing by yourself. He breathed deeply through his nose, pulling his chest up and his shoulders back. The smell of pine trees in the rain had something acrid in it. Burnt plastic, wood, something else.

The *Caravel* knocked gently at her moorings as men clambered over the decks. Its timbers were burnt black, segmented into little blocks of charcoal. Planks ended jaggedly, some burnt all the way through. It seemed odd to Barry that the charring started at the gunwale, well away from anything mechanical.

From there it had eaten into the foot of the cabin, up the side to the roofing, across the deck and over the equipment, bubbling the plastic covers into crazed stalactites. There were open holes in the hull like a cutaway diagram. Near the centre of the blackening, the timbers were still smoking faintly.

Between two of the men on board lay the rigid form of a dead man. He wore ordinary jeans, but they were burnt up to the hip on one side and to the mid-thigh on the other. His legs were blackened, the socks melted at his ankles and burnt away over the feet to reveal the snapped-off remnants of toes. The top half of the body was largely unmarked, and Barry could see enough of the face to recognise young Mags, the rough-cut eldest orphan of Dennis and Trish Lanegan. *There you go*, he thought. He'd always assumed it'd be the younger brother, the hair-triggered Patrick, who would come to a gruesome end in the rain.

A thick puddle of shiny black blood had congealed under the Lanegan boy's right ear, stretching itself into a bloody string as the men on the deck lifted the body towards a blue tarpaulin. The sight raised a low murmur from the crowd. Above the puttering of the rain, the voices rose as the body disappeared inside the tarp. It was clear to all present that this was not an accident at sea.

More men were recruited from among the crowd to assist with the lift over the edge of the vessel and up onto the wharf. A small man in a heavy woollen jumper tried to press the arm down. Recoiled in fright when it resisted him. Barry looked over the crowd. Laurie from the sports store and his wife Sue, partial to a quick drink before dinner some nights, but never among the revellers later on; four or five of the drunks from the Normans Woe, who always were; a couple of holidayers in loud Gore-Tex, one of whom pointed a phone camera at the tarp until the man in the jumper barked at him; two kids on BMXs. And Mick McVean. *Bastard*, thought Barry. No friends, no manners and aside from that, no interests. He was a loner who said little and appeared both unoccupied and constantly agitated. His only regular work was running errands for the Murchisons; at nights he'd fill a stool at the Normans Woe and stare at the women, working slowly through pots of light beer. He was tall and thick, as though he had settled into the shape that would take him to sixty: rounded shoulders and heavy jowls. Hair thinning in a deep vee over each temple, leaving a clump marooned above his forehead; belly slung low over the belt of his jeans.

As Barry watched him, McVean took a last look at the tarp and wandered off, fiddling with his phone. His eyes did not meet anyone's as he shouldered through the gathering on the wharf, heading further out on the planked decking rather than back towards the vehicles. Meanwhile the body was being lowered into the rear of the divvy van. Tight funding dictated that ambulances in these parts were reserved for the living, divvy vans for the drunk and the dead. The doors were slammed shut. A few onlookers remained to peer at the boat, as the van rolled carefully through the crowd, its blue and red lights fracturing prettily in the raindrops.

Barry sat on a pile of craypots and studied McVean, who had walked directly to the Murchisons' boat, the *Open Quest*. Barry loved to know people's business and, as far as he could see, McVean had none out there at this time of night. The big man had stepped from the wharf onto the deck of the *Open Quest*, a higher and much bigger area than the *Caravel*'s. The vessel rocked slightly under him. One of its mooring lines slapped the surface. McVean was looking for something. Lifting hatches, feeling through bunches of netting. Stopping to check tubs of equipment, dislodging lids with bearish sweeps of his broad hands.

Heaving himself up the ladder to the roof of the wheelhouse, he squatted over a black plastic spotlight on a mounting bracket. He produced a shifter and started to wrench away at it. When it came free, he stumped forwards to the wheelhouse, his heavy footfalls ringing on the narrow gangway. He stopped at a blue plastic barrel clamped to the wheelhouse wall, put the spotlight down and unscrewed the lid of the barrel. He peered inside. Barry's fascination had momentarily stopped his breath.

Then McVean replaced the lid and moved to an area on the wall next to the barrel where an empty steel clamp hung open. He held the clamp in his hand for a moment as if deep in thought. Then without warning, he lashed out with considerable violence and sank a boot into the cabin's steel wall. His hands flew up reflexively to restore his balance, and then rested on his hips. He swung a second kick at the spotlight, and sent it clattering across the deck. Then he looked back towards the carpark, and his eyes met Barry's.

'What are you lookin at, cunt?' he spoke across the thirty metres that separated them, his voice carried by the wind.

Barry rose from his perch on the craypots and started towards the carpark without a word. With his back to the wharf, he waited anxiously for the sound of McVean's booted feet.

Again on the wind, without any rising of effort. 'That's right, Egan, keep fucken walkin.' McVean was moving towards him, striding over the wharf timbers and onto the concrete apron, coming straight for the ute.

Barry swung onto the torn vinyl of the drivers seat, slammed the door and turned the key as he jabbed the accelerator. Nothing. Transmission in park? Yes. He looked up again. McVean was picking up the pace, mouth slightly agape, breathing harder. Barry's hands darted over the dashboard. What? *What?*

The bloody interlock.

He grabbed the handset and heaved a panicky breath into it. Why wasn't anybody else looking at McVean? *Fuck fuck fuck.* After a long and cruel silence, the display on the interlock lit up and the ignition fired. McVean had reached him. He lifted one paw into the air and slammed it down on the bonnet with a loud *whoomp*, staring at Barry through the grubby windscreen. Barry listened gratefully as the little ute revved into life, jolted into reverse and drew away.

CHARLIE JARDIM WALKED the streets of Melbourne, lugging his heavy leather bag inches above the puddles. The late February heat had been swept away by a cold front, bringing squalls and flushing the grease and dust of the city's summer down the soupy gutters. He stopped to pick up a coffee, looking down Lonsdale Street at the long queue of meat wagons in the clearway. Remand prisoners, due in court for the morning's hearings.

As the lift rumbled to the eighth floor, still full of cold morning air, he was deep in thought. He didn't glance at the noticeboard at the back of the lift. Had he done so, he would have seen fresh obituaries for two of his colleagues. Men with grey hair and long familiarity with the cycle of victory and defeat. Whose heart and liver (respectively) had quit in disgust.

Charlie had spent two weeks on the brink of professional ruin. The two nights in the police cells were no great problem—in fact the cops passing through had been variously supportive and highly amused. His Cadaverous Honour Maurice Lefcovics fined him, but with little enthusiasm. Standing before him, Charlie suspected Lefcovics actually pitied him, chastened as he must be by the exercise of raw magisterial power. He walked out $2500 poorer.

It was after the hearing that the walls started to close in. A notice from the regulators: he'd been cited for misconduct. A letter from the OPP: he was stood down from prosecution work until further notice. A request from his indemnity insurers for a written statement on the incident with Lefcovics.

Charlie was tired, in a way that gave him a dangerous edge of indifference about the whole thing. Part of him wanted to make a fight of it, but there was a growing apathy too. Maybe it was just that he'd been found out at last: a harbourer of petty rages, unable to contain the personal within the professional. The grief, the hypocrisy seemed unending and Charlie was increasingly sure he wouldn't survive as an advocate. He couldn't hide his visceral reactions. Jesus, he had to clench his teeth to avoid crying some days.

And then there was Anna.

Just another pop-out commercial law drone, he'd assumed. Until she surprised him, kept surprising him, with her wit and gentle irony. Anna, who'd come in a great wave of love and acceptance, evading every self-destructive attempt to push her away. Who'd listened and responded to his tantrums and his fears.

She was too good to be true, of course. If nothing else there was her patient dedication to her own career. She didn't struggle against the lower-court grind like he did. Broadmeadows, Heidelberg, Melbourne Magistrates; weekends on a cycle of coffee up and booze down, reading the papers, then Monday's brief. She didn't slump into a Sunday-afternoon funk knowing she had to get on a tram next morning to do it all again. She would take months, years, the larger part of her life, and draw herself towards whatever it was that constituted fulfilment.

He didn't have that. Did he envy it? Was that why the mockery was always there, brewing and occasionally erupting? He'd made last night's conversation difficult; but how do you make a thing like that easy? He should call. Yes, and say what? Was that why people used text messages for these things?

The lift slowed. His mind lurched to business, the call last night after Anna left: an incoming brief, something significant. His clerk, working late when the courier delivered it, had thought of Charlie's situation and got straight on the phone. He wondered now if this

23

would be the brief that would change everything. Make the lift and the coffee and the dry retching and the trams and whole shitty game fall away from the foreground like cardboard theatre sets, revealing something that would expunge the futile ritual of his weeks.

He assumed initially it was a defence job: it seemed unlikely the prosecutors would send him anything of consequence so soon after letting him know in writing that he was not wanted. He wasn't part of the defence community with their ritualised talk, their double standards on drug use. No one he knew would sling him a murder defence.

So all right, maybe it *was* a prosecution job. A Crown brief for murder could mean months of steady work, relief from the one-day Magistrates' Court brawls. Government money, straight up, and no catfights over fees.

And such a brief, in the cold summer of his exile, could only come from Harlan. If it was Harlan's name on the backsheet, Charlie knew what to expect. He'd wind up covering the miles for the crazy old bastard, leaving Harlan responsible for the genius and the big moments. Fair exchange, he thought.

The lift ejected him and his gust of street air on the eighth floor. He strode through the foyer to the door that bore his name. Throwing his overcoat at one chair and his bag at another, Charlie studied the trolley in the far corner of the room. Every other object in his office—Anna couldn't stand him calling the room 'chambers'—answered an unconscious call for him: the filing cabinet, the back of the hard drive, the law reports, the row of framed certificates.

But the trolley stood there with its load of folders like a defiant stranger. He didn't know a thing about the world inside those folders, beyond the two printed names he could see: Murchison. McVean. *The Queen vs Murchison and McVean—Murder.*

The ring binders were wrapped in white prosecutors' ribbon, the first one marked with Harlan's name as lead counsel. So he'd swung it somehow. The index volume bore the six-pointed star of the

Victoria Police. The witness list: a dozen unfamiliar names, followed by some he knew—investigators, scientists, the photographer.

Charlie ran a thumb down the edge of the photo booklet, bound in the royal blue of the forensic science lab. Establishing shots, the back of a fibro house, a boat. Another boat, this one burnt. Plastic tubs, sitting on thick green grass, unlike the stuff of Melbourne, but more like, what? Ireland. Something slimy-looking—shellfish meat?—lined up in orderly rows on a white plastic sheet. A disposal skip. A shot of the inside of the skip, some sort of electronic instrument with a blank dead screen, above which was embossed the word *Navmaster*. A manhole in someone's ceiling, then insulation batts, a black object lying partially concealed under them. Charlie turned the booklet slightly, trying to identify it. Stuff in bins, so often the forensic treasure. Weir had once said to him that the criminal law is obsessed with discarded objects. A pair of upturned hands, the palms deeply fissured and callused.

Sometimes, in their effort to capture a particular evidentiary feature—a tiny graze, a crease in the skin, the smashed panel work of a car—the forensic photographers would accidentally strike compositional gold. The upturned palms seemed to be pleading. Without an accompanying face, without context, the hands asked for something on behalf of the unnamed and the overlooked.

Next, a police photo of a male face, sleepy, rough and creased. A sullen mouth, stubble darker in the valleys of the jowls. A wide nose separating dark, heavy eyes. Shaggy brown eyebrows and receding hair. Charlie checked the index: this was accused number one, Michael John McVean. He looked as mean as hell.

The face of the other accused, Toby James Murchison, had the childish look of military photographs from old wars. A full mouth, a ruddy blush on the cheeks like a public schoolboy hauled off to fight, still perplexed by his change in fortune.

Next, a family's photograph of their lost son.

It was strange, Charlie thought, how people who'd died

immediately looked different in the photographs taken while they were living. Lost. He wondered if anyone had ever done a study, taken a hundred mixed photos and asked people to nominate the living and the dead.

He flipped photos and tapped the end of a pencil on the top of the desk clock. It was Anna's gift to him, the clock, when he got his first prosecution gig. The bright optimism of the brass dial spoke of stoic cheer, nobility, something—but it reminded him daily that by tiny ticking increments, he was becoming an old man. More than any other object in the room, it was a reminder to him that he was badly out of touch with the way others, Anna in particular, saw him.

He watched the clock take three minutes of his life. Dropped his gaze back to the photo book.

The sheen of a mortuary table. A dead guy with burnt legs, naked and washed, mottled with livor. Close-ups, like an uncomfortable introduction. Slack face; pale lips, a week's stubble and the eyes of shopwindowfish. Young, grotty-looking. The police would've picked this one for a *scrote*, but having just seen him dressed, a little younger, Charlie felt a wash of sadness.

A round puncture wound over the right temple. No doubt there would be a pathologist's report among the ring binders that would refer to 'a circular defect in the right temporal region': the language of objective examination. Someone had plugged the boy. He leafed onwards. More images of the body on the bench, the right forearm slightly aloft in half-hearted protest.

Charlie snapped the book shut and slotted it back into the top shelf of the trolley. He took out the first of the fifteen numbered volumes, carried it to the desk and flipped it open. Well, sorry men, he said to himself: let's have the story.

STATEMENT OF PATRICK HUGHES LANEGAN,
4231 SOUTH COAST HIGHWAY, DAUPHIN VICTORIA.

I was born on 23 January, 1991 and I am a commercial fisherman. I am the brother of Matthew LANEGAN (DOB 11/6/89) who was also known to me as Matt and Mags, and I have a sister and twin brothers. Their names are Milly (15), Ben and Jack (both 8). My parents are both deceased.

I know a man named Toby MURCHISON, although he is known to me as Skip. Everyone just calls him that. Toby and I went through high school in the same year, and his family run the Normans Woe. They also have an abalone licence, meaning they are able to take 2.3 tonnes of abalone from Victorian waters each year. This is called their quota, and they have to sell it through the co-op and record all the amounts. The Murchisons boat is called the Open Quest.

My brother and I have a shark boat in Dauphin, the Caravel. It is a steel hull, about 8 metres. We have run it as a squid boat a few times in recent years because the shark numbers have been down.

On approximately three or four occasions in the past I have bought one pound blocks of dope off Skip and resold it. Other times I have taken dope to Melbourne for Skip and received payment from him for doing the trip. By dope I mean cannabis. I think the cannabis was hydroponic, although I don't know where it was grown. The times when I have resold the dope, I would break it down to a couple of ounce lots and some one gram deals to sell. I would keep about an eighth of the block to smoke by myself.

In about June last year I had a chat with Skip which I think was in the bottleshop at the Normans Woe. I was walking through to get beers, and Skip was working out there. He does this sometimes at night since his eco-tourism business shut down. We just talked about general stuff, fishing and that. Then he mentioned that they were going way over quota and they could use a hand getting rid of some extra abs. I sort of laughed it off at the time, but I mentioned it too Matt when I got home.

Matt brought it up a few times after that and he was really keen to do it. I think it was matt that went back to Skip and said yes. It definately wasn't me.

Nothing much happened about it for a few weeks after that, and then there was a stretch of good fishing weather and everyone was out. This was approximately the first week of June. Matt got a call on his mobile, I think it was Skip or his mate Mick McVEAN, saying to meet up at a point which they gave him off the GPS. This was roughly three nautical miles south of Boulder Point.

We went there and met up with the Open Quest. It was just Mick and Skip on board. They gave us three plastic tubs of shucked abalone, that means the shell and gut were taken off. I would say this was about 450 abs. They told us to deliver them to an address in Melbourne which I do not wish to provide. The agreed price was $2000 and I think Matt had sorted this out already, but I don't know if it was during the phone call.

This job worked out without any problems and we got paid in cash a few days later by Mick in the front bar of the Normans Woe. After that, we did about four or five more jobs like the first one, always at the end of a stretch of good diving weather. We sometimes had fish we didn't want to sell through the co-op, so this was no problem. We would take up a few tubs for Skip in with the shark fillets or whatever else in the refrigerated van.

We did a job for Skip Murchison yesterday. It was me and Matt and Mick in Matt's van. Skip wanted Mick to go with us because he said he was worried about whether we were skimming some of the abs and selling them off somewhere else. This was not true, and I know Skip and Matt had had an argument about it because Matt was dirty about the whole thing for a few days before we did yesterday's run. He also had the shits because Skip and Mick were getting behind with there payments. He said at one stage that he was going to stop doing runs for Skip, but he changed his mind because we needed the money.

We took the abalone to the Melbourne address as usual. I know Matt was expecting Mick to pay us on the spot, once the delivery was done. He figured if Mick was with us, then he should have the money. Mick didn't have it and the two of them were bluing about it all the way back. At one stage, at a servo on the Geelong Freeway, they nearly had a punchup and I had to get between them.

By the time we got back to town it was getting dark. We left

Mick at the wharf at about six o'clock and went home. Matt was getting more and more angry about the money and in the end he rang Skip and it turned out he was heading out around then to go fishing anyway. He said to come out and meet him at the same spot as usual. He said he was going to fish that night and if Matt was so keen for the money that he couldn't wait till morning, he was welcome to come out and Skip would fix him up.

I dropped Matt at the wharf about eight pm and he said he would go out to get the money from Skip and then see me at home. I sat at home and watched a DVD by myself. Because it was a Saturday night, MIlly was out doing stuff and the twins were asleep. By about eleven I started wondering if he'd come back in and gone straight to the Normans Woe, so I went down there looking for him. His phone was going to voicemail. I come home from there, and I was just turning off the car in our driveway when Robbo turned up in the divvy van and told me Matt had been shot and the Caravel was on fire. I was asked to come down to the lockup and identify Matt's body.

I do not know who shot matt. I was at home all through that evening, except for about ten minutes when I went to the Normans Woe looking for Matt.

Patrick James LANEGAN

Statement taken and signature witnessed by me
At 1:06am on 11 August 20--
at Dauphin in the State of Victoria

Neil Robertson
Detective Sergeant 258447

CHARLIE WRESTLED THE overcoat on as he slammed the door of his room. The family lawyer next door was deep in negotiation mode, feet on his desk, loud, breezy and profane; as comfortable selling real estate as children. Charlie passed the stale flowers at the empty reception desk—a constant sore point for the one commercial lawyer on the floor who doggedly arranged *Harper's Bazaar* and *Vogue* on the waiting room coffee table only to watch them gather coffee rings.

Across the street at the prosecutors' chambers, Charlie found that the card he'd been issued was no longer recognised by the scanner on the door. He waited until a woman in earphones swiped in, and darted through the doors behind her.

Harlan Weir SC was perched regally behind a big plain desk in his fourth-floor office. Among the neat piles of paper, each crowned by a glass paperweight, Harlan cut a large, shambolic figure, not quite aligned in his chair, silver hair swept over a wide forehead, suit jacket crumpled. He was polishing his glasses vigorously with the end of his tie.

'How come I got this brief?' asked Charlie, before he'd even sat down.

Weir ignored the question. 'What'd you think?'

'It's interesting. Sad bunch of people. You been there?'

'Nope. Looks vulgar to me…kelp and lighthouses. Fish.'

His lips momentarily caught on his teeth, in a comical

death's head grin. 'I think I'm an inlander.'

Weir held the glasses up to the light to inspect his work.

'Have you ever studied the Beaufort Scale, Charlie? Beautiful piece of writing. It's a technical document, of course, but from a time when you could write technical stuff with your heart, when it wasn't so bloody soporific. Beaufort was a Pom, and he wanted to—' Weir squinted as he replaced the glasses on his nose. 'He wanted a way to relate wind strengths to the appearance of the sea. Subjective exercise really. "Crests of glassy appearance" and so forth.' He studied his thumbnails momentarily. '"Rolling is heavy." Dear me. Isn't that beautiful? *Rolling is heavy*…You can't describe anything scientific in those terms anymore. No verbs at all now, let alone at the front end like that. Or if they do have verbs they're the ones they develop in a test tube by reconfiguring noun DNA. Do you know I heard a man say "baselining" the other day?'

'In court?'

'No, on the television.' Harlan rolled one of the paperweights in his left palm. 'Talking about football of course. And while I'm on that, tell me this—why are they so obsessed with accountability on the field, which to my mind is such an obscurity that none of them actually knows what it is—and yet they appear to be accountable to no one at all when they go out at night? You employ it as a sports cliché and it's apparently more important than life itself. And yet, used the way the Queen intended—that is, as a moral standard—it baffles them to the extent that they see no problem with urinating on a police car.'

'Which queen?'

'What?'

'Which queen intended it to be used that way?' Charlie had become adept at pulling the handbrake on these tirades.

Weir sighed. 'You've read this, this Murchison brief?'

'Enough of it.' He tried again. 'How come I got the gig?'

'Why on earth wouldn't you?' Weir had leaned forward very

slightly, and he studied Charlie with gentle regard. A phone rang distantly outside the room. Charlie found himself looking at the spines of the books behind the desk.

Weir was still watching him. 'Now tell me how we're going to run it.'

'Okay. You've got these two families, the Lanegans and the Murchisons. The second accused, McVean, he's just hired muscle. Lanegans have got a tribe of kids and both parents are dead. They're in the fishing game but a bit on the periphery, well-known trouble-makers in the town. They get an approach from the Murchisons, who own just about everything in the main street. They're also into fishing and they've got an abalone licence. The Murchisons say, we're getting more abalone than we can legally sell through the co-op or whatever, so if you take these extra abalone to Melbourne so we can move them through the black market, we'll give you a commission.'

'Why don't they take their own abalone to Melbourne?'

'Licence is worth a couple of million dollars and they're not going to risk it. Fisheries do roadblocks, all sorts of stuff to catch these people. So they're better off putting a couple of expendables on the road and just denying everything if they get caught.'

'What, with shellfish? It's not exactly Burmese heroin.'

'It's very expensive stuff. There's only a dozen or so of these licences west of the cape, and there's an insatiable export market. I rang their fishermen's board after I'd finished reading the brief, and I got talking to this guy. He described it as swimming along scooping up hundred-dollar bills. Anyway, those boats are only sharing about twenty-five tonnes of product for the year, so the quota quickly cuts 'em off. And the co-op, the central clearing house for the abalone, it issues a docket which has to stay with that consignment of shellfish pretty much all the way to the table. Makes it very hard to fool the system once the abalone catch has been declared.'

'So you don't declare it in the first place.' Weir nodded. 'What about the murder charge?'

32

'I think at a gut level a jury would buy it. There's clear physical evidence of deliberate homicide, the way the wound looks. There's motive: the Murchisons were behind in their payments and the victim was getting lippy about it. He'd complained to people at the pub, he'd made scenes at various times in front of others. It's a small town and people have a mind for other people's business. If the town witnesses stand up, then none of that's going to be too difficult. There's opportunity—the accused have got access to a boat. The phone records show some contact during the day between accused and victim, and then again about an hour before the fire's first spotted from shore, so that all ties in. Neither of the accused has got much of an alibi, and one of them, I think McVean, can be placed at the wharf; he accessed the security panel at exactly the right time. Murchison is by all accounts slightly smarter than McVean, but he was silly enough to answer a few questions in his police interview— made a bit of a mess of it. McVean's dumb, but different kind of dumb. Knows enough to give a no-comment. Anyway, the police version is very plausible: they arranged to meet at sea, either for the accused to provide more product to the victim, or so they could set up an ambush. There's a disagreement out there, or the whole thing was prearranged. They shoot him then and there on board the Murchisons' boat, throw him over into his own boat and set fire to it in the hope it'll burn to the waterline and—'

'Why? Why not weigh the body down and dump it at sea? Why not sink the boat with the body in it?'

'I guess because that area's not very deep, according to the local coppers, and someone would eventually come across the boat. You know, snag it on a net or a craypot or something.'

'All right. Why not tow it out to sea and then do it?'

'Yeah, why not? That's the best of all worlds. Take it ten miles out and do it...you've got sonar so you can make sure it's deep. Maybe they just panicked, but if they set the killing up from the very start, why would they fall at the last hurdle like that?'

'What do the cops say about that?' Charlie could see Weir laying out a matrix of thought that stretched well ahead of the question.

'They've got no problem with calling it panic—they reckon these boys are both a bit thick. They're also pretty fond of the idea that the gun only came along for intimidation. Whichever of these two was holding it, he's just lost his composure momentarily and bang. Course, that makes it a felony murder for the other, so it doesn't much matter who was who at the time. Everything just unravels for them after that and they decide to torch the boat without thinking. Too late once it's alight.' Charlie slapped his hands onto his knees and exhaled.

'What about the weapon?'

'Search and rescue picked it up easily enough. They drew a straight line between the area where the witnesses place the boat on fire and the harbour mouth, then they just dived a grid both sides of that line, and there it is in about ten feet of water. Bolt-action twenty-two. Ballistics are a match. Silly bastards didn't even think to go and dump it somewhere else.'

Weir had the glass paperweight under the end of one finger and was rolling it on his desk blotter, firing sparks of refraction at the walls. 'So what's the problem?'

'The brother.'

'What, the, er...' Weir lifted a volume from the shelf behind him and leafed through it. '...Patrick?'

'Yeah. Firstly it doesn't make sense that he'd spend the day with his brother doing business with Murchison and McVean, they get into a dispute with them, and Patrick lets his brother head off knowingly into a dangerous situation while he stays at home to watch a movie. Why didn't he try and talk the victim out of it? He says it himself—it could've waited till morning.'

Weir watched him, fists bunched under his nose, elbows on the desk. Heavy enamelled cufflinks protruded from his coat sleeves.

'Second thing is, it's the better explanation for the failure to dispose properly of the body. Whether they intended to shoot Matthew Lanegan or not, Patrick's got away from them, meaning that they had to deal with him rather than deal with the body.'

'So what about the fire?'

'They reckon there was an accelerant. Deliberate arson. So you say to the jury, they shot Matthew, Patrick was there but he got away from them, they're in a complete flap and they can't afford to risk Patrick making his way back to shore while they're towing the evidence out to sea. They need to be safely back in harbour and off their boat by the time the brother makes it home and raises the alarm. Quickest thing is to slosh the Lanegans' boat with fuel and light it up.'

'Why not shoot holes in the thing?'

'Because you're back where you started—the boat's on the bottom in shallow water and easily recovered. Fishing boats don't just sink on a calm night. Mind you, I think that's assuming too much insight where these fellers are concerned. I'm all for the panic theory.'

'And there's no panic without Patrick out there,' said Weir. 'Otherwise they've got all the time in the world.'

'Patrick's got his own reasons for wanting to say he wasn't there, presumably.'

'Presumably he has. But he's going to have to do better isn't he?'

'He's given his version.' Charlie shrugged. 'We can't influence him to change it.'

'I'm not suggesting we influence him. He may have made his statement under some kind of pressure, maybe still grieving. There might've been threats—god, we don't know what goes on in these places. The first part of his statement rings true, so he's half-implicated the accused. He just didn't go all the way. We need to work out why he said this stuff when logic would suggest it isn't true. He doesn't have a clear motive for lying, this kid.'

'So we send the local copper around with instructions to get a second statement?'

'The local copper might be part of the problem.'

Weir lit up his most beguiling smile. The glasses rode up on the wave of creases across his nose. 'I was thinking we might send you.'

Charlie knew he'd been had—Weir had been circling him invisibly for the last ten minutes with his feigned bafflement, closing the gates around him until he was trapped, a victim of his own analysis. He owed the man his professional survival, and Weir, for reasons only he knew, was going to exact a price. The old swindler was gazing, affably enough, straight into Charlie's eyes. The smile faded slowly, leaving the faintest line of amusement curling at the corner of his mouth.

THIS IS A TAPE RECORDED CONVERSATION BETWEEN DETECTIVE SERGEANT NEIL ROBERTSON AND TOBY JAMES MURCHISON OF 22 CASPIAN STREET, DAUPHIN IN THE STATE OF VICTORIA, CONDUCTED AT ST KILDA ROAD POLICE COMPLEX ON MONDAY 24 AUGUST. ALSO PRESENT IS MY CORROBORATOR, DETECTIVE SENIOR CONSTABLE BRYAN GOODALL.

Q1   Toby, do you agree the time by my watch is 10:13 pm?

A   Yeah.

Q2   Okay. Just get my things organised here. Toby, just for the purposes of the tape, can you state your full name and address please?

A   Toby James Murchison, 6 December 1976, and, sorry you didn't need that, did you. Um, 22 Caspian Street, Dauphin.

Q3   Right, now Toby I intend to ask you some questions in relation to the death of Matthew Francis Lanegan. Before continuing, I must inform you that you are not obliged to say or do anything, but anything you say or do may be given in evidence. Do you understand this?

A   Yeah.

Q4   I must also inform you of the following rights. You may communicate with, or attempt to communicate with a friend or relative to inform that person of your whereabouts. And you may communicate with, or attempt to communicate with, a legal practitioner. Do you understand those rights?

A   Yeah.

Q5   Do you want to call anybody before we ask you further questions?

A   Nah Robbo, that's all right.

Q6   You don't want to make a phone call?

A   No. No thanks.

Q7   So you don't wish to exercise any of those rights before we commence?

A   No.

Q8   OK, I think you gave us your date of birth, now are you an Australian citizen?

A   Yes.

Q9   Are you a permanent resident in Australia?

A   Yes.

Q10 And are you of Aboriginal or Torres Strait Islander descent?

A Nah.

Q11 Okay, Toby the purpose of us talking to you here today is in regards to a phone call you made to us yesterday, do you agree with that?

A Yeah. I called youse, yes I did.

Q12 And so the reason you're here today is in response to that, or is because of that, is that correct?

A Yeah. As I said, there was a fair bit of talk in the town and I wanted to come in and clear the air a little bit.

Q13 So you attended at the Dauphin police station last night, is that right?

A Yep, and they gave me the number to ring youse, which I did.

Q14 Okay, and we asked you to come up to Melbourne and talk to us here today, and you've been good enough to attend here tonight on your— on your own volition, is that right?

A That's right, yes.

Q15 Well we certainly appreciate it. Are you okay with work and every-thing? Did they give you tomorrow off?

A Oh yeah that's all fine, it's just dad, so that's—that's right, yeah.

Q16 It's just sometimes, in our experience, people come in to talk to the police and their employer gets—you know—gets the wrong idea and goes jumping to conclusions about things ---

A Nah, dad's a grumpy bastard at the best of times, ey. He'll be right, he just wants this out of the way, you know, just get it cleared up, like I said.

Q17 You're referring there to your father, who's Alan Murchison, is that right?

A Yes.

Q18 And Alan is the owner of the Normans Woe Hotel, and he's also the president of the local, er, abalone board?

A Yes.

Q19 Okay, so you're currently employed as a bistro manager at the Normans Woe Hotel in Dauphin, is that right?

A Bistro and events, yeah. We've got an events company going too, and I take care of all that. Like, race days and weddings, that sort of stuff.

Q20 And how long have you held those positions?

A   Since '03, for the bistro, and, ah, last winter for the events management.

Q21 And what about before that? What were you doing then?

A   Well every season I do abs on our boat, the Open Quest. Like, I do a bit of decky's work, and also transport the product up to Melbourne, to the markets, and I do the contracts with the cannery, and just help keep it all running. But I ---

Q22 What about the, er, the eco-tourism?

A   Yeah, I was going to say, I had the eco-tourism business before the events thing got going.

Q23 What was that all about—the eco-tourism?

A   Oh, we had a van, like a four wheel drive minibus, and we just showed people the beaches. You know, if there were whales in, we'd try to get them out to the lookout above Gawleys at Antonia's Beach there and give them a look. We did camping out in the dunes, had some blackfellas on the books who'd come out and do a bit of a cookup and talk about the area, like dreamtime stuff and that. Kayaks too, on the flat days. Um, learn to surf. That's about it.

Q24 All right. Now you know that we're here to talk about events that occurred last night, don't you?

A   Yeah, I understand that, but I don't ---

Q25 All right, in particular that a young fella named Matthew Lanegan was shot last night at sea on his boat the Caravel and ---

A   Yeah I heard about that ---

Q26 - and that his boat was then set on - appears to have been set on fire. Now firstly, is there anything you wish to tell us about that incident, or those incidents?

A   I don't know anything about them, no.

Q27 Okay, what were you up to yesterday?

A   What, all day?

Q28 Yes.

A   Well, I did an oil change on the four wheel drive in the morning, then I took the drum of old oil out to the tip. Um, had lunch in the bistro at the pub. In the afternoon, I went to a clearing sale with dad up at the Rosslyn's, came back, dropped in at the pub and did a roster -

Q29   What time would you have returned to the pub?

A   Oh about four thirty.

Q30   And I should just ask for the sake of clarity, when you say 'the pub', you're referring to the family business, the - the Normans Woe Hotel in Dauphin.

A   Yes that's right.

Q31   Okay, so four thirty you're doing a roster. Now can I ask you, you know a man named Michael John McVean?

A   Yes I do.

Q32   And how do you know him?

A   He works for dad, does odd jobs around the place. He's kind of, I suppose you'd say, just a general employee of the family business.

Q33   So by that do you mean the pub or the boat or the other ventures you mentioned just before?

A   Well, all of them. Whatever needs doing.

Q34   Do you know where he was yesterday?

A   Ah, I think he was taking a load of seafood up to Melbourne to the markets for us.

Q35   Why would he be doing that? Aren't you on a contract with a buyer who collects it all for you?

A   Yeah we are, but now and then you get a special order, maybe a restaurant or that, or maybe you catch something unusual and you want to run it up there fresh. It's good for relations, you know?

Q36   Who did he go to Melbourne with?

A   As far as I know he went on his own.

Q37   Are you sure about that? You're not aware of anyone who was travelling with him?

A   No I'm not.

Q38   Well Mr Murchison, one of the things we check on when there's a death like this, a suspicious death, is we look at the deceased's phone records, you understand?

A   Yeah, that makes sense.

Q39   And here, we've had a look at Mr Lanegan's phone calls, and he talks to you three times, at er, let me look at this, at 12:31 pm, 12:36pm and

5:12pm yesterday afternoon. Now can you think of any reason why you two would be talking yesterday afternoon?

A   No. No I can't. Unless he was ordering something from the pub or -

Q40 No, I don't think you're following me, Mr Murchison. Those calls went through phone towers—you understand that mobile calls can be located by the nearest mobile phone tower ---

A   Yeah yeah.

Q41 - and those towers were at Werribee, for the first two calls, and then Geelong for the later one. He wasn't in Dauphin, I suggest to you.

A   Oh right, yep.

Q42 Can you see -

A   - I don't -

Q43 - how that makes it -

A   I'm not sure -

Q44 - look a lot like you were talking to him while he travelled?

A   Yes I can, but I have no recollection of doing that.

Q45 You don't know how that could be?

A   No I don't. Could I -

Q46 You must agree that it looks a lot li -

A   - make a phone call?

Q47 Well, who do you want to call? I mean, er, I've offered you your right to call a lawyer, but you can't, for operational reasons I can't have you calling anyone else right now you understand?

A   Yep. I do. I'll call me lawyer thanks.

Q48 All right, we'll just pause the recorder there for a minute. Mr Murchison do you agree that the time by my watch is 10:33pm?

A   Yep.

Q49 All right.

INTERVIEW SUSPENDED.

DETECTIVE SERGEANT NEIL ROBERTSON:

Q50   Now Toby do you agree the time by my watch is 10:56pm?

A   Yes I do.

Q51   All right. Just before we get underway again, I'll just recap where
      we've got to.

THIS IS CONTINUATION OF A TAPE RECORDED CONVERSATION
BETWEEN DETECTIVE SERGEANT NEIL ROBERTSON AND TOBY JAMES
MURCHISON OF 22 CASPIAN STREET, DAUPHIN IN THE STATE OF
VICTORIA, CONDUCTED AT ST KILDA ROAD POLICE COMPLEX ON
MONDAY 24 AUGUST. ALSO PRESENT IS DETECTIVE SENIOR CONSTABLE
BRYAN GOODALL.

Q52   So we'll just do your name and address again please Toby.

A   Yes, Toby James Murchison, 22 Caspian Street Dauphin Victoria.

Q53   Before continuing, I must inform you that you are not obliged to say
      or do anything, but anything you say or do may be given in evidence.
      Do you understand this?

A   Yep.

Q54   I must also inform you of the following rights. You may communicate
      with, or attempt to communicate with a friend or relative to inform
      that person of your whereabouts. And you may communicate with,
      or attempt to communicate with, a legal practitioner. Do you under-
      stand those rights?

A   Yes I've done that, thanks.

Q55   Okay, now while the interview was suspended, Toby, do you agree
      that we haven't discussed this matter at all?

A   That's right, yep.

Q56   And we put you in an office with a phone by yourself there.

A   Yes.

Q57   And you've spoken to your solicitor?

A   Yes I have.

Q58   All right. Now the last thing I was asking you about was the phone
      records that we've got, and they indicated you and the deceased in
      this matter, Mr Lanegan, were in contact by phone yesterday. Now
      do you want to tell us anything further about that?

A   On legal advice I have no comment to make.

Q59 Were you at sea last night on your vessel, the Open Quest?

A   On legal advice I have no comment to make.

Q60 Okay, Mr Murchison, are you intending to make no comment responses to the remainder of my questions?

A   On legal advice I have no comment to make.

Q61 Understand that Mr Murchison, but you can actually answer that one. I just need to know for the recording here—

A   No comment.

Q62 Righto. I now propose to conclude the interview. Do you agree that the time by my watch is 11:02pm?

A   No comment.

Q63 Interview concluded.

DAUPHIN

HE COULDN'T GET comfortable until he was well onto the Geelong road, set up in one of the left lanes so he could let the Saab find its own rhythm. He drained the last of the coffee he'd brewed at chambers before he left, and threw the cup on the passenger floor. The coffee grit sat dry on his tongue. Fantastic. Furry teeth and four hours of panic coming up.

He fed a CD into the stereo, fiddled with the cruise control. Aircon for a few k's, then open windows. Anna had made one of her welfare calls before he left. She'd been quite specific—don't drive straight from work. It'll be hell on that road, everyone headed down the beach for the long weekend, she'd said. And you'll be driving into the evening sun. But now there was a heavy bank of cloud rising from the western horizon. The sun was beaten, reduced to a brilliant rim on the cloudbank after the sticky heat of the day. Charlie leaned forward to air the small of his back and wished he'd changed shirts.

The old workers' suburbs, red and orderly and flat in the tired light, gave way to the steel flanks of the factories, giant signs telling him who to fly and where to merge. *I'm supposed to be in the conflict business*, his head was saying. *I'm not an advocate, I'm a long-haul babysitter.* The factories yielded to tilt-slab housing—boxes, boxes, boxes. Neo-Georgian, faux-Victorian, pseudo-warehouse-conversion. No trees. Off the plan, on the block, financed by the collective debt of swooning young punters.

Anna would call him a snob and ask him by what accident of history he had been set up in judgment, but there they were, hand in hand: gazing up at the anaemic eaves of their little palaces, gym-honed and pouring westwards over the paddocks of old Italian sharecroppers, with their home theatres and courtyard pavers. Plasma screens for the long evenings, jetskis for the weekends.

Dusk fell around him and headlights streaked in the oncoming lanes. The storm cloud, lit by faraway lightning, had crept up to fill the whole windscreen. The housing estates were gone now and he was well into the paddocks. He closed the windows, opened the fresh air vents and was immediately struck in the face by a stream of airborne grit. He found a square of chocolate in the console somewhere, greasy with the heat and inexplicably hairy.

The road narrowed and grew rough. The choices presented by the outlying towns were behind him: now it was just a matter of keeping the car on the road until it got to Dauphin. He had nearly four hours to work through the whole Annie situation, and yet he was filled with childish resistance. With effort, he constructed a couple of good sequences. Annie had never been in love with him: she was just *determined* about him, like she was about everything. He was there to be mastered, grappled with and brought to heel. He pictured her friends, watching their toddlers on a plastic slide somewhere, silently thanking their lucky stars that they hadn't settled for such a maudlin prick.

What he suspected, however, was less easy.

She was probably good. Not in a churchy, virtuous way, just good in her bones. The type of person who was capable of doing the right thing when no one was watching.

His eyes felt sticky. Two towns and a radio news bulletin had passed without him noticing. The engine was screaming; he'd left the car in third as he emerged from the second town. Two-thirds of a tank gone. He slowed down to eighty for a place called Regent, watched a servo go past on his left and a war memorial on his right.

They were just lights now, downlights, uplights. An avenue of honour, skeletal outlines against a dark and angry sky.

They weren't connecting, that was it. Not even when he'd faced her over some café table, wherever, locked his eyes onto hers. They were always ten degrees off square, just like the other night. Maybe it's a natural state, he thought, to be dissatisfied but plugging on, grimly trying to make each day slightly more honest than the last. One day, if they'd kept going, and found out what would hold them together by sheer attrition, he might've closed the void between them.

Tennis courts, a footy ground, third, fourth. He hit fifth as he passed the 100 sign. A green sign listing towns he didn't know. Then, the souvenirable yellow sign with the black kangaroo, and almost immediately—a second later? A minute?—in the dull compression of road time there was a flash of movement on the road and a loud bang.

The seatbelt bit. Charlie felt the car drift left, grip briefly, start spinning. As it floated through its arc he had time to imagine the savage finality of the tree, the pole, the oncoming B-double, whatever hard object was about to shatter this weightless world. He tried steering, in the expanded seconds of the spin, and knew it was futile. He couldn't tell if he was braking or not. Half-clenched, half-resigned, he waited.

But the car just faded into silence. Momentum gone, it juddered and bounced once before coming to rest in a cloud of smoke. The front wheels had found a culvert of some sort on the grass. The rear end sat out in the roadway. He'd stalled it.

Somehow the stereo had given up in fright, leaving silence. He could taste the coffee, smell the burnt rubber. The headlights daubed light on a paddock fence. Insects drifted in the smoke, lurching pinpoints in the sick yellow glow.

He got out and wandered around to the front of the car. The drivers headlight was gone, leaving a gory smashed eye socket. The front quarter was caved in almost to the wheel, and a streak of something fleshy led back towards the drivers door. There was a clump of fur lodged in the battered bodywork. He walked an aimless circle around the back of the car, heard the first, fat rain-drops striking the hot metal.

Doonk...doonk. Slowly at first and then in a rapid staccato, fizzing and popping, whacking the asphalt. For a brief instant, every drop missed him entirely, as though he wasn't part of this night. Then he wore one on the right eyebrow, another two on the top of his head. They jabbed into his shirt, again on his face, and again, then they were at him in squadrons; face shoulder ear head chin head chest shoes, and the storm came roaring down on him, drumming on the car and pattering on the road, leaving him deaf and insensible to anything other than one thought. He'd hit something. He needed a reckoning with the object, it must be an animal, that had strayed into his path.

In the distracting curtain of rain, he was at first only aware of the wide, unfocused sound. And then another noise. Thumping, dragging, scraping. On the roadway, back towards the car, his eye snagged it in the arc of the headlights. A big roo, tilted over its left flank and lurching to keep a distance. As he approached, the dark eyes followed him, big and soft and wounded. Fresh, sticky blood was raised to a ghastly froth on its snout, and its heaving breath crackled like fire through twigs. It was wrecked, shattered. Watching him quietly.

What happens now? asked the eyes.

It would be all right to get back in the car and go. Thousands of these things out here...they're pests in some areas, he'd heard. It's not a person, it's not your fault. *Let nature take its course.*

The roo made a movement, lurched again, exposing its other flank, and Charlie flinched. The left leg was snapped, hanging only by matted fur. He backed away, wanting more than anything else to escape those eyes. The animal tried to hop away and the mangled leg flailed around in a deranged circle as it overbalanced. Pedalling madly with the good leg, it stood again, heaving and wobbling. Continued to watch him.

Charlie went to the boot of the Saab. His potential weaponry comprised a suit carrier, a soft bag of clothes and six boxes of ring binders. Trading as he did in the aftermath of violence and not its delivery, he was a traveller without blunt objects.

But not quite. He reached into the tyre well and felt around until his fingers closed around a thin steel rod. The winder for the jack. He brought it out and gave it an experimental swoosh. It clanged into the back bumper of the Saab, jarring his hand and sending the damaged roo scuttling into the shadows.

He changed his grip on the jack winder. As he approached, the roo broke cover and tried to bolt, breaking the leg off entirely and dragging the exposed end of the bone along the asphalt. It left a chalky yellow streak on the wet road. The roo's breath was tight and hissing now, its gait jerky, futile. Charlie dropped to his haunches and threw up. He rested with both hands on the wet road, staring into a puddle of vomit pocked with raindrops. Waited for his fingers to stop their mad buzzing.

The animal had retreated to the shadows again. The eyes were harder to discern, though he could feel them still, imploring him. If it wanted deliverance, then his conscience was clear. The use of the rod would be right and good. But did it? Was it hoping for mercy? Help?

He crawled forward. Curled and uncurled his hand on the wet steel. He was within reach of the animal now. He braced, left hand extended for balance. Pictured the soft brown fur at the top of the skull and thrashed downward as hard as he could.

Whatever he'd expected in a lifetime of never having tried to kill anything, he did not expect the dull, damp thud he heard now.

The kangaroo's one good leg seemed to buckle, and the ungainly prop of splintering bone gave way. The animal collapsed on the grass, gagging and twitching, and Charlie struck it again and again, feeling the strain in his shoulder as he brought the rod up for the third and fourth times and the sharp sting in his wrist as the rod met bone, again and again. The rain was hammering down on him now, and flecks of blood spat upwards at him as he struck. *Just be gracious and die*, he thought. *Please stop twitching now.*

It persisted, though, and Charlie felt a flash of irrational fury. He pushed the knowledge away. Nobody flogging a wounded animal wants to own up to anger. For a mad second, he thought of Harry in a fishing boat, watching with him as a little flathead flapped away against the hull. It's just the nerves, Charlie, he'd said. *The nerves* couldn't feel sorrow or pain. There was no panic or fear in them, no frantic desire for escape. *The nerves* didn't cling desperately to life. They were an abstraction of sorts. Surely the insistent kicking of the busted legs was just nerves. Surely the soft-eyed animal had left long ago.

It wasn't until the head was a misshapen, purplish mat that the animal was finally still. In the places where the fur was not caked with blood, it bowed beneath the attentive raindrops. Charlie stood there, heaving for breath, before running the rod through the wet grass a few times until all the blood was gone. He then carefully replaced it in the spare wheel cavity, slammed the boot and slumped into the drivers seat. He gripped the wheel, staring dumbly at his spattered knuckles for a long time, and began to cry.

THE FIRST THING that struck Charlie about the Normans Woe was the smell. Even as a gust of the brutish southerly wind whipped in the doorway behind him, he caught a waft of old cooking oil, boiled cauliflower, something slightly rancid.

The pub was old. Not just in its architecture, but in its mood. No one had spent anything on this building in many years. The doorway carpet was shiny and it clung slightly to the soles of his shoes. Bar to the right side, seating to the left. A dining room out through swinging doors, with the lights dimmed. There were about eight people in the room if you included the bartender, and they were all staring at him.

The bartender was a big man without sharp edges. He occupied a space between bar and wall that seemed made for someone smaller. As Charlie entered the room, he was bent almost double, scrubbing away behind the dishracks where the plywood of the bar had turned soft and mouldy. There were racks piled on the floor beside him and he was squirting jets of pink cleaning fluid into the dark cavity as though targeting a spider.

The jaws of a long-dead shark grinned down from the wall above him as he scrubbed. Flanking the jaws, a few framed shots of grinning fishermen, a beer ad, a novelty Jim Beam mirror, and a dogfight of beer-can planes hanging from fishing lines. Stubby holders, beef jerky, pictures of stunned-looking greyhounds with elaborate ribbons around their necks like pageant queens. All of it tinged with a golden patina of ancient nicotine. Behind the cooking smells, Charlie could discern the ghost of the long-ago smoke. Sometimes he thought fresh smoke would be better.

Three old men and two honey-coloured backpackers were deployed around the bar. The backpackers' beers had gone flat—they were engrossed in writing what Charlie took to be diaries. He made a mental entry on their behalf: *stuck in windswept shithole.*

One of the old men struggled to scoop his change from the folds of the bar towel into the front pocket of his cardigan with a clubbed left hand. A shit-brown cancer had parked itself on the man's cheek, and as Charlie watched he dabbed at it with a handkerchief, a tiny counterassault on the forces that seemed to be decomposing him where he sat.

The old boy headed for the door. The bartender stumped off to the storeroom and returned with a pile of clean folded tea towels. Charlie stood in silence at the bar as he began unloading them. Eventually the bartender regarded him with a puzzled look, smiled through his beard and plonked both fists on the bar.

'Yes mate?'

Charlie ordered a beer and took up the stool that had been recently vacated by the old man. It was still warm. The other drinkers were eyeing him now. The bartender flipped the draft tap and swung a pot glass beneath, watching him too. Charlie took his wallet out and began pulling it open in various directions in a vain search for cash.

'Not to worry,' said the barman. 'I'll open a tab. We got eftpos.' He went to the sink and brought back a clean dishcloth, rinsed it under the tap and placed it on the bar in front of him.

'You might wanna…' he pointed vaguely at the blood.

Charlie took the cloth and started wiping in an arc around his jaw and across his nose. Neither of them spoke.

The bartender picked up the remote and flipped to the news. The regional weather girl, so pregnant that her belly obscured the whole of Gippsland, said the rain had three more days to run. Charlie raised the pot glass and drained it; stared back at the bartender, who picked up the pot glass without further prompting and began to refill it. There was silence for a moment as the beer swirled in over the foam tracks of the first pot. He spoke in a quiet, slow rumble.

'See it's Friday night and it's pissing down out there. You walk in alone, wearin a business shirt looks like a Swans jumper, all that blood and shit round your neck. You've even got smudges on yer cuffs where you wiped yer brow…'

'I hit a kangaroo.' Charlie raised his eyes and looked straight at the big man, searching his face.

The bartender passed a look over the blood-spattered shirt. 'Not an axe murderer, then.' He placed the pot in front of Charlie, froth spilling over one edge and forming a pool on the bar towel. 'But you got that bag at your feet and every time someone's moved, you've checked it like there's a bomb in there. The clothes are very Melbourne—well, apart from the blood—and you got indoors skin. Indoors hands too. College hair. Youngish, but you weren't a footy player. And you speak…very…carefully.'

He moved in towards Charlie, grabbing the beer taps for emphasis. 'So you'd be the guy the cops were sending about the Lanegan boy.' He grinned and moved off down the bar towards the till where he busied himself changing a receipt roll. 'How'd I do?'

Charlie swallowed deeply and put the empty pot on the towel again. 'My name's Charlie.'

'Good,' said the bartender, taking the pot to the taps once again.

'And you are?'

'I are Les.' He proffered his hand and Charlie shook it. By now the old blokes along the bar had given up pretending they weren't listening. They watched Charlie without any self-consciousness as he lifted the new beer and took a chunk out of it.

'Leshter,' called a little man in a beanie. He had no teeth, and his bristly white stubble was stained to sepia under his nose. Les ambled over and the old man prodded his glass with an index finger. Les attended to the refill as the drinker poked coins out of a pile towards him. 'He here 'bout the Murchishon thingy?' he croaked, apparently happier to direct the question to the bartender than to Charlie himself.

'Yep, I think he is,' said Les.

'*Haph!*' barked the old man. Charlie couldn't pick it for scorn or phlegm, but the small eyes under the beanie were firmly fixed on him now. The knotty index finger came up off the bar towel and was pointed directly at him, the eyes sighting him along the knuckles.

'Doan you go believing anything that Lanegan cunt tells ya, lad. I tell you now...' he swept the finger along the bar as though gathering consensus from unseen allies, 'he's a lyin dog. An' whatever he tells ya, it's all fuggin malarkey. Ya fuggin come ere an ya... ya come ere thinkin we'll juss be sayin "oh hello missa policeman, can we help ya wiff sommen?" an' all the silly ol country fuckers'll be linin up'—the hands swept expansively around him now—'sayin, oh yeah, it was this bloke what did it, or this bloke or whaddever.'

'Easy, Mick,' said Les. He picked up Charlie's empty and poured again.

'I'm not your lad,' said Charlie quietly, half-inclining his head towards the old man.

'Whah?'

'I said I'm not your lad.' Charlie stared straight back over the rim of the glass at him.

The old bloke's eyes widened. For a second he seemed to be making a choice.

'Nah nah nah. You know it,' he turned on Les. 'You know it ya big prick. Issa good pub. He's jussa cunt.' He turned his palms upwards, as if to invite a counterargument. 'An' he was up to no good, an 'is brother got shot. Why you wanna go takin down good peeble who a running a good pub. Huh? Fuck yas.'

'Last warning, Mick.'

Mick rose and drew deeply into his lungs, hawking up a big ball of snot. He opened the door half an arm's length and shot it into the night. The cold air swirled around them again and Mick fell silent like a sullen child.

'Sorry,' said Les to Charlie, who had slumped an inch or two on his stool.

'Guess you people've got me pegged, eh.'

Les assessed him with a faint smile. 'Mate,' he looked down the bar and lowered his voice as he leaned in towards Charlie. 'In my job you can't go judging people. You take that poor old bastard who just left. Got nothing in the world. Got no one. I can tell you exactly what he had in his shopping bag.' He counted off the items on his fingers: 'Tinned sausage, Lipton teabags and antacid. If today was Thursday, there'd be a carton of Winnie Blues. Government gives the old guy a pension, takes it straight back off him in sales tax on the smokes. Hey? Fuck me.'

'Nasty looking cancer on his face,' said Charlie.

Les shook his head. 'Been watching that thing growing for weeks. It's creeping up towards his eye. Started to weep, did you notice?'

'I did.'

'You wonder why he fucking bothers at all. Why wouldn't you just wander off into the scrub like a crook dog and, you know, lie down? Warm, dry spot somewhere in the leaves and the twigs...' He shook his head and shrugged.

Charlie thought for a moment. He tapped away at the side of his glass, collecting cold condensation on his fingertip. 'You were right before. I need to talk to Patrick Lanegan.'

'Oh yeah,' chuckled Les. 'Not much of a talker. He's in a bit of trouble, eh?'

'Depends on how you see it, but no, I don't suppose he is.'

'He's already spoken to the cops hasn't he?'

'Well, I can't really discuss that, but I'm not the cops anyway. I just need to have a chat to him about things.' Charlie was getting himself in a hole and he knew it. 'Can I have another beer?'

Les walked off with the glass. 'It's *leeegal*, is it?' he tossed over his shoulder.

'You're very nosey aren't you.'

'It's not about bein nosey. See, if it's legal stuff, you don't want to go to his house. The welfare, the cops, that's how *they* do it. Lob up to the front door and start bangin. He absolutely fucken hates it. And wouldn't you?'

He flipped the tap shut once again. 'If I'm just *nosey*, then I'm sure you don't need to know that Paddy the boy will be at the footy tomorrow and you can try hassling him there.'

'Thank you.'

'Fine mate,' he replied dismissively. 'He prob'ly won't talk to you anyway.'

Two hours passed without further discussion between them.

Charlie steadily drained the pots that were placed in front of him, relishing the dull glow that was slackening his mouth and slowing his mind. Every half-hour or so the beer would send him to the urinal, where he'd stare at the tiles, breathe in the sharp disinfectant stink and study his blurred face in a chipped mirror. He tried washing away some of the animal blood around his eyes, but only smeared it further into the creases.

Les called time at one. Charlie fumbled the card out of his wallet and placed it with exaggerated precision on the bar mat in front of him. Les sighed through his nostrils and walked to the back of the bar. He swiped the card forcefully through an EFTPOS terminal.

'What's your PIN?'

'Sorry?' Charlie raised his eyebrows.

'WHAT'S YOUR PIN NUMBER?'

'You're not serious.' said Charlie. 'You want me to yell it out?

Bring the bloody thing over here.'

'Cord's not long enough.'

'Mate, you're not having my PIN. Thass a—' Charlie broke off, corrected himself. '*That*'s a breach of the bank's regulations, and you could be…anyone.'

'I *am* anyone, pal, and you're not leaving here till I get paid. What's the number?'

Charlie ran both hands through his hair. A light dusting of bloody flecks had formed under his forearms on the bar, rubbed from his skin by the pull of his sleeves. At least two of the old farts had stopped their conversation and tuned in. 'Tip the cunnupside-down an' shake im Les,' offered Mick from under his beanie.

'I'll come round the bar and type it.'

Les placed the EFTPOS unit back on the bar and put his hands on his hips.

'Been very patient with you tonight, young fella. But you're not coming round my bar.'

His face was resolute. 'How 'bout I cancel that and put it through as credit. You can sign the slip over there and we're all square eh?' He offered a smile.

'I doan have credit. You seen the interest rates on those things?'

'Well,' said Les. 'This is a hotel. People sometimes pay for their beers with plain old cash.'

There wasn't a word being spoken in the bar anymore. Les squinted with frustration. He put both hands on the bar and drummed his fingers.

Charlie had his head down. Out of the unexpected silence, he yelled at his feet.

'Five six six three six six.'

The old farts set up a chorus of emphysemic laughter and one began to clap. Charlie wobbled as he leapt from his stool and confronted them.

'Yeah yeah. Five six six three six six…easy one isn't it? Even a couple of deadshits like you two oughta be able to commit that'—he pointed viciously at his temple—'to memory. Huh? Get it through ya thick…fucken…heads? It's London, it is. I met her in London, an if you type the fucker into a keypad you'll find it says *London*, so OKAY?' He swivelled around and took in the remaining drinkers with a wild look. 'FIVE SIX SIX THREE SIX SIX any FUCKEN questions?'

Silence returned and Charlie ran the back of one hand across his mouth.

'I dinner think so.'

Les wordlessly placed a page from the waitress's pad in front of him. In a neat cursive, he'd written 'Charlie—bar tab—March 6', and then listed the beers. Charlie took it and swept it into his pocket without speaking as he fumbled in the other pocket for his keys.

Les shook his head. 'You're not driving.'

For an instant Charlie was caught at a childish post-tantrum crossroads, unsure if he was going to resume hostilities or crumple.

'You asking me or telling me?'

'Telling you. Where are you staying?'

'I wanted to ask you about a room and I got sidetracked.' He was now very much in retreat. He didn't care: after a couple of days he would never see these people again.

'We don't have rooms, mate.'

'Well what's going on upstairs with all the little attic rooms you can see from the street?'

'They're not rooms.' He pointed at the ceiling tiles. 'Might've been once. Now it's just a false ceiling and roof joists.' Les was rolling the bar towels up as he walked the length of the room. 'Barry Egan's dog got loose up there one night, little highland terrier thingy, before he got the staffy. Chased a rat up the old staircase and ran around on the top of the false ceiling, tiles going *whoomp whoomp whoomp* as he ran…see the three white tiles over there?' He pointed to a pale spot above the cigarette machine. 'That's where he fell through…dog, rat, ceiling stuff, whole bloody show come crashing down on Don Whittle and his missus. Absolute pisser.'

His eyes fell as he realised Charlie hadn't broken his stare.

'You're tired, eh.'

Charlie didn't respond.

'I can put you in a place till you work out what you're doing.'

From behind the door he produced a set of keys on a green plastic tag and flicked a hidden bank of light switches to black out various patches of the room. Charlie's drunken stare had rested on the bright colours of the Casablanca Lucky Envelopes machine. Les reached behind it with a grunt and killed the happy blipping. He opened the main door, and the cold air curled around them both.

'Come on.'

In the street, puddles had formed around the wounded Saab. The gutter was blocked by milk cartons and shredded cardboard. Les had taken off at a reasonable speed for a big man, but as Charlie watched him from behind, he could see a limp that originated at the right knee. He was heaving the right leg completely straight through each stride, so that his head veered from side to side as he walked.

'You done your knee?' Charlie called tactlessly to his back.

'Long time ago, yes.'

They were heading south, the houses thinning out and gradually giving way to scrub. The footpath lost definition, trickling out into a smooth track, greasy from the rain. There were no gutters, Charlie noticed. He made a mental note to take issue with this at some later stage when things made more sense: where the hell were the gutters?

Les walked ahead of him, the wet scrub now brushing his ample flanks as he passed. They'd topped a rise and the wind hit them with renewed force as the dark mass of the ocean appeared. Les was muttering disconnected words every few steps. Charlie missed the first few, then caught one.

'Heath.'

'What'd you say?"

'I said *heath*.' Les stopped. 'That's coast beard heath. It's what makes this whole coast look dark green. Gets little white berries on it in summer. They taste like granny smiths.' He started along the path again, waving an abstract hand to his left. 'Coastal daisy. Polygala. Dreadful shit. Introduced. Saw-sedge. Poa. Pigface.'

'Thanks, Les,' called Charlie, failing to conceal an edge of sarcasm.

Les stopped. 'Don't you want to know what all these are?' he asked, blinking.

'Why would I want to know that?'

The question seemed to strike Les as impossibly trite. 'Why *wouldn't* you want to know that?' He shook his head gently and walked on in silence, visible to Charlie only as a faint silhouette against the dark sky.

'What are those lights?' asked Charlie, trying to rebuild whatever he'd just crushed.

'Where?'

Les stopped and followed Charlie's gaze out to sea, to where a series of vague glows lit the horizon. There were nine of them, stretching from one end of the visible sea to the other, evenly spaced.

'Squid boats. It's the season. They're out every night at the moment.'

Under the loose canopy of the ti-tree, a timber fence appeared. Les turned in at the gateway and crossed a small yard before lumbering his way up a few steps onto a deck. Their footsteps were louder on the boards. The house, barely visible against the thick sky, looked to Charlie much like the holiday houses he remembered from summer holidays of the past. Fibro. Bits of odd plumbing sticking out of the walls.

Les rummaged in his pocket, found a key and swung the door open. Charlie was struck by the familiar waft of seagrass matting and old curtains. The bare bulb illuminated a basic living room—vinyl and checked cloth armchairs radiating from a pine coffee table with a ceramic tile surface. The curtains he'd smelled were repeating patterns of sailing boats in horrific burnt orange. There were metallic lamps screwed into the far wall. The main windows of the living room faced perversely inland, while a modest window above the kitchen sink looked over the ocean. A laminex counter divided the armchaired room from the little kitchen.

The counter caught his attention and held it. The hypnotic arc of a hand sweeping crumbs off its surface, the wedding ring's scouring sound as it looped across. Comfort in routine. *Your brother's gone to heaven.* He'd learned a new word while the police sat around in his parents' lounge room, drinking his parents' coffee and writing things down.

The cunt never even stopped, he had overheard. The hand sweeping nothing off the counter.

Where's Harry, you cunt?

He looked away, saw a framed poster tracing the history of the Leyland P76 and a pine bookcase crammed with paperbacks. Each spine had faded down slightly to a bluish tinge and bore the linear scars of having been put down open.

'You can bring your car around and park it in here in the morning,' said Les.

Charlie felt suddenly the completeness of his exile.

'If I turn up at the footy tomorrow, how will I pick him?' The tacky after-effects of the beer tripped his tongue.

'Patrick? Well let's see, eh? Tallish. Thin. He'll be the only bloke at the footy who's had his brother shot by the guys who own the pub. He's the bloke who's on first names with the local magistrate cos he's got so much form, and he's the one trying to feed twin eight-year-old brothers and a sister cos both his parents and his big brother are dead. So if I were you, I'd look for the guy who *doesn't* look like he wants to chat.'

Les looked around the room with a final air of assessment. 'I'll figure out the rate for you. S'pose the Queen pays the bill, eh?'

Receiving no reply, he turned towards the door. 'Have a nice stay.'

As the door slammed behind him, Charlie slid into one of the armchairs and dropped his head into his hands.

HE BEGAN WALKING soon after the sun came up.

He'd showered the muck off himself, but wiping his teeth with a square of toilet paper did nothing to expunge the sour taste. The bathroom cupboards had mouse shit but no aspirin. His hands were light and shaky, and he could feel the early gnawing of a gut ache he knew would plague him all day. The wind outside had slowed, and played lightly over a world washed clean and still damp in the cool air. Slamming the door behind him, he wandered up the rise of the dune and squinted at the great bowl of the ocean below.

In the distance, out towards the horizon, it looked the way it always did when he summoned it in his mind: foreign, secretive. A blank sheet over what had gone before and what continued to occur beneath. His eyes passed over the water, anticipating some thing, some object, that would break up the conspiracy of nothingness. A fin. A breaching whale. Something floating.

Fixing his sight on a point on the surface, he tried to picture the colossal blue cathedral of depth beneath, the first and mightiest truth that the ocean hid. Huge creatures, huge agglomerations of tiny creatures, had passed through this column of space. Silent giants and gelatinous microbes, the chrome-sided everyfish passing through the dim light with all of their eyes, all of their thousands of eyes, fixed ahead on the ineluctable business of sex and predation.

When they were little, he and Harry had believed that one day, scanning the surface like this, they'd see the mournful drift of a dead man trailing the shreds of his clothes in the face of a wave.

But the flat sheen of the ocean, lying glossy under the morning's still air, offered him nothing.

Except nearer to shore, where black boulders stretched out and joined in a loop to form a wide lagoon. Inching away from the beach and across the lagoon was a small wooden boat.

Charlie could see, even from this distance, that the man who sat steadily rowing the boat was very old. His movements were concise, but there was no power in his stroke. After a couple of dozen strokes he stopped, both fists resting on his knees. Then he resumed, steady again: another two dozen strokes, and another rest, repeating the sequence until he reached the rocks on the seaward side of the lagoon. Charlie watched him turn the little craft through ninety degrees then rest it, beam-on to the rocks. He reached out one hand from the boat, leaning slightly, until he was holding a rock, resting his hand on it while he looked further out to sea.

He sat like that for a long time, while the birds came and went, the waves rose and fell in gangs of four or five. Then, without any other movement, he let the rock go and the boat turned itself in a familiar way towards shore. When its nose came to be pointing directly at the beach, the old man took up the oars again and began to row.

Charlie, who was not inclined to any activity that involved effort for its own sake, watched all of this in silent scepticism. His first reaction was to assume the old man was disturbed in some way. His second was to admire the simple beauty of the little ritual.

He stood, dusted the sand off himself and began to retrace the previous night's steps towards the centre of town, down through the scrub off the back of the dune, onto the flats and into the marked streets. The footpath reappeared, followed by the houses.

Someone had got to these people with a metal cladding scam. In cemetery rows behind the trunks of Norfolk pines stood the sober weatherboards of the interwar years, all of them converted into tin cans. He imagined the salesman at the door, in a slim tie and hat, explaining patiently to women in floral aprons that their husbands would never have to paint again. He saw the nervous touching of earrings, the resting of wedding bands on the doorjamb; the brief, immodest thought of inviting him in.

The lawns were unlike anything he'd ever seen. Thick, spiky, pale couch grass shredded into submission, edges cut to a humped right angle against the footpath. The only softening touch was agapanthus, livid green and rude with health. Snails ventured from under the protective clumps and spotted their way across the footpath. Charlie took care to tread on every one he saw.

He passed a milk bar with a plaster pie suspended above its awning; two doors further on, a fish and chip shop had a grey plastic shark. The trickle of isolated shopfronts, still dark and silent, became a strip: a video library, then an op shop in which everything appeared to be crocheted, a churchy-looking bookstore full of images of Jesus looking like a menswear salesman. A shop called Marg's Beads 'n' Things; hardware, a coin laundry, a supermarket. He passed the Normans Woe, saw his car awaiting him with its smashed panels. A waft of sour beer struck him from the open door of the building, the unmistakable smell of a pub at low tide. Two doors down, a barber in a white coat was unloading cartons of cigarettes from the boot of an XD Falcon, assisted by an old man in a cardigan.

Charlie sat down on the cold concrete plinth of the war memorial at the top of the street. It was an equestrian statue of a very severe-looking man and his equally severe horse. The dead were listed alphabetically in neat capitals. Half a dozen Lanegans. Below them, four Murchisons. The main street stretched before him, wide and empty. The silence pressing for his attention the same way noise normally would. He could see now that the east side of the street was taken up almost entirely by a series of shopfronts strung

together under one awning marked with confident capitals—
MURCHISON AND SONS FURNITURE AND TRADING
EST. 1983.

Outside the milk bar a girl in polarfleece was putting out a
sandwich board. When he got there she was inside, stacking news-
papers under the rows of magazines. He ordered a coffee and she
wrestled the machine into hissing compliance, producing a surprisingly good espresso that he clutched in his warming fingers as he
continued northwards, away from the beach and into the paddocks.
He was following a road that had fallen into disuse: the edges broken
into little fragments like pack ice. He saw a length of fencing wire,
pieces of a dead rabbit, stubbies with bleached labels and a plastic
hubcap. Grass—thick, vigorous clumps of the stuff—climbing all
over everything.

He came to a house, set well back from the road behind a bank
of cypress hedges and four car bodies in varying states of decay. The
verandah was painted in undercoat and a cluster of pine framing
sprang from the back, weathered as if the project had long since
defeated the residents. He'd slowed to an amble and was studying
the place when he realised he was being watched. A small girl had
made herself a nest at the farm gate. She had a group of stuffed toys
arranged on blocks of wood in the overgrowth behind the brick
gateway. Her hair was matted but her face was bright and forthright.

'Hello,' she said evenly. She'd lost her top front teeth.

'I like your friends,' said Charlie, nodding at the furry ensemble.
He always felt he was acting the part of someone else when he spoke
to small children. He was fairly sure they could pick it.

'They're at the movies,' the girl replied happily, sucking a fast
breath so she could crowd her sentences forward. 'They're watching
a nature film. Mum took us to watch a film. It had a volcano!' Her
eyes grew wide as she mimed an explosion.

Charlie leaned both arms on the gate. 'How old are you?'

Her expression changed, and she was silent. She looked down

at her chest for a moment, then peered carefully at him. 'You look sad,' she concluded.

'Do I?' In Charlie's world, such exchanges worked responsively. Questions, even antagonistic ones, had related answers.

'You got sad eyes. They're like a elephant's.' She nodded solemnly, closing her own eyes for added gravity.

'Really?'

'Elephants are very big,' she explained, her voice falling away as she spoke. She returned to gently adjusting the animals with tiny strokes and nudges of her perfect hands.

Charlie hurried on, surprised and stung.

Beyond the house he passed large agricultural sheds, a saleyard and a CFA depot. It was low land, even to Charlie's eye, pocked with boulders and thistles. The smell of cowshit and wet grass was lifting warmly off the paddocks now that the sun had begun its arc over the town. More rows of dark cypress, pasture and foliage, deeper and shallower greens.

He'd reached the eighty sign on the edge of town when the sorrow overtook him. The land was arranged in a code he couldn't decipher. He had left the language of his world behind and this place would offer him no translation, merely reflecting his troubles blankly back at him.

Bruised sky, sodden earth, razor wind between. What a fucking dreadful place.

THE SIGN ON the gate said seven dollars, five concession.

Charlie thought that was pretty steep for local footy, but he didn't have a better plan for his Saturday. Les had told him the panelbeater wouldn't look at the car today because he had a swap meet to go to. Charlie pulled the bent guard out of the way of the front wheel, and it seemed to go okay.

He parked behind the grandstand and took in the sentimental smell of wet turf as he got out: childhood footy, jarred fingers, rows of anxious parents. He'd hated every minute of it, didn't even envy the ones who did it with ease. Even as a kid he knew they'd get caught by time. Their knees would go and they'd be left with nothing but team photos and arthritis.

The game was well underway. Charlie leaned on the rail and watched for a while, conscious that the crowd had moved away from him and had recongregated closer to the clubrooms. Mostly he saw their backs, with just an occasional glimpse of ruddy jowls. Even the kids seemed to know to avoid him, sensitive to the negative polarity of the outsider. Or maybe they were caught up in their own worlds and completely unaware of him. *Don't be so paranoid, Jardim.*

Within moments of his arrival the siren sounded and the players moved in bovine procession towards the rooms under the grandstand.

Once they'd all filed through the changeroom door, a handful of spectators followed. Charlie wandered in behind the last of them, dealing out small nods of appreciation as shoulders parted to let him through. The rooms were crowded around the fringes. In the centre, the players were trotting small circles, boots making small popping sounds on the rubberised floor. Kids in hoodies slumped on the changing benches; above them, handwritten signs dished up motivation in butcher-shop capitals. DISCIPLINE, said one. RESPECT. COMMITMENT. Then a jarring verb: RUN.

The players, slap-cheeked and wild-haired from the cold, talked as automatons, not to each other but to the group. 'First at the contest.' 'Forward pressure.' 'Two-way running.'

The coach's voice rose over the room, exhorting, pleading. He wanted more. He wanted direct play, down the guts, numbers at the ball. He wanted them to look after each other, to keep presenting. The slogans sounded to Charlie like a mutation of management jargon. If you talk this way to people who expect to hear it, he figured, you can get them to do things that are no good at all. The circles were increasing in pace and tightening like a whirlwind, the drumming of the boots rising in pitch and volume. The older blokes around Charlie in the doorway began to grunt encouragement at players they knew. Drink bottles were cast aside, and they slapped each other on the backs, the backsides. The tight cluster began to surge through the doorway and back out into the light of the day until only one player remained, still jogging slowly, but in a staggering ellipse that took him close to the civilians around the edges.

The runner approached him and dropped his tray of drink bottles in a show of concern. 'You right, mate?' The player started to wobble towards the door. 'Concussed!' yelled the runner over his shoulder as the player bounced hard off the doorjamb and fell back in to the arms of the trainers. Charlie looked away, turned and followed the crowd back outside.

He watched the game grunt its way up and down the ground, then realised a figure had joined him at the rail. Middle aged, scruffy beard, heavy-set. Can of Coke in hand. Beanie, farmers boots with

71

the tags protruding front and back from the hems of his jeans, the jeans themselves slung low under his gut and halfway down his arse. There was a dog at his feet, an overfed staffy that jerked at any burst of action on the field but never left its post beside the man's boot. The man looked at Charlie in a way that was somewhere north of hostile but nowhere near friendly.

A string of passes along the wing ended as the ball spilled out of bounds and rolled under the pipe railing. It was collected by a small boy who threw it to the boundary ump.

'Aah, send it down the *guts* will ya!' the fat man yelled. He looked at Charlie, as though pleading his case.

Charlie responded only by compressing his mouth into a brief smile.

The fat man's face changed slightly. 'You're the prosecutor bloke, aren't you?' He stuck out a stumpy hand. 'Barry Egan.'

Charlie shook it without conviction. 'My name's Charlie.'

'You doing some research on it all, eh?'

'On what?'

Egan scoffed. 'The Murchisons.' He pointed his can up the ground. 'Little fella goal umpirin up that end's a first cousin of your accused.' He swung the pointing can downfield. 'So's the forward pocket in the helmet. Big lady working the scoreboard—see her there?—she's Murchison's uncle's de facto. She's only got one left eye.'

'We've all only got one left eye.'

'What?'

'Left eyes. Everybody's got one. You mean she's only got one eye left.'

Barry Egan looked confused. 'Yeah. She's missin an eye. That's what I said.' He returned to the railing and didn't speak for some time. After another slurp from the can he pointed a finger obliquely towards Charlie, ready to resume. 'Anyway, makes your job tricky, doesn't it? All these relatives all over the place, whole town talkin about it an' that.'

'I don't know what you're…'

'Ha! Course you don't. You've got to get the Lanegan boy to fess up, and he's keeping mum. Poor bugger's faced with Murchisons everywhere he looks.' He drained the can and tossed the empty in front of his feet. Another soft drink materialised from the pocket of the coat. S'pose you don't want to talk to me about all that, do you?'

Charlie turned back towards the game.

Egan didn't seem even slightly put off by the lack of response. 'Why didn't they give you a guvvie car if you're working? I mean, sorry, I'm pretty sure a smashed-up Saab with bald tyres isn't gub'ment issue, hey?'

'Well, I'm doing the government's work, but I'm not really government,' replied Charlie testily. 'I'm sort of an independent contractor. How do you know that's my car, anyway?'

'Cos I know it isn't anyone else's car. And it's got a Melbourne dealership sticker on the back window. And you can't get them takeaway coffee cups in Dauphin that you got rolling around on the passenger floor. And it's got an e-tag. You want me to go on?'

He took a slurp from the can. 'I was hoping I might get to talk to you.' The umpire's whistle blew in the middle of the ground. Egan nodded towards a figure seated on a car bonnet with his feet on the fencing rail. 'You're after Paddy hey?'

'Is that Patrick Lanegan?'

'Yep, that young bloke on the car.'

Charlie followed his gaze, and took in the youthful slouch, dirty runners, scruffy buzz-cut growing out. He was dressed in tracksuit pants and a bomber jacket, and seemed unaware that he was being observed, focusing steadily on the game. Charlie could see the car was an old Holden, maybe a Camira.

'He was definitely out there, you know. Patrick, I mean. I heard the cops got a statement from him and he reckons he was home watchin a video movie.'

Charlie turned full body towards him. The man was watching

73

the sky above the grandstand. 'See, I reckon youse missed a couple of important bits.'

Charlie was unsure what this meant, and decided to ignore it. 'Do you know Patrick?'

'Nah. Never met. But you sort of know who people are, even if you don't *know* them. You know?'

A fight had erupted on centre wing. Players ran in to throw haymakers. The crowd bellowed and surged forward. Someone was prone on the ground under the feet of the brawlers. On the boundary line, a wiry man with white hair roared and jabbed his finger at the umpire. His voice only partially carried over the distance, but Charlie clearly picked up his accented *fook you*.

'He's pretty worked up,' Charlie observed.

'Father Bill?' Egan seemed taken aback by Charlie's sudden laughter. 'Got a terrible temper. He was a bantamweight in his younger days. Still does all the conditioning coaching for the footy club. They have to get him to sit in his car some weeks.'

'What business has a priest got with punching people?'

Egan seemed affronted by the question. 'Bible doesn't say nothin about boxing, far as I know.'

The brawl continued unabated.

'Have you given a witness statement?'

'Me? Shit no. I'm a pretty simple feller, Henry.'

'Charlie.'

'Yep. I'm pretty straightforward, just potter about. No one's innerested in what I think.' The can was emptied with another lusty gulp. 'So why don't you go introduce yourself?'

'Why don't *you*? You're living in the town with the bloke. If you know so much about him, seems a bit rude that you haven't met.' Charlie noticed that the young man Egan had pointed out was not among those bellowing at the fight. He was standing very quietly, observing the observers.

There was no prospect that the annoying Egan would wander

74

off, or that Charlie could approach Patrick Lanegan while he remained in the vicinity. Charlie decided to follow the smell of frying food towards the grandstand, and found a small canteen window in the old weatherboard wall under the grandstand stairs.

Inside there was a deep fryer under a rangehood, the stainless steel baskets submerged in fizzing oil. Off to one side, a man in a white coat sat on a plastic chair by a drinks fridge, his cheek resting on a fist while he stared out at the ground. His face was drawn, bony and faintly European, ringed by white hair around the base of his skull. He took no notice of Charlie's approach to the counter.

'Could you do me a couple of dimmies?' asked Charlie.

The man didn't answer, but slowly climbed off the chair and scooped two frozen lumps from a chest freezer, tossing them in the frying basket.

'Two bucks.'

Charlie found change in his pocket and placed it in the outstretched palm, still slightly chilled. The change disappeared into a till drawer, and the silence descended again. Seeing the burger menu offered a 'Jim's special', Charlie felt inclined to try his luck.

'So. Are you Jim?'

'Yeah.'

'Right. Okay. Good,' said Charlie. 'Been in the frying game long?'

'Frying game? Oh. Forty-one years.' He lifted the basket, thumped the dim sims out onto a sheet of paper and tonged them into a bag. 'Soy?'

'Yes please.' Charlie gave him the biggest smile he could find. 'What's the best local fish?'

'None of it. All comes down from Melbourne. Frozen. You want anything else?'

'That'll be perfect. Thanks so much.' He threw the man of granite a wink, purely to give him the shits. There was no response.

Returning to the boundary line, Charlie found Barry Egan

had left his boundary-line perch and was now deep in conversation with the goal umpire at the far end. Lanegan remained solitary and unmoving on the front of the Camira like a Rodin hood ornament. It was a tricky opening, but Charlie had to start somewhere.

He drifted over and leaned on the fence in front of the passenger headlight, glancing casually back at Lanegan.

'How's it going?'

Lanegan studied him in silence for a moment, one eyebrow cocked warily. 'Goin fine.'

'You get down to the footy much?' *Shit line.* Charlie winced inwardly.

Lanegan's eyes darted over him, took in his clothes, his indoorness, his otherness. He made an assessment and gave it voice. '*No,* I don't get down to the footy. Much.' His lip curled in open ridicule and he turned his back, climbed into the car and started it up. It clunked and smoked as Lanegan engaged reverse and pulled away. Charlie couldn't even bear to look back.

The footballers had visibly slowed as the weight of mud impeded their movements. The ball was making a heavy thud off the boot and the strain of the last quarter was audible in the breathless calls from downfield. He had seen and heard enough. The town had revealed itself to him by giving away absolutely nothing.

CUT ADRIFT FROM the routines of his life, Charlie Jardim was slightly surprised to find when he read the paper Les had left on the bar that it was Saturday night. The pub was quiet. The difference, according to Les, was that the usual Saturday night band had been moved to Sunday because of the long weekend: with Skip on remand Les was now in charge of booking bands.

The punters stood and slumped and sat. An effete student of maybe twenty demonstrated a drop punt to a heavy woman in crushed velvet and beads. Two men with broken skin and wire hair laughed gently while a bored girl watched the air between their chests. A small, sad-looking man on a stool with heavy glasses and greasy comb-over was encircled by four concerned listeners, the words drifting across in sharp fragments.

'Did you ever shoot anyone?'

'I shot *at* some people.'

Charlie had secured the same position near the wall at the end of the bar where he'd wound up on the previous two nights.

The sad man wasn't quite done. 'There was one bloke I'm pretty sure I hit...'

Les kept taking the empties away along with money from the little pile on the bar towel, so that Charlie had no idea how much he'd drunk. Thoughts wandered casually through his head like strangers at a bus terminal, lingering momentarily before being conveyed away to somewhere else. Les was talking to him.

'It wasn't always like this, you know.'

'Like what?'

'The town wasn't always this, um…' he searched for the word. 'Dormant.'

Charlie had his head propped on a fist on the bar. 'Now why would it be dormant? The shit climate? The swamps out the back? The lack of any discernible civic history?'

Once again, Les looked pained but chose to press on.

'They found gold up the river in the eighteen-hundreds. Dragged a fortune in wool down the main the street and out onto the wharf. Wheat, rock lobster, federal ministers…jeez, we had a state amateur tennis champ, lived in the same street as that house you're in.'

'Gosh.'

'Yeah, I know. You've seen it all, haven't you young fella. This place goes back a long way, goes back *deep*. And it'll outlast you and me.'

Les leaned forward on the bar, closing the space between him and Charlie. 'I'll tell you the thing about *you*, right. You and this town. Okay?'

'Go on.'

'See, in the spring of 1963—I was just a little tacker but I remember—there was this terrible southeasterly gale.

'Just blew and blew and it brought in five inches of rain on Melbourne Cup day and the swell threw boulders up onto the road, it was so wild. The whole coast and all the ports on it are shaped to cope with the sou-westers, so when it comes up hard from the other way, it gets right into everything. Rained so hard, the water came up out of the river and the entire place was knee deep in frogs. Whole thing lasted about three days all up, wrecked everything. People were wandering around dazed when the rain stopped, least that's the way it felt to me as a child. The holy and apostolic Roman Catholic Church weren't above exploiting that either, I'll have you know. Most of the adults I knew were looking into their laps for fear of raising their eyes to the lectern, by reason of their various sins, and I was asking my little self what else could He inflict upon us? And it was later that Sunday that they found it.'

Les paused for emphasis and refilled Charlie's pot. He shoved it neatly back across the bar.

'Thanks,' said Charlie. 'Found what?'

'It was well known that you could pick up all sorts of useful stuff after a big blow—timbers and ropes, stuff that's come adrift from the boats. You have to understand about Gawleys, there's a wash through that bay. They call it the longshore drift. All the shit sweeps through from the river mouth towards the northeast—winds up down at the eastern end of the beach. Always working away, moving everything through, constant as gravity. The floats, yeah the timbers, like I said. Dead things, people's crap, all splintered and washed up in the high tide line down there. Anyway, someone found this thing along Gawleys and word went racing through the place—'

'Well?' Charlie was aware, despite the insulation of the booze, of his role in the drama. 'What was it?'

'It was a *mine*.' Les's lips pulled back as he uttered the word. His cheeks had pulled both brows down over his eyes as though his face were sprung with unseen cables.

'War'd been over for near twenty years, and here's this German sea mine. Six hundred pounds of ammonium nitrate. *Unstable* ammonium nitrate. They laid em all along the coast from Cape Otway to the border. Y'don't think of the Germans lurking around out there, do you? All the way from Europe, pokin around, just out there. Least I never did. They dropped em in the ocean anchored to a bloody great chain, ship-size chain. And there they sat, mostly. War ended, everyone shook hands, but no one told the mines. And it turns out they could drag the chains. Big enough swell, they'd break loose, drift towards shore. In the dead of night.'

He took a glass from the rack and poured himself a beer. Drew a thoughtful sip from the top of it.

'You think about that. Cover of darkness, the world asleep, and these wicked bloody things creeping towards the shore, inch by inch, hour after hour. Sometimes, over the years, they'd detonate on their own chain if the links came into contact with one of the horns. Sometimes they'd take out a fishing boat—poor bastards'd just fail to come home, and people would say, you know, maybe they drifted off course or they hit a reef or something. We used to shit-scare each other at school; about how the cops were called out from time to time to collect pieces of them, blown to bits, headless, burnt. Down the end of the bloody longshore drift like everything else.'

He shrugged. 'But as I say, this was over years and years. The war was long gone when I was a kid. Then this thing turns up on our beach. It didn't feel random, coming when it did. It felt like a curse on the town. They put a fence around it while they waited for the people to come from Melbourne who knew how to defuse it. We were all told to stay away, so of course I skipped school with a couple of mates the week after they found it and we went down there. It was sitting up with all the kelp, covered in barnacles and bits of weed. Horns like spider's fangs, hateful-looking things.

'We'd got under the little fence pretty easy and we just walked up to it. It was taller than we were, and the thing I remember now is we were whispering. I think we all thought that if you talked too loud it'd go off. I can still see one of the others walking around it with his mouth hanging open and his hands in front of him like *that...*' He spread his fingers before him as though feeling forwards in the dark.

'He had his fingertips maybe two inches off the surface of the thing. I was so scared I was shaking, I couldn't suck a decent breath outta the air. Then this other kid, he produces a ruler from his bag, and the minute he took it out I was thinking, no, don't, but

I didn't say a thing because the whole trip out there, it was like a dare, you know? Who's the toughest. So he taps it on the hull of the bomb before we could stop him. It just made this little *tink*, and in that instant my heart stopped and I thought I was going to be torn into scraps of shredded meat, the bits all sandy, and they'd never quite find all of me. The seagulls'd be fighting over the little bloody shreds o' me. *Tink*. I ran for me life, didn't stop running till I got home. I was so frightened I told my parents everything and I got a hell of a beating for it but I didn't even care, I was so glad to be away from the thing.

'Anyway that was that. But thing is, the fear in the town got to a point that they actually stopped the men from Melbourne, when they got to us. Wouldn't let 'em out there to do their work because they were so afraid they'd accidentally detonate it and take us all out. The mine was a couple of miles out of town, for godsake, but they wouldn't see reason. These men must've been dumbfounded— they'd driven all the way out here, probably expected a pretty fond reception, coming to eliminate the menace, so to speak. But no, not this lot.

'I don't get that at all,' said Charlie. 'That's ridiculous.'

'No, it sounds ridiculous to you because you're seeing it from the outside. Look at it their way: first the storm, then the mine, then this crew turns up, city people, wanting to fix the problem.'

'Well the locals were hardly going to fix it, were they?'

'Doesn't matter. They'd take...well, paralysis—doin nothing— over some risky intervention from up the highway. The problem was *theirs*, and they weren't going to cop outsiders pushing a solution on them.' He leaned forward. 'Sound familiar at all?'

Charlie didn't respond.

'So they ignored em at first, wouldn't put em up or sell em a drink. Rudeness, just like you're gettin. Bomb fellers wouldn't leave, the Atchesons parked a tractor across the beach access down there, someone else messed with the army truck. Stupid, juvenile stuff—just harassment really—so they had to work at night, under big lights...

'Only took them about half an hour in the end, though. I saw it on the back of the truck in the main street. Just a harmless ball of rusty iron after all that. Heavy thing, mind you. They had it lashed down to the bed of the truck to stop it rolling around, which only made it look more like some beast they'd had to subdue. The locals wouldn't even look at it, wouldn't acknowledge the army blokes. They just wanted to see it gone. They wanted the army blokes gone and they wanted the mine gone. It affected people around here very badly.'

His tone had softened as he spoke, and now he fell silent.

'Why the hell are you telling me this?' asked Charlie after a little while.

'Because you don't understand what you're dealing with here. There's a deep core to this place. There is in any small town. People in close confinement. Sure, there's plenty of the outside world here now, but a part of this community is still looking out through their venetians at people like you. They associate you with bad things. Taking a spanner to their mine. Everyone knows those boys, the ones who done it, and Paddy's brother, the dead one. Everyone feels like they're on trial.'

He snorted and waved vaguely at the interior of the pub. 'Everyone needs a Murchison, one way or another. So they want you to start up your truck and leave.'

'What do I do?'

Les had his pot glass tipped on an angle, regarding it with a worried look. He drank the remaining beer and poked the glass into another tray with a sigh.

'Do it his way. Don't do it your way.'

A group of newcomers walked in the door and Les resumed his public face, beaming and taking orders. Whatever it was in the man that had just surfaced was now hidden from view.

SHE TRIES TO make a decent fist of it under cross-examination. Woollacott does a serviceable job for the other side without breaking a sweat: there are enough problems for Hayley Swan to explain that it doesn't take any great feat of advocacy to tie her up. The older kid's got Asperger's. The little one's fine except for a bit of eczema. They'd have got on, struggled through, because she loves them fiercely. But there are peds circling their lives like sharks, waiting without expenditure of energy for a swimmer to tire. Her mother's de facto, for one: the one who likes to call himself a step-grandpa, the one with the knowing look behind his creepy little santa-claus smile. The social workers can't say for sure that he's breached the feeble walls of her protection, but there's a sense of inevitability about it. If he hasn't already, he's going to. She's been living at her mother's, with the old bastard in a caravan out the back due to orders made years ago which prevented him associating with minors. And the aluminium shell of the Jayco isn't going to hold him back forever. She watches over them but she falters; she'll fall for men who tie her off and ease the needle in, send her nodding while those children sleep. So they sleep, hair askew and mouths open in peace, and one of those men, or the one in the caravan, will move watchfully in the night, will slip into the room that smells of schoolbags and stale bedding. Creeping and feeling forwards in the gloom, murmuring reass-urances. Slumping against the woodgrain plastic of the stereo, she will never know. The promises and threats they weave around her children will ensure she'll never know.

So she's trying to tell the magistrate that she's done the course. She's been to the office where she's tearfully explained the smack and the men who visit and the need she has for the two forlorn little shadows she tows through life. She's told him the social workers are impressed by her efforts, but everyone knows they aren't. She's told him she's completed urine screens, learning to use the clinical jargon rather than talk about pissing in a cup. The language in the social workers' reports is not for Hayley, it's for the consumption of others, even though the reports are built from the aggregate of her admissions, the very enzymes in her piss. To Charlie, over the course of four hearings, the language has remained clear in its intent: this girl cannot go on as a mother. Biology is beside the point. No one can conceive at fifteen and again at seventeen in the midst of multiple, all-consuming addictions and a deviant cavalcade of sexual partners, each of them enmeshed in separate tangles of lives and courts; no one can walk the streets and no one can hawk their skinny ribs to the prodding fingers of strangers and be a mother.

So little Hayley Swan stands there in her tracky dacks and pulls at one side of her hair as Charlie takes her through her evidence. Yes, she washes the children. No, nobody else does, except occasionally her mum. Yes, she tries to wash their clothes when she has coins for the laundry and can get a machine to herself. Yes, she cooks a bit, and yes, the kids get takeaway when they're good. Yes, she receives a single parents pension, and yes there have been times when she's had a de facto living with her and shouldn't have qualified at that rate. No, she's never bought drugs with the children in her care. No, she's never denied buying drugs, and yes, the drugs are mainly meth and mull, but there have been periods on smack as well. Yes, she's been given cash by people who've stayed with her and her mother, and yes, she's had sex with some of those people, but it's never been discussed, the sex and the money. It's just money that helps cover the cost of these people being there. The sex, she agrees, is independent of that. It just happens. Most of the time she agrees to it happening.

Charlie leaves her to the Department's lawyer for cross-examination, thinking she's given herself a slim chance, where before she'd had none. If dull honesty can feed the machine the same way bureaucracy does, then the machine should be sated. Each problem he's handed her from the report he holds in front of him, she's wrestled into a response with her awkward language, wrapping her thin words around it until it seems she's smothered that one, the next and the next. Sometimes she sounds feisty; she's got explanations for some of the barbs in those reports. The social workers are perched on their generous arses in the gallery, looking grim. Charlie knows if they fail today they'll be back within months. A new report, another twenty urine screens and another chance to prise the children from Hayley Swan.

But the moment the cross-examination begins, it's clear they've already won. As the morning wears on she's tiring, and worse than that, she's hanging out. Charlie knows the lost concentration, the picking at the skin, the repetitive drumming of the fingers. She's looking at the clock while unanswered questions hang in the air. The magistrate is losing patience and he's a bastard at the best of times. Underneath the cheap lace edging, her top may as well bear the words 'Need to score urgently'. Time is slipping away towards the lunch adjournment, when she'll be on her own for an hour, and he can do nothing to hasten the cross-examination, which by now is raking over things that interest no one. The magistrate keeps feeding questions to the cross-examiner, fuel for the bonfire. 'Ms Woollacott, I don't think you asked her about the urinary tract infections…' When the old turd adjourns for lunch, Hayley bolts from the building without a word, Charlie following in time to see her heading east down the laneway in the rain. The social workers cluck around him, talking over each other in their eagerness to condescend. You gave it a shot dear. She's gone. It's for the best.

He wanders out with the rain speckling the shoulders of his coat, then working its way under his collar. Makes his way to Russell Street, looping through video arcades, an alien in a suit. No one looks at him. None wears any sign of having passed her a foil and taken her cash. She's gone, swallowed whole by the city.

He circles back towards the court, and as he reaches the stairs he can see her sitting there. The damn bag she hauls everywhere, piled by her side. In it, the photo she presses on those who challenge her. He's seen it many times: her in the full blush of health, heavier, smiling and bathed in sun, a baby clutched to her shoulder and a stumping toddler in the foreground, reaching towards the camera. The optimism caught in that instant is unbearable: the impossibility of a child and her children.

He rushes up the first few steps and hauls her to her feet. 'Where did you go? We were getting somewhere...' But her head is limp and heavy. The fury wells up in him and he grips her chin, yanks her face up. There are tears gathered in her eyelashes, pooled and not falling, and the eyes are not hers anymore. A sucking, choking horror consumes him and he looks down at the arm he's taken, at the crook of her elbow, where a bright spot of blood sits in the smooth white curve of her skin.

On the nights when the dream doesn't come back to him so strongly it is the only transmission he receives: just that arm, that skin, that tiny prick of blood.

The banging came distantly through his sleep. He felt it had been going on for a long time before he'd heard it. He opened one eye and looked at the clock on the bedside table. In bloody red numerals it said 3:24.

The banging was harder than polite but not quite smashing. Groups of three, evenly spaced.

'What?' he called. The knocking stopped then resumed, this time on the glass.

It was still windy outside, and he could hear the roof creaking as gusts caught the eaves. He sighed, reached the kitchen and turned on the outside light. Next to the laundry sink he paused for a moment.

'Who is it?'

The knocking stopped.

'Can you just open the door?' came a female voice.

Charlie waited again, head down and listening, as the light fed back into the room through the gaps in the curtains.

He opened the door sharply and startled a girl, who was midway through the motion of hitting it again. A pretty girl, badly dyed blonde hair pulled back, her body indistinct in a heavy jumper and scarf. Teenager. She watched him for some time before she spoke.

'You the prosecutor from Melbourne?'

Charlie rubbed his eyes wearily. He'd collapsed after half a dozen more beers, staggered back to the house in the early evening and finished up snoring in front of infomercials in the banged-up armchair. Only the incessant clattering of the wind outside had roused him enough to reach the bed.

'Uh huh.' There was nothing but ocean and wind out there. Where had this girl come from?

'I think I can help you with…what you're doing.'

'What's that mean?' He stood aside in the doorway. 'Do you want to come in?'

'Nah. But I, um, I want to talk. To you.' She motioned slightly with a tilt of her head, and Charlie stepped onto the doormat.

'About what?' he began. There was a sound to his right and he looked that way just long enough to see a figure running from behind the hot water tank, straight at him and the girl. He couldn't register why someone would be doing that, where this person had come from, whether it was him or the girl who was in danger. But he knew it was danger of some kind.

He was able to form that thought plainly in the instant before there was a massive bolt of pain from his ear, and he fell. He felt weight on his ribs and looked up to see a male face under a baseball cap. Young, maybe a little older than the girl, and twisted with fury. His shirt was loose and it flapped wildly as he raised a fist and punched him in the eye.

'Fucker,' he spat, and slapped Charlie across the face. 'You like that, arsehole?'

'Get *off* me,' Charlie blurted. 'What do you want?'

There was no answer, but his assailant got up and grabbed him by the front of the T-shirt, punching down hard onto an area between Charlie's cheek and his nose. As the stinging and the tears cleared, Charlie could feel blood starting to run warm down the side of his face and into his ear. He felt a kick in his ribs, then another and another.

'Leave him,' came the girl's raised voice. Charlie could hear panic in her tone. She seemed to be hitting the person who was hitting him, because his body rocked towards Charlie's a couple of times. The male face appeared close to his, and for the first time he took a long look at it—a thin nose, high cheeks and pale eyes. He had a light, wispy stubble and a cold sore in the corner of his mouth. The mouth was open and moving but he needed time to follow the words.

'Stay the *fuck* away from Paddy Lanegan. You listening? Leave him fucken alone.' He pointed straight between Charlie's eyes. 'Fucken idiot.'

The man jabbed a short punch into the fibro wall behind Charlie's head, breaking through the surface with a loud clatter. Charlie could hear his light footfalls as he skipped off the timber decking and was gone, the girl with him. He lay on the doormat and coughed painfully.

So Patrick Lanegan had an ally after all. He felt a need to lie where he was, pinned under the deafening chorus of pain, his eyes turned up towards the eaves. Bugs had gathered around the globe above him, swirling round and round in endless, pointless circles.

FROM THE ROAD, the property looked like a picture of rural tranquility. Small and functional, with hedges of dark cypress on the windward side. A lush bed of green pasture fenced with barbed wire and redgum squatted directly in front of the house. Three listless-looking calves regarded Charlie's approach. The driveway was marked by a cut-open white plastic tub that served as a mailbox. A childish hand had written '4231' on it in thick black texta. Charlie picked his way over a cattle grid at the gate and walked towards the house.

As he got closer to the house, the disarray revealed itself. A child's bicycle lay in long grass where the gravel met the over-growth. Sheets of corrugated green plastic had been used as shades around the front door of the house, casting a sickly green glow on the cement sheeting exterior. A rusty dark green Camira wagon was parked on the drive, the same one he'd seen parked at the footy the previous day.

Seeing no buzzer on the front door he rapped loudly on the metalwork of the flywire. He could hear children inside the house. There was a thump and the deeper growl of an adult voice, followed by the sound of nearing footsteps. The door swung open to reveal the thin features of Patrick Hughes Lanegan.

'Jesus,' he blurted. Charlie had forgotten about his face. A boy of primary school age peered out from around Lanegan's hip. 'What happened to his face Paddy?' he asked, staring.

'Shut up Benny,' came the curt reply. Lanegan swung the door open and stopped it against its springs with his booted foot. He raised his chin.

'Yeah?'

Charlie knew there was no easy way to start this conversation. 'I'm Charlie Jardim,' he began. 'I'm—'

'From the footy. You think I'm stupid? You're a prosecutor.' The whole of Patrick Lanegan's lanky frame prickled with hostility.

'What do you want?'

'I'd like to talk to you about your brother's death.'

The boy grunted something at him as he said these words and kicked his small foot at the screen door. Lanegan aimed a back-hand swipe at the side of his head. 'Fuck off Benny. Go an find the others.' The kid aimed one last vicious look at Charlie and disappeared into the gloom.

'I've already told the local coppers what happened. Go ask them for a copy, okay?'

'I just need to go through it again quickly, if you don't mind,' said Charlie. He was about to lose this bloke, but his face hurt and he wasn't going to give him the pleasure of begging for an audience.

'Then go get a copy and go through it. I'm done with the coppers. I'd prefer it if you got off my fucking property. Please.'

'Well,' sighed Charlie. 'I will, but I tell you what. I've driven a fucking long way to get here and smashed up my car on the way. I've tried to be polite but I've had nothing but bloody suspicion and rudeness everywhere I've gone. Leaving aside Les at the pub, this has got to be the meanest, most paranoid little shithole I've ever been sent to...'

Lanegan didn't respond, so he went on.

'What is it with you people? It's like you're under siege for christ's sake. Some dickhead turns up on my doorstep last night and punches me in the head, apparently because I'm here to talk to you, and it's not even like I'm gonna pull you in for something—I'm here to help you out for fuck's sake. Jesus.'

He guessed from the silence inside the house that the kids in there were eavesdropping. 'So okay, I'll leave. I'll turn around and go home, and I won't give this joint another thought. But I reckon you should do me the courtesy of at least listening to me.'

'Yeah, yeah.'

Lanegan regarded him in an exasperated way for a long time.

'Who gave you the floggin?' he said eventually. He rested his chin on the sleeve of the arm holding the door.

'I don't know. Young bloke, had a girl with him.' Charlie's hand went up unconsciously to the lazy bulge of swelling over his left eye.

'That's odd,' said Lanegan flatly. 'Come in.'

The kitchen was crowded with food in various stages of its life: groceries not yet unpacked from plastic bags, bitten sandwiches on the benches, fruit in a bowl and strewn across a tabletop. Smeared dishes were left where they'd been attacked. The smell of old meals in the room was distantly comforting.

Charlie took a seat at a table surfaced in linoleum and edged with rusty chrome. Lanegan had put a kettle on the stove and was looking for mugs. Two boys now stood in the doorway, their curiosity beating out their shyness. They were more or less identical, even dressed the same, their straight, reddish brown hair bowl-cut over a spray of freckles. One of them held a figurine at Charlie's eye level. 'It's a Transformer,' he said gravely. 'It's mine.'

Patrick brought him the coffee he hadn't asked for and the boys scattered again in response to some unseen cue. Instant, pale with milk and made in a heavy, chipped mug. Charlie accepted it gratefully, though he'd intuited enough to the ways of this town to know that being given coffee was no sign of warmth. It was the proper observance of ritual and nothing more. The silence mounted.

'So, the twins are eight, hey?'

'Yep.'

'And you're, what, twenty-three? That's a fair spread.'

'Mm.' Patrick was fiddling with a plastic robot at the other end of the table, prising at a battery cover with a small screwdriver.

'Folks must've started early, hey?' Charlie cursed himself inwardly.

Patrick's brows lowered in irritation. 'No, not really.'

The silence descended again, broken eventually by Patrick.

'So what's up?'

'Well you seem to know who I am,' began Charlie. 'I work with the Office of Public Prosecutions. I'm a barrister, a freelance lawyer if you like, but I'm doing a job with the OPP at the moment. That job is the murder trial of the two men who killed your brother.'

Patrick redoubled his focus on the robot. 'Aha.'

'I'm working with a senior crown prosecutor on this matter. We divide up the various things that need to be done and—as you can imagine, there's a fair bit of work to do, especially when you've got two defendants, two sets of lawyers and so on...'

'Mm. Must be full on.' Patrick had got the screwdriver into the innards of the robot, which now cleaved open with a loud plastic *snap*.

'We've got a lot of evidence to get through, Patrick. There's all the police work, the telephone intercepts, the searches of cars and houses, the pathology on your brother's...on your brother. There's the other forensics, like the weapon.'

'Yep.'

'And there's your evidence.'

Charlie's words were drowned by a loud clatter as the boy from the doorway reappeared, running through the kitchen chased by someone larger. Charlie's gaze shot from the boy to his pursuer as she came through the doorway.

Blonde hair, roughly dyed. Big, dark eyes. Prettier than he remembered, and younger; maybe fifteen. Definitely her.

She stopped abruptly in the doorway and stared at him. He could feel her gaze wandering over his face, the comically bulging eye, the graze under his chin. Then she was gone, leaving the kid to scuttle after her somewhere in the gloom at the front of the house. Charlie looked back at Patrick, immediately filled with suspicion. He was still probing at the robot.

He looked up, fixing Charlie with a very direct gaze. 'What happened to your face anyway?'

'I told you. Someone came over last night and gave me a flogging.' He stared back until Patrick returned his attention to the toy. Charlie could detect no sign that he had any idea of what had just happened.

'Who was that in the doorway?'

'That's my sister, Milly. Say hello, Milly,' he called over Charlie's shoulder towards the door. The response came from somewhere in the front half of the house. Nonchalant.

'So,' resumed Charlie. 'Your evidence. I don't want you to take this the wrong way, but both the senior prosecutor and I, we read your statement and we think it isn't right. That is, we don't think you've told the truth.' He watched Patrick carefully as he said this.

Patrick's face didn't change. 'What makes you think that?' he asked.

'Look, it's not a criticism of you, okay. We see this sort of thing a fair bit. Sometimes people are protecting someone else, sometimes they're under pressure from somebody, sometimes they're trying to do what they think is right. But usually the logic in the statement just isn't there, and that's, that's what we thought when we read yours. I don't believe you would've sent your brother off into danger that night without supporting him. I don't think Murchison and McVean would've taken off in a hurry as they did, leaving the *Caravel* burning, unless they had a more pressing concern, and I think that concern was that you had got away. That's a pretty reasonable assumption isn't it?'

'I've said what I've said. The rest is your problem, mate.'

'Well yes, it is for the time being. But the thing is, the defendants' lawyers are going to see through it just as easily as I have and they'll be coming from a different angle. They'll be saying *you* did it.' He drained the coffee. 'Then it's *your* problem.'

Patrick put the robot down and swiped it with his finger so that it spun on its back. 'I'll just have to take my chances on that front. Are you done?'

'I'm done,' said Charlie, with an air of surrender. He scooped his mug and placed it on the sink. 'Thanks for the coffee.'

As Charlie headed for the front door, down that dark hallway that filled him with unaccountable sadness, he sensed Patrick was close behind him, shepherding him in his haste to get him out of the place. As if he was an ill omen or a harbinger of misfortune. Patrick closed the front door firmly before Charlie was over the doormat.

He was reaching for the car door when a voice from the side of the house stopped him. The girl, Milly. She was breathless as she approached, nervous. Charlie felt justified in letting her squirm.

'What?'

'I just wanted to say sorry.'

'For what?'

'For last night. Like, I didn't know he was gonna do it. I thought he just wanted to warn you off, y'know. I mean I thought he'd—I didn't think he'd hit ya like that.'

'Yeah? Well, tell him from me he's a fucking savage. And seeing as you got me out there so he could do it, all I can think is you're a dirty little mole and you don't know any better.'

He expected she'd fire up, which, he figured, is why anyone calls a mole a mole. But her reaction surprised him: her face crumpled and she began to cry.

'We're just—trying—to—look after him,' she sobbed. She was leaning on the back of the Saab now, clenching her jaw in an effort to stop the sobbing. 'He's good, Paddy. *Good*. You don't under-stand what he's dealing with—it's you, it's the welfare, the bloody Murchisons, it's where the money comes from, it's who looks after the little ones. He's not coping. He's gonna be the next one to go at this rate. It'll do him in, I swear. This fucking family'—she heaved a great ragged sob from somewhere in her throat—'it's a mess. Been a shitstorm for years. Why do you have to pile up even more crap on us? Why can't you all just fuck off and leave us alone?' She was beseeching him. Charlie had no idea where to look. He certainly couldn't look back at her.

'Arch was a fucking idiot to give you a belting like that. I don't expect you to believe me, but he thought he was helping us. I'm, I'm sorry,' she sniffed.

'Yeah. Right.'

'He's me boyfriend,' she said softly. 'Sort of. Has been for two weeks anyway. I arksed him to come along when I went to your place because I was too scared to go on me own. I didn't know he was gonna do that. I never would've been a part a that. The fucken idiot was tryin to impress me.'

Suddenly she stuck her hand out, offering it to Charlie. He must have stared at it for an uncomfortably long time. Where he came from, girls in motocross T-shirts didn't shake hands, didn't lift their reddened eyes to a stranger they'd ambushed and expect compromise. He was, yet again, a fumbler in a foreign land. He took the hand and shook it. It was warm and strong, and the first comforting thing he could remember in a long time.

THE BAND WERE doing a sound check in the public bar. The chrome rims of the drum kit caught the lights as a skinny guitarist plugged a lead into his amp, the pop and hum causing nearby drinkers to clutch at their ears.

Charlie's phone had gone dead, as it frequently did when he needed it. He leaned against the heavy stone pillar behind the bar and dialled Weir's home number on the pub's phone, another small courtesy extended to him by Les. The big man's generosity had him baffled. As the guitarist ran the edge of his pick down a guitar string with a metallic *thrring*, the line clicked through, and he was surprised by Weir's voice, raised to a holler and echoing.

'Yairse.'

'Harlan, Charlie.'

'Hello lad. How are we faring?'

'Sorry, I'm just having a little trouble with the line here. Are you hands-free?'

'Better than that. I got a bloke in and he's wired the phone through the stereo. I can just walk around the house talking, see, and your voice is coming to me in surround sound. I change rooms, I've still got you. Infra red, I think. Bluetooth or something. I'm in the living room now.'

'Call me a Luddite Harlan, but why the hell would you want to do that?'

'The pursuit of applied thought.' There was a hint of mock

pomposity; he knew how he sounded. 'You filter out the distractions and you're thinking without impediment. I did a plea deal the other day with the Bearded Basque, never left my kitchen bench. This is that thing in Pascoe Vale—you know it?—I was chopping coriander. Anyway, his bloke'll nod to reckless endangerment and we'll drop the culpable, and I had a whole laksa slapped together by the time I got rid of him. I don't know what the Basque was doing at the time, probably guzzling scotch in chambers under that bloody great portrait of Ignatius Loyola. So me, I've got my hands free, but the sound quality's beautiful, that's the thing, and you don't have to have one of those idiotic real estate spruiker things attached to your ear. You can gesticulate, pace up and down. Hey? And I've got a better sense of your inflection and so forth. Booming out of the ceiling. But I'm sure that's not why you rang, is it?'

Charlie imagined him in the living room he'd only ever seen once. Neat, orderly and functional, a repudiation of his seniority. Fishing photos. A big Rank Arena telly from the eighties. Couches in a floral pattern the dear departed Pamela had picked out. Lampstands, art that was tasteful, even progressive, and evaded any suggestion of Weir's role. A detailed litho of a wattle bird in a thin gilt frame. Seascapes done in thick, gloopy oils that made no sense at five paces, but resolved into photorealistic clarity from across the room. Framed portraits of his daughters, and Pamela, standing conversationally together in a recess on the bookshelf. A room that spoke of man without a need for fearsome projection, a man who at home became a hermit with a TV guide and socks.

'Wasn't the laksa a distraction?'

'Goodness me, no. There's no better stimulus to clear thought than semi-sedentary activity. Something your body can do without cerebral oversight. Walking, for instance. Now tell me'—Charlie had the feeling he'd stopped pacing and was standing under one of his ceiling speakers, in effect peering at him—'what's happening down there?'

'It's not looking good, boss. I've been to see our witness and he's damaged goods. He's seen me coming a mile off, and he doesn't want to co-operate. Half the town knows what I'm up to and you've got a few who support the Murchisons and reckon Lanegan got what was coming to him. There's others who reckon Patrick's mad and there's a few who support him and think I should fuck off.' Charlie picked at the stonework absently. 'I'm not sure how we're going to go, to be honest.'

There was a long silence at the other end.

'How are you coming across to them?'

'What do you mean?'

'I mean…don't take this the wrong way, hmm? But it's going to take some, er, *humility* to break through.'

The picking finger stopped in its tracks and Charlie felt a hot pang of shock.

'I…um. Harlan, are you suggesting I'm up myself?'

Weir's tone immediately softened. 'Not for a second. But you're trying very hard and that means you come over in a particular way. These people are not like you: you understand that don't you?'

'Tonight's my third night drinking at this bar. Believe me, the differences are stark.'

'There you go again—that's where you're going to have trouble. You're an outsider and there's going to be some suspicion that goes with that but you might not be meeting them halfway. Those people *have* to deal with outsiders to some degree, like tourists and bureaucrats and retirees, but it doesn't come easy to them. In the Pitcairn Islands, you're either a local or you're from *away*. How about that for an idea…You either grow up on a speck of rock in the middle of the ocean, or you're an alien. To some lesser degree, lad, you're encountering the same dichotomy. Go easy on them.'

'Harlan, I'll be honest with you. This isn't what I do. I stand up in court and argue, just like you do: all right, obviously not as well as you do it. I don't come from the country, and I'm not going incognito. Fuck, I wear slacks, okay? You sent me down here to talk to a witness to see if the bloke's going to give evidence—*truthful* evidence…' Charlie found himself jabbing his forefinger in the air for emphasis. Heads in the bar had noticed, and he pocketed the offending hand.

'Now there's a fair bit a resistance around the place and I can reliably report that he's not coming through with the goods. I've spoken to him and I don't think he's well. Psychiatrically, I mean. So there's your answer. My car's smashed up, I've been in a fight, I'm talking to myself quite a bit and I've got a few domestic spot fires of my own back home. How about we call it a day on this one, eh?'

Silence filled the line, and somehow Charlie again knew how Weir was standing: hands on hips, staring at his feet with his brows pushed over his eyes. It was a pose he'd adopted on the few occasions Charlie had seen him deeply troubled.

'You need to keep going.'

'Why?'

Charlie felt the idiocy of the whole venture crowding in on him. 'If you tell me to try harder and I start really pressuring this bloke, he's just as likely to blurt it in cross-examination and you and I are going to be flushed out in court as having influenced him. Is that what you want?'

His hands were again making agitated thrusts. A hairy forearm curled around the pillar, placed a beer on the woodwork, then disappeared.

'Let's go back to the plan, eh?' Harlan offered gently. 'You know and I know that the boy knows more than he's said, hmm?'

Charlie could hear his footfalls on the faraway carpet.

'So I can have him brought to court under subpoena, and what will he do? He'll resent us for starters and he'll be out of his element. So he'll revert to type and stand there like a drongo. We can drop him altogether, but the defence are going to smell a rodent and demand that we call him for cross-examination. Besides, we can't just work around him—what sort of jury is going to give us the thumbs up on a circumstantial case with a plainly absent eyewitness?'

'Maybe if he's not going to do it then that's the end, Harlan. Maybe you've just got to accept that it's not going to work. What you've got me doing here is not only fucking annoying, it's also not my line of work and it's potentially impro—'

'Oh get your hand off it, Charlie.'

'Pardon me?'

'You're being paid a daily rate and I got Accounts to cover all your travel expenses, including whatever you rack up in that…hotel of yours. There's a man called Lewis in Dauphin who does smash repairs. I want you to find him and get your car fixed. I've made arrangements to cover it. You've got a little window out of your life over there, lad. No pressure. Isn't that what you've been after?'

Charlie leaned back against the pillar and studied the grotty ceiling tiles. A glass broke somewhere in the public bar. He sighed deeply, the expelled air fanning down from his nose and making a noise in the receiver.

'How much longer?'

'However long you need. If it gets past May, I'll start cooking up adjournments.'

'Mm.'

'Charlie, when this works, and it *will* work, you will have made it happen. One day this kid's going to thank you for getting him into the starting gate. He just doesn't know it yet.'

Charlie took a deep gulp at the beer. It was cold and it felt disturbingly like an old friend. There was no sound from Harlan as he swallowed, exhaled, and leaned heavily on the stonework once again.

'You know, I've got no idea what I'm doing here…'

'None of us know what we're doing. And I mean that in the

big sense. Let's just stumble on in this direction for a little while, shall we?'

Seized by the impulse to retain a shard of defiance, Charlie clicked the phone gently back onto its hook without a further word and immediately felt mean. He picked up the beer and wandered back towards the bar as a sour-looking woman read meal numbers into the bistro microphone.

THE GIRLS HAD said it would be the last place on the left as you walked towards the TV antenna. They'd been eyeing him as they danced in front of the guitarist, flirting and throwing their hair. He sat through the ritual, unmoved. Their cheap clothes, the lithe bodies, that hair; all of it was new enough to flaunt in the full confidence of youth. For now.

'Where ya from?'

Charlie smiled weakly as the taller of the two leaned down into his face, enveloping him in a cloud of perfume. She had freckles, and a silver sleeper through her eyebrow. 'My mate wants to know where you're from,' she grinned, as the other girl swung a kick at her backside and shrieked, 'Argh! Bitch!'

The tall girl hooted with delight and extended a hand. 'Dance!' she yelled, just as the band rang off the end of a song.

Heads turned and Charlie panicked. 'I'm right thanks.'

She stuck out her lower lip and feigned disappointment, then just as quickly brightened again and told him about the party, only just down the road, and all the booze was laid on because the pub guys would take care of it and the host—Corey? Cody?—was *sooo* hilarious. The band started up again and the room resumed its rhythm.

The girls bumped off across the crowd on some other orbit, leaving Charlie castigating himself for being such a bore.

So he found himself, later, walking alone in the dark, up the street and away from the coast, away from his borrowed home. He was following a cluster of other drinkers, who meandered from the fence line out onto the nature strips, laughing and cursing loudly enough to echo off the fronts of the houses. They swerved into a driveway, between a column of parked cars, all wagons, and up to a brightly lit front door. Charlie followed close enough to hope that he could slip in after them, far enough away that he didn't have to introduce himself.

Up the concrete steps and in the door, painfully collecting the sharp edge of the springloaded flywire screen across his achilles. Tight, cramped hallway. People moving in and out of the doors along the hall that must have led to bedrooms; a bigger crowd down the end where the fluoro lighting suggested a kitchen. Faces he recognised from the pub. The girl who'd made him a coffee. Two or three of the footballers. They were all loudly engaged in their own worlds and their own conversations. He took a left at the bathroom, found the bath full of ice and added the beers he'd brought in a plastic shopping bag.

Taking one in hand, he was headed out towards the party when a couple came in with a loud clatter. They were laughing at something, a joke they'd brought into the room with them. It took them some seconds to register Charlie's presence, by which stage the girl had closed the door.

'Hey!' said the boyfriend. 'Prosecutor guy!'

Charlie was sure he hadn't met these people, but they seemed harmless enough.

'Got a business card?'

Charlie obligingly reached for his wallet, found a thin block of cards inside it. He plucked one out and handed it to the girl.

Charles J. Jardim, Barrister at Law. She read it with mock seriousness.

The two of them set to work on the bathroom vanity, licking and laying out papers, then tipping a generous handful of greenery from a sandwich bag onto the papers. The card was ripped in half lengthwise and coiled into a tight cylinder at one end.

'Is that appropriate?' protested Charlie.

'Mate,' laughed the roller, 'you didn't think I needed a...' he read the remaining half of the card, '...a *rister*, did you? What's a rister anyway?'

'*Bar*rister Dale, ya mong,' giggled the girl. 'He's a barrister. Ya hafta be a barrister to be the prosecutor guy. Der!' She pointed at her temple and stuck her tongue out.

Dale had finished rolling, and he made a great fuss of handing the thick joint and the lighter to Charlie.

'Please sir,' he intoned, all mock-pompous. 'Seeing as you donated the roach...'

Charlie took the joint, dismissing a faint instinct that this mightn't be an intelligent move, and lit up. It was beautifully rolled and it drew well. He took three deep pulls, holding the smoke until it emerged to form a thick cloud around his head. With a sheepish grin he handed it over to Dale.

Then it kicked in.

He grabbed at the vanity for support as his hands and feet became impossibly heavy. His head was drifting, his tongue a giant foreign object in his mouth. The sound of the other two laughing became an indistinct fuzz, yet he could clearly pick up individual words being spoken in the kitchen on the other side of the closed door. There was nausea, but it felt like someone else's.

The girl was talking from far away.

'Oooh,' she was saying, rubbing the small of his back and peering at him. 'Shoulda said. It's hydro. You right?'

He tried taking deep breaths, not wanting to be conspicuous about it. But the surges of new oxygen just fuelled the headlong rush. He braced himself on the vanity, both hands, studying a person looking back in the mirror who wasn't him. Toothbrush, toothbrush, soap. Cosmetics talking to a can of deodorant. Grimy sink. There was a distant roar, a wave breaking in his mind, the calm grin on the face in the mirror indicating an experience he wasn't sharing. His new friends were opening the door, heading out into the crowded kitchen, and he realised with a cold jolt of panic that he was surrounded by complete strangers, stoned out of his mind.

With some trepidation, he removed his clenched hands from the edge of the vanity and directed them to turn the cold tap on. He splashed his face, missed, threw a large handful of water past his left ear. The second handful hit the target. He squinted helplessly and groped around for a towel. Once he'd dried his face, he shuffled slowly out of the bathroom and into the crowd in the kitchen.

Photos on a fridge door—the ones he'd expect to see, pissed people waving beer cans, girls posing up their air-kisses and hugs. Someone's dog, a formal lineup of blokes under the wing of a light aircraft. But then there were the ones among them that he couldn't fathom: cliffs, sheets of layered limestone, waves without surfers, a seabird photographed from below so that the sun penetrated the image as a series of refractive circles. He was disoriented by the idea that the owner of this fridge, the tenants of this house, set as much value on these images of the outside world as they did on their friends.

Charlie stood and pondered, tangled up in a complex scatter of thoughts about whether the appreciation of inanimate things belonged to higher intellects. He couldn't decide, though he felt well-disposed towards these people and there was a warm feeling in his leg muscles.

He surveyed the benches—empty stubbies and wine bottles forested the available surfaces. Pizza boxes in greasy stacks. Faces appeared and retreated from his vision—he smiled where he felt the eye contact was long enough to warrant it. Otherwise he pretended to be looking at a point in the near distance, as though his progress through the kitchen was taking him somewhere in particular. This strategy, of course, had its limits. He'd soon pushed through the kitchen and into a small sunroom at the back of the house, and had to turn around and go back.

As he turned—and somehow he felt this was inevitable—he came face to face with Patrick Lanegan, sitting on the kitchen bench. There was a girl beside him. He had an arm around her waist and she didn't seem to have noticed Charlie. She was short and her features were dark, fine black hair swept glossy over her ears into a loose ponytail. She was dressed in every way as though she came from this place; the jeans, the boots, the heavy jacket; but her face seemed to come from somewhere else, the wild progeny of Scottish crofters or a black Irish uprising. Her skin was flawless. Charlie could feel himself staring, but wasn't able to stop.

Patrick took his incredibly heavy hand and gave it a shake, laughing as he did so. 'Charlie, Charlie…are you okay in there?'

'Yeah, yeah, I just got a flogging from some bastard last night.' Charlie raised a reassuring hand.

'I know you did, ya clown. You told me that this arvo.'

'Oh yeah. Hello, Patrick.'

'You're all right then?' Into his eyes.

'I'm fine, thank you,' insisted Charlie.

'Charlie, this is Kate. Kate, Charlie.' And she turned her caramel eyes fully towards him, taking him in with a noncommittal air. After a short appraisal, she looked away, sighing.

'This is our first night out in a little bit,' said Patrick. 'Isn't it?' He squeezed at her waist affectionately, but she wriggled out of his grip and jumped off the bench, disappearing down the hall. Patrick's voice was raised slightly to compete with the conversation in the room, the dull thump of music under it. 'Sorry. She's not real happy about things. We hardly ever get out, you know.'

'Why not?' *You're swaying*, he told himself. *Stop swaying.*

'All the others, mate. You met the crew—I got a little sister and two little brothers. The twins mate, if ya don't watch 'em all the time, they'd rip the house down.'

'Can't you get someone in to help?'

'Can't afford it. Milly looks after the little men now and then. She's fifteen. But I try not to get her doin it too much, you know. She's got to...' he made a sweeping gesture with his hand. 'She's gotta get out, see people. So it's just me doin the home stuff most of the time. I get the old lady from across the road sometimes, but the young lads, they run fucken rings around her. Anyway, not much fun for Katie—"Come on over and we'll watch a video while the kids run amok." Never mind. Hey, you want some fish?'

He shuffled to one side, revealing a huge sheet of tinfoil on the bench. On it were the remains of a whole fish, pop-eyed and open-mouthed. Its flank had been opened up, pieces of the roasted flesh spilling onto the foil under a colourful scattering of lemon and herbs.

'What is it?' asked Charlie.

'Blue eye. Deep sea fish. Very nice.' Patrick reached into the ice-filled sink. He tore two tinnies off a six-pack and handed one to Charlie, who was still examining the fish.

'Brilliant. What do I—is there a fork?'

'Fucksake,' muttered Patrick. He shovelled a hand into the flank of the fish and scooped out a chunk of flesh, proffering it to Charlie.

'It comes from the trawlers. They go right down the west side of Tassie. See the big guy over there?' Charlie followed his pointing finger across the kitchen to where a heavy man of about fifty stood talking to two young whippets who could only have been surfers. He was grim, built for weather, or by weather. He laughed at something the whippets said, and he seemed to do it reluctantly.

'There's all these rules about their catch limit and the bycatch and all that,' continued Patrick. 'They have to chuck the extra back unless it's buggered. 'Not viable,' they say. So they bring those ones back here,' he shrugged. 'Everyone wins, eh?'

Charlie peeled back the gun-grey skin from the shoulder of the fish and broke off a larger lump of meat. He was suddenly hungrier than he could stand. He stuffed it into his mouth while his other hand opened the beer can. He took a slurp at it while he tried to focus on Patrick's conversation.

'How's your face?' continued Patrick.

'Mmm. Fine.' Nothing was hurting at the moment. Charlie accidentally spat a fleck of fish. 'Gave me a fright though. Doesn't happen all the time in my work.'

Patrick laughed. 'No, I don't s'pose it would. Milly told me it was her new fella. Fucken idiot. I don't expect you to understand this, but it's kind of…it's loyalty that made him do that. He was tryin to help in his own stupid way.'

Charlie couldn't think of a response to this, so he just smiled. His eyes felt heavy.

'You gonna hang around until you get what you came here for?' asked Patrick. His tone had changed very slightly.

'Don't have much else to do at present,' he replied. 'The bloke I work for, he thinks I need to change my approach. Says I'm up myself. So I'll just blend into the scenery till you don't know I'm here.'

'That may take a while.' Patrick slid off the bench and clapped Charlie on the shoulder. 'I'm gonna go find Katie, get meself in some more trouble. I'll see you later eh?'

He eased his way through the room and disappeared up the hallway. Charlie leaned back against the bench, wondering from where any further conversation might materialise. *Everyone in this room is staring at that mouse over your eye,* he told himself. *Everyone's talking about you. Fucking blend in will you?* He took another swig at the can. As he lowered it, felt the fisherman's eyes on him. It was a neutral look, neither friendly nor aggressive.

'You had a good go at that fish?' he called across the kitchen, just above the ambient noise. Charlie nodded amiably in return, raising his can in an idiotic salute.

'Right. Then fuck off.'

THE RAIN HAD started drumming on the tin roof before dawn, easing Charlie out of a heavy sleep. He yawned and surveyed the mildew on the ceiling battens above him. His eye had opened up a little further overnight. Two mosquitoes lifted off the wall above the bed, bumping their way towards the ceiling. His knuckles itched madly and he drew his hands above the bedclothes to find the white-topped mesas of their bites.

From his faraway childhood came a feeling, lying in bed on summer nights after a day on the beach, his brother on the top bunk above him, his body faintly registering the waves of the day, still rocking him in the glow of sunburn and the cool of the sheets.

Now he felt the previous night washing over him and the sensation was nothing like nostalgia. Bloody Weir and his management by decree. The beer, the party, the ill-advised joint. Patrick Lanegan, his very lovely girlfriend, his idiotic resistance. What was he trying to prove?

Charlie rose and stumped his way to the bathroom, feet cold on the vinyl floor. The mirror was blotchy and dull. He traced the pink and yellow arcs around his eye where the colours were leaching slowly out of the bruise. The cut on the bridge of his nose had settled into a dark scab, and the swelling had come down, alleviating the mad-clown effect of yesterday. On the floor beside the handbasin the bloodied clothes he was wearing when he hit the roo lay in a pile. He'd need to wash them at some stage. Not right now, with the remnants of last night sloshing around in his head and his gut.

Twenty minutes later he was out walking the streets, following a photocopied map he'd picked up from the bakery counter. Between puddles, he traced the series of downhill lefts and rights that led to the commercial wharf. The road ended at a carpark with a bank of shopfronts to his left, provedores and stevedores, coolstores, fuel stores. On his right was the cyclone-wire fencing that indicated the water's edge. He walked towards it, took out his phone and dialled her number.

Raindrops pocked the heavy grey surface of the water as he leaned against the wire, taking in the coloured hulls of the fishing fleet, the antennas and lightpoles against the sad steely sky, the timbers of the wharf, the heavy cylindrical uprights that held it inches above the high tide. The phone rang a fourth time and cut abruptly to voicemail. Her voice was calm and slow.

Hi, flat and disembodied. *You've rung Anna Murdoch. I'm sorry I can't take your call right now. Please leave a message.* It was just removed enough from who she was, from the girl he knew her to be, to satisfy the requirements of the clients and colleagues who expected that clinical mantra. The rain had shone the boulders of the breakwalls to rich glossy browns and blacks. The voicemail delivered its starting line bleep and he realised he had nothing to say. Things that he felt and needs that he had, but nothing to say. He fumbled with the silence, wanting to launch some conversational satellite, however flippant, into the frozen void. But he had nothing to offer. He stabbed at the button and slid the phone into his pocket.

In the distance, further along the seawall, he could see the blackened outline of the vessel he'd come to find, the lettering on the stern standing out from the pale blue of the hull.

Caravel.

Under that, smaller, *Port of Dauphin*. The boat was a leper, cast out from among the ranks of the working, the seaworthy, the undefiled. The cabin and superstructure were coated in birdshit, the metal fittings dull with corrosion. The deck area was charred, breaking away and tumbling inwards near the sides of the boat. A long, angry streak of black ran up the cabin wall, blistering the paint as it went. Charlie recognised all this from the forensics lab photos, felt he was in the company of a longstanding acquaintance. He now stood directly opposite the boat across a short stretch of water, and he could see through the grimy cabin windows to where the instruments had been unscrewed from their housings, where the refrigeration unit was gone from its steel base. Rust was slowly burning what the fire had spared. As he looked down at the water-line, he could see a thick forest of weed swaying slowly in the current from the points where it had taken hold between the timbers. A rainbow of oil seeped along the water's surface from the stern.

He pushed his way through a gap in the wire and sat on a boulder with his feet hanging just above the water. With the phone in his hands again, he breathed deeply and tried to focus his thoughts. The rain was gradually soaking him. Birds called over the water, over the poppling of the rain, but the world was otherwise empty and silent.

He bought up Weir's number and knew immediately that he, too, wouldn't be answering. On Sunday mornings he played the cello for hours at a time, by himself, with his front door locked and his phone turned off. Dvořák, Elgar and Haydn, over and over, repeated and refined to an exquisite degree. Charlie only found out about this side of Weir after he'd banged on the kitchen doors of his house in frustration that one Sunday, when they were supposed to be drafting appeal submissions together.

So he let the phone ring, waited for the tone, and this time he knew what he wanted to say.

'Harlan, it's me. Sorry I hung up on you last night, but I needed time to think. I saw our boy again after we talked…saw him at a party. What are you doing at parties, you're going to ask me. I don't know. Probably indicates I should get out of here. Whole project's a dead loss, so…I'm sorry. I'm going to take the car to that panel-beater tomorrow and get something done about the front end so it's safe to drive, and then I'm going to hit the road back to town. I reckon I'll be in chambers Wednesday morning if you want to have a talk about it. Um, yep, sorry. Call me if you want. Okay, bye.'

The rain was getting heavier. He retreated under the awning of a tin building marked CO-OP, and scanned the phone, looking for evidence of an outside world. Weather. A frontal trough. Rain today but clearing tomorrow. A southwesterly swell decreasing overnight to one to two metres by tomorrow.

Charlie was surprised to be interested in this. For as long as he could remember, his physical environment had been subject only to the minute variations of airconditioning: the weather accounted for little more than incremental changes in the light. Here, now, the weather altered the very appearance of the world, by turns stripping and bleaching, shading and saturating the town's colours. The wind, idle at the moment, was nonetheless integral to the shape of the trees, the mood of the sea. His static surrounds had hidden this reality from him: the world was in a state of incessant upheaval.

The phone rang in his pocket. Anna. He grabbed for it, but no. It was a private number. The voice on the line was hesitant, unfamiliar.

'Er, is that Charlie?' He was young; there was wind in the background.

'Who's this?'

'Oh yeah gedday, it's Patrick Lanegan. How you going?'

The petulant strain in Charlie's character surfaced, demanding that he make this difficult. 'I'm fine,' he said shortly. 'Bit dusty after last night maybe.'

There was a gentle laugh. 'You were having a hell of a crack at that fish when I left ya. How's the rain, eh?'

'I thought you get lots of rain here.'

112

'Well, we do, but not straight downwards. Normally it's going sideways.'

'How'd you get my number?'

'Got it from Les…is that okay?'

Jesus Charlie, snap out of it. 'Yeah, of course it is. I guess I'm just wondering where Les got it from.'

There was a faint chuckle on the other end. 'Les works in mysterious ways. He can get you all sorts of things if he feels like helping. You like the pub?'

'I do. I like the pub. I didn't think you would, though. Isn't it part of the Murchison empire?' Charlie had no idea where this conversation was going.

'Yep, but if I took that view, half the bloody town'd be off limits.'

There was a brief silence. 'What can I do for you Patrick?'

'Well I just—weather's gonna clear up tomorrow, and I figured no one's shown you round the place, have they?'

'Nope. They most certainly have not.' *Although people connected with your family have shown me a comprehensive beating.*

'Okay then, you wanna go snorkelling? Milly said she'll take the kids after school, so I'm going anyway. You're welcome to, like, tag along if you want.'

'That'd be great. What do I need?'

'Nothing. I'm guessing you can swim all right?'

THEY'D BEEN DRIVING for a while on gravel when Patrick slowed and started watching the fence line on his left. A high run of dunes had materialised to the south, at the end of the paddocks, the deep concaves of the western sides collecting pools of sharp afternoon sun. Pockmarks of boxthorn and rusty pump equipment scarred their smooth flanks. At intervals a fence line ran up towards the foot of a dune, disappearing into the sand shortly after it began its rise. Charlie wondered whether the fences had run at the dunes, or the dunes were creeping north over the paddocks.

Patrick slowed the Camira and turned left, towards the coast. He came to a gate and plucked a key from the scatter of objects in the console, passing it wordlessly to Charlie. An old windmill clanked away beside the gate as Charlie dealt with the padlock. A new-looking poly tank stood at the foot of the mill. Beside it slumped the shot-up remains of the previous corro tank, and lying on the ground beside the corro was a pile of rusty shards and flakes that could only have been the tank before that one.

The way was reduced to wheel ruts now, and they bounced in and out of holes at a pace that suggested Patrick had no great fondness for the Camira. A final gate at the end of the track signalled the transition from paddock to dune. Swinging it open, Charlie felt a jolt of fear as he realised that Patrick fully intended to keep going. 'You're not going to get this thing through there,' he said by way of question and statement as he climbed back in.

'Why not?'

'How's it gonna go on sand?'

Patrick appeared to consider the question seriously for a moment or two.

'I dunno.' He revved at the engine until it rattled at the high end, and then surged forward through the clumps of marram grass. Charlie could feel the top of each hummock as the floorpan flexed under his feet, could smell the seeds of the grass inside the car. They topped a low headland, and the sea burst into view, flat, dark and serene in the heavy air. Below them on the right, a beach curved away to the west, littered with driftwood and backed by scrub. Dried kelp formed linear tangles along the high tide line, scattered with worn plastic relics—tubs, bottles and baskets.

Patrick had the revs up again, and the car plunged towards the beach, still nosing its way along the wheel ruts. Scraps of vegetation made poonking noises on the headlights and the front panels, and the springs squeaked over the bleeding engine. In a gap in the scrub, Charlie saw a pile of shells as high as the car window. He knew by now they were abalone.

And then without warning they were out and streaking across the soft sand at the top of the beach, the car tilted down towards Charlie's door as it ploughed ahead. Patrick was hunched forward over the steering wheel, elbows high. The front tyres bit once or twice, and the back end developed a lazy drift, made more alarming by the presence of small boulders here and there in the sand. Patrick cackled as they collected a boulder under the front passenger wheel.

'The trick to it'—his eyes darted across the beach looking for a line—'is to keep the revs up. If you slow down, you're fucked.'

The curve of the beach pinched tighter at the western end, and the space available for the car to continue its high line was shrinking fast. Without warning, Patrick swung it violently downwards, crunching through the kelp and fizzing out onto the damp tidal flats. The end of the beach was approaching fast, where the reef took over and the headland met the sea. He looped extravagantly across the sandbank and slowed to a stop, then reversed straight up the slope of the beach until the depth of the sand prevented any further climb. They were perched about ten feet above the water level now, and armed with a good enough forward run-up to allow easy escape.

As the Camira settled on the soft sand, burning grasses smouldered in the engine bay. There was a sharper smell too, possibly brake linings. Charlie decided not to sniff too deeply. From the boot of the car, Patrick started pulling out diving equipment made of old-fashioned black rubber: a sleeveless wetsuit that did up over the shoulder, long black fins, a steel-rimmed mask. He made two piles of gear and quickly dressed himself from the first pile, throwing a heavy weight-belt around his waist and his mask and a pair of gloves—they looked like gardening gloves—into a catch bag.

Charlie stood at the tailgate, which Patrick had wedged open with a piece of radiator hosing, and pulled on the old wetsuit. The sun emerged from behind the slow-moving haze in the northwest and the sea lit up as though a dial had been turned. The forbidding grey-green hue moved through a spectrum of turquoise to a brilliant emerald green as a warm glow fell on his back. Charlie looked up to see birds circling in the sun. Not seagulls as he'd expected them to be, but larger, heavier birds with cruel-looking beaks and mottled plumage. Their wings stretched nearly as wide as his arms, swept back in a predator's arc. As Charlie watched, one bird suddenly angled itself straight at the shallows, metres from the dry sand, smashed violently into the surface and disappeared under the boil of whitewater. It re-emerged with a hand-sized crab in its beak and hauled itself heavily into flight. The crab pawed frantically as the bird lifted it higher, one clay-orange leg probing at the bird's eye, trying to prise an advantage in the unequal struggle, until the bird took it over an outcrop of rock and let it go.

Charlie felt a strange urge to involve himself, but he could see from the raised ground beside the car that the crab had disintegrated on impact, and now the killer's squawking competitors were fighting over the scattered fragments. The brawling settled quickly as the birds devoured their spoils on separate rocks, but the image wouldn't clear from Charlie's mind: the legs windmilling forlornly against the sky as the crab was taken up.

He shuffled down the beach after Patrick, worked his way from boulder to boulder, looking up only when he'd reached the water's edge. The mask felt foreign as he fitted it, the strap yanking painfully at his hair. Remembering summers forever ago, he took it off again and spat in it. Repositioned it, with another painful tug.

Patrick had slid into the water without a word while Charlie was fiddling with the equipment. He marked Patrick's direction of travel by the trailing wake of the snorkel, and flopped forward off the rock. He coughed some water free of the snorkel, surprised to find the mouthpiece had stayed in position, and waited for the water's aerated fizz to clear.

The sound had changed. The birds, the gentle lift of air around his ears, the faraway waves, gone. There was no less sound in here, but it was unearthly—an orchestra of gloops and tinkles, even the highest registers somehow blurred. The water had a wobbly translucence, unlike anything he'd seen in the air, and he found he couldn't grapple with it—his mind didn't have a word, a corollary, anything. It was like an incomplete mix of oil and water, or hot and cold, swirling within itself and confusing his sense of distance, his understanding of colour.

His breath was loud in his ears. One ankle popped and rolled reluctantly as he finned his way over the shallows and the straps of the fins cut into the sides of his feet. It took a moment or two to find Patrick, reduced in the middle distance to a pair of pulsing black fins leaving stabs of silver bubbles, chattering consonants among the blue-green vowels of the reef. Charlie tried to keep him in sight, craning his neck forward as the sea floor fell rapidly away.

Once when he and Harry were little, they'd discovered the contrast control on the family TV. They turned it down slowly until the objects on screen drowned in a darkness that robbed them of definition, merging everything into cathode grey-black. Something like that was happening below him. There were fish moving around down there, dark and secretive, nosing their way to nowhere in particular. Either the arrangement of their eyes was such that they were unaware of him hanging in the sky above them, or they knew somehow that they were beyond his reach.

Still Patrick's fins receded ahead and the darkness grew below. With the weak sunlight angling in from in front of his right shoulder, Charlie knew Patrick was headed for the near edge of Gawleys. At some stage, the rocks had to come into view again when the reef appeared. His bone-deep connection to dry land kept promising him this. He'd thought there'd be a bond between land and reef: that the outcrops would be more or less a continuation underwater of the tumbledown rocks at the foot of the cliff. But right at the deepest point of the crossing, Patrick suddenly plummeted vertically down, kicking hard but otherwise relaxed, hands resting near each hip. He stopped just at the point when the depth had stripped the colour out of him, and grabbed momentarily at his mask. Then he continued downwards, until he became another bluish shadow at the limit of vision.

He was gone for long enough that Charlie decided to follow. He drew an oversize breath down the snorkel and began to swim down. Once his fins had penetrated the surface and he was fully inverted, his ears began to hurt. Something about water pressure, he knew, and it involved his nose. As he continued kicking downwards, he reached up to the facemask and pressed hard at the point where he thought his nose was. It broke the seal against his skin, and the mask instantly flooded. He lashed out with both hands, disoriented, blinking frantically—panicked by the instant and total loss of control over his environment. The snorkel came loose. The bubbles that were his breath tickled their way over his ears, around the sides of head, away to the surface. He wanted them back. His brain tried to tell him he could blink the blindness clear. He knew his legs were running now, and he grabbed at the mask, trying to free himself of the unseen enemy. His lungs began convulsing. In a final surge of fear, he got the mask off and let it go, the world around him a contiguous blur as he fought his way back up towards the light. When he finally broke the surface, he tore the ragged air into his lungs too soon, taking flecks of seawater down and sending him into spasms of coughing. The coughing subsided and he was alone on the surface, far enough from shore that the exposed rocks of Gawleys were the nearer landfall. He waited there, feeling his legs gently paddling to keep him upright. The light changed over the shore, and the sea lost the last energy of the day, gently reflecting the sky. His mind gradually slowed down and wandered. He was Nolan's black square Ned Kelly, suspended in an alien world. His companion had enough physical grace to fit in here. Charlie's body was as dumb and foreign as driftwood.

When he broke the surface beside Charlie, Patrick wore a look of exasperation. He had Charlie's mask in his hand. 'Found a cray,' he croaked in the middle of a deep inhalation, then disappeared again.

Charlie put the mask back on his face and watched him descend, once more disappearing from view. He reappeared with hands by his hips again, this time with a bright spark of orange in one hand. The creature was heavy, prehistoric, armoured. Marked with bright splotches of gold and vermillion like a treasure of some kind.

ONCE HE'D DRIED and changed, Charlie felt a great wave of drowsiness come over him. He lay on a warm boulder near the back of the car, and watched Patrick watching the cray. He picked it up from the rock where he'd left it and ran a finger over its carapace.

'See the way all the spikes point forwards? The legs are hinged forwards as well. All the crap you can't eat is up the front—the good stuff's down the back. So the defences point out from its hidey hole. They're useless at runnin, especially forwards. But they can snap backwards real fast. And they've got a mean grip. If you get a finger in there'—he pointed at a long conical spur in the joint of the cray's front leg—'it'll push that spike straight through it. Saw that happen to a guy once.' He flipped it over, the legs treadmilling blindly. 'See those leaves along the underside? The way they cross over, it's a female. She keeps her eggs under em. On the males, they don't meet in the middle like that. The females have got little pincers here'—he brushed at the ends of the hind legs—'so they can hang on when they get a root.'

Charlie was watching the eyes—bright black beads suspended on the ends of stalks. They seemed alert and, to Charlie's mind, distressed.

'How old is it?' Charlie wasn't sure why it mattered.

'Dunno. Few years I s'pose. She might be ten.' Patrick fell into silence, occupying himself with the kindling.

Once he'd got a fire going, he produced a blackened iron pot from the back of the wagon and filled it with water from a plastic drum. He took the cray and held it up for a moment, glowing orange in the last of the sun. Then he flipped its tail upwards from beneath and dropped it neatly into the pot. It pulsed violently once or twice as the fresh water flooded into its body, and then it was still, the graceful whip-like antennae protruding from the pot.

'Isn't the water supposed to be boiling?' ventured Charlie.

'I'm drowning it. Cos it's not salty it sorta puts em to sleep. I don't agree with boiling em alive. You want a drink?' Patrick returned to the back of the car and produced two plain beer bottles, longnecks with no labels. He jammed them both in the back bumper of the wagon to prise the lids and handed one to Charlie.

'What's this?' he asked, sniffing the top.

'I think it's a Newcastle Brown. Les's mate Bernie Harris brews em. He's a stickler for sterilisation, so don't worry about the muck on the outside. Also makes a whisky outta barley, boils it all up in an old hot water tank, but it's not very, um...' he looked out over the water with a smile. 'Not very sociable stuff.'

The beer was fizzing over the top of the bottle. When it had stopped, Charlie slurped the froth off it and was struck by how real it tasted, something he couldn't describe, but which immediately had him thinking he'd drunk too much commercial beer until now. It was warm, but it didn't seem to matter. His hand gripping the bottle had dried salty and rough from the seawater, with the exception of the two fingertips where the beer had run.

They drank for a moment in silence. Flies buzzed around the catch bag where the cray had expelled some sort of slime. The shallow bay in front of them had finished its dealings with the sky, and now lay like darkened glass. Charlie watched Patrick carefully for a moment: he was content, or maybe just distracted. His movements were slow and his eyes fixed on some point in front of him. He produced a snaplock bag from his coat pocket and started rolling a smoke.

'Is that grass?' asked Charlie.

'No, mister prosecutor, straight baccy. No more of young Dale's hydro for you.'

'It's just that it didn't come from a packet as far as I could see.'

'That's cos it's chop chop,' returned Patrick, raising the finished item to his tongue to seal it.

Charlie smiled. 'The beer, the cray, the smoke...Does anybody actually pay retail around here?'

Patrick had the smoke in the coals at the edge of the fire.

'Depends if you can afford it.'

Leaving it there would leave the afternoon untrammelled, Charlie thought. Pressing ahead was bound to end in trouble. It always did. 'What happened to your parents?'

Patrick looked at him quietly for a while, considering.

'Who cares?'

'Just interested.'

Patrick took in a deep breath and released it slowly.

'Well, Dad was a drinker. He'd been warned by the doctor enough times. He had trouble, I think it was his pancreas. He'd take himself away for a few days at a time, just go off his head out in the bush. He'd drive over to the Otways, park the car deep in the scrub somewhere. I don't know what was botherin him, but something was just eating him up. He wasn't a bad drunk. Just went quiet, and we all stayed away from him. It wasn't that we were scared of him. Just felt like he was deep in the middle of somethin and you knew you couldn't, um, intrude. Does that sound strange? Anyway, that was how it felt. It was his private stuff, and we didn't know any different so we all worked around 'im.

'He had plenty to be angry about, I s'pose. He was always broke, even though everyone thought fishing was a job where you could make as much as you wanted. He just wasn't good with the money. He paid too much for things, he wasn't ruthless. He had bad luck, did bad deals. Couple of the boats over the years turned out to be dogs. There was somethin wrong with his neck. He got…he got hit by a hatch cover in a big sou'westerly one night. He had a few stitches and he got over the concussion all right, but it did somethin weird to his neck. He didn't have any kind of insurance, like an idiot, so he couldn't go and see specialists about it. Never discussed it with us, but you could see it in his face when he'd lift things. It's one of the things I remember real sharp from my childhood, every time he reached for his seatbelt he'd make this grunting sound. I don't think he even knew he was doin it.

'So if you'd asked Mags, he'd have said that Dad never got on top of the pain. Just drank to take the edge off it. But I don't know if I bought that—I mean, that'd explain the steady drinkin of a night—he'd have the three or four before dinner, and then he'd hit the cask over his food, and then back on the beers afterwards till he fucken passed out in his chair. But the big sessions by himself out in the bush, they were like somethin else. As far as I know, he never went out in the boat pissed. He must've had some shockin hangovers, and the funny thing about Dad, he used to get really seasick. You'd think a bloke who'd spent his life on the boats woulda got over it, but he'd throw up for hours out there. An his bloody pancreas'd fire up again, and round we'd go. Same cycle all over again.'

Patrick was prodding at the fire with a thin length of steel, his eyes fixed somewhere among the burning driftwood. A delicate spiral of embers rose from the disturbed coals.

'Anyway, I was about thirteen I think. In year seven. How's that, fucken year seven. Anyway, Dad'd been gone three days, and I was crook at 'im because he wasn't there to take me to footy but nobody'd ever say anything when that stuff happened. Someone'd turn up and give you a lift and it wasn't discussed. And he turned up at his mate Wal's place in Lavers Hill, was the word we got back. Wal reckons he come tearin up the drive and pretty much crashed into the carport. He got out and he was smashed, falling all over the place, but the way he was roarin and grabbin at his guts, Wal thought he'd been shot. They took him in to the hospital and there'd been some kind of rupture, they said, and we all got marched in there to see him and I'll never forget it. I'll never forget it. Mum was pregnant with the twins at the time. She'd tried to pick a day when they all thought he looked okay, even though he was half dead, and we were all taken out of school and we kinda filed in there, and there he was on the bed, and he was just grey, and there were the tubes, you know. He was sleeping with his eyes a bit open and I thought he was gone, I thought he was dead. There was a box, I remember this, there was a box of those man-size tissues on the side table, the red and black box with the train on it. I've never seen those fucking things anywhere except beside a hospital bed. And then he started sorta coughing and he jerked up in the bed and he was throwin his arms around and this blood just started gushing out of him, just pouring down his front. And he was grabbin at the tubes and Mum had a hold of him but he was thrashing away at her and we were all just standin there starin, you know how kids when they're watching something really bad, they just stare.

'Someone must've marched us out eventually, but the last I saw of him was just the blood and the sheets were going everywhere, and the last thing I caught as I turned away was his eyes, and it's the bit that's stuck with me because they were just bulging, just popping out of his head and he looked so fucking scared. It was more than the pain, you know, you could look right through it, and he wasn't bad with pain, he'd been hurting for years, but this was somethin else. He was petrified, the poor bastard.

'So that was it, and he died six or eight hours after that, and they told us in the mornin. We were all sittin along the kitchen table, this big long table, and we used to make walls with all the cereal boxes, you'd kind of pen yourself in there. And Mum come out and she didn't need to say much. No one had spoken anyway that morning. And I remember after a long time I looked around the side of one of the cereal boxes and I could see Mags, and he was just sobbing away to himself. I s'pose he was that little bit older and he knew Dad like the rest of us didn't. Later on, it was the thing he had over us. He could always trump everyone else with a Dad story, or you'd say somethin about Dad and he'd correct you. And he'd give us the shits because he'd put on these airs about being the man of the house, and I used to think it was pathetic and we had a couple of ripper punchups over that, but it's funny as the years go on and I think I understand what he was on about now. I reckon he acted that way because it kept Dad alive for him, like he saw himself as Dad the Sequel or something. You know how that stuff goes. You got brothers Charlie?'

Charlie looked at the fire. 'I had a brother.'

A pause.

'Well, you know then. Like, Mags was right in a way with all that carry-on. I didn't really know Dad as well as he did, but I used to think about him out there in his car. I wondered whether he got any kind of peace doing that. You know, these days, you'd do that if you could, wouldn' ya?'

Patrick turned his head from the fire and looked straight at Charlie. Receiving no response, he continued.

'But the thing that still gets me about Dad dyin was that it was so um, it was rough, you know? It was fucken gruesome. I always thought hospitals, I mean this was only nine years ago, and I thought hospitals were places where everythin could be managed, and if someone was in strife they'd come in in their white coats and just bump up the drugs, or they'd knock em out or something, but people weren't flailin around with their eyes hangin out of their heads. It was a bit of a wake-up to find that you could die real... real *violently*, right there in a modern hospital bed, while the guy in the room next door watches telly, and there's mums down the street doin the shoppin, and here's this guy with all this medical care and he's drowning in all this blood and spraying the shit everywhere and throwin punches and stuff while his family watches. I still don't get that. We put all this spin on it, but it's primitive isn't it? It's still guesswork. I think back to that, and in a lot of ways I don't reckon Mags suffered that much compared to the old boy.

'So anyway, that's Dad. Mum hung in there for another five years. I remember I had my eighteenth at the footy club, an' she died a few months after that. Still don't really know what happened, but she'd wandered out into the dunes at the far end of Antonias. God knows what the hell she was up to, but she was a fair way from the house, like five or six k's away. Anyway, they sort of worked it out afterwards, after they found her out there. She was lyin in a little scoop between the sandhills, on the clear sand where the marram grass wasn't growing. She'd been there for three days and we were all just freakin back at home, had search parties out everywhere. I even went and pulled a rake through the dam. You have to understand, Dad mighta nicked off pretty often, but Mum never did. She was just chained to the house with all them kids. So there she was. Fishermen found her. Not a scratch on her. But she'd left these marks in the sand all round herself—I don't know what you'd call em. Swirls, half circles. In the end we figured she'd had a fit of some kind and her hands and feet made the marks. Personally I think she had a feeling. A premonition, whatever, and she'd taken herself out there to die. But there wasn't too much point speculatin about it eh? She was dead. No one else had done it—there were only her tracks leading to the spot from one direction, and the fishermen's tracks in from the other. It was sad all right, but I s'pose we were all a bit over it by that stage. We were having money troubles and Mum was never the same after Dad died, so you know, it was more just a case of get on with it by then. Mags took her rainjacket off before the undertaker took her away, and Milly still wears it around the place.

'But you gotta die at some stage, hey. Mum'd had enough, and you compare it to what Dad went through an'…anyway. That's that.'

Another long silence. Another chance, thought Charlie, to let it rest. Later there would be time to ask himself why he pushed it.

'What are you going to do about all this, Patrick?'

'About what?'

'About your evidence.'

'Fuck. Right down to business, eh? I've told you what happened.'

'I don't think you have. You've been through a lot and I don't want to be disrespectful, but I think what you've told us is probably bullshit. Which happens a fair bit, but in your case it's a pity because if you don't fix it up, you're going to wind up in the witness box and they're going to tear you to pieces. These two cretins are going to walk and, shit, in those circumstances you'd have to say it'd be largely your doing.'

'Righto. Suppose for a minute you're right. Let's say I was there and I saw everything and I give you a new statement or whatever you want, and I get in the witness box and I tell everyone what I saw. What happens then?'

'They're likely to be convicted.'

'And then?'

'They'll go to jail—they'll do—I dunno—fifteen, seventeen years.'

'Okay, so they go off to jail, right. What happens to me? What happens to my family? You go on to your next one, and the one after that, and one day you could be a judge or whatever. The witness welfare lady, she'll find a rape victim or somethin and good on her. Someone else'll shoot someone else. See, the whole circus moves on. You're all obsessed with getting this one over the line, but it's just the match of the day, isn't it? And after I've bared my arse in public for you people, I still don't have a brother, no fucken parents, and life just goes on, doesn't it? Still a leaky water tank, still a busted-arse car, kids' lunches.' His voice rose and cracked. 'Ha! Kids' lunches…'

He flicked the dying smoke in his hand at the back bumper of the Camira. 'So really…why bother?'

'Because it's the right thing to do.' Charlie groaned inwardly.

'Right thing to do. Pretty fucken cold comfort, isn't it?' Patrick's agitation was mounting again, and Charlie was now worrying that he hadn't plotted an exit from this conversation.

'I'll give you the other side of it. I get in the box, I tell it exactly like it is in my statement and I walk away at the end of the day. Still be a shitfight back home, but at least I've got around the cross-examination bit, I get no fucken nonsense round the town from the Murchisons. And ya never know, they might get convicted anyway...' The anxious darting of the hands had returned, his eyes starting to oscillate sharply from side to side. He poked viciously at the file with the metal rod.

'It'd be perjury.'

'Hang on, I thought this was hypothetical. I didn't say it wasn't the truth.' Patrick gulped at the beer.

'It isn't, mate. We both know that.'

There was a long silence. 'Well if I was lyin, why would I put all that stuff in me statement about the drugs? Wouldn't I just pretend I didn't know anything about it? See, it's you that wants me comin up with some big story about how I saw it all and there's the guy that done it and all that. I'm not stupid, man. I know you got sent over here and someone's expecting you to come home and say yep, he's gonna co-operate, and I talked him round and ra ra ra...'

His face darkened.

'That shit's all about *you* isn't it. It's a bit fucken rude sayin it's about truth and justice like yer a superhero that goes round rescuing kittens from trees. You call me mate and you talk as if this is you and me working out some problem we both got and you're here to help, but that's not what's going on. You still got yer lawyer head on in there somewhere, and to be honest I'm half expectin that everythin I say to you is gonna wind up in some statement. And the first thing the coppers are gonna do when you get a new state-ment from me is take it to those fuckers in remand and say, "Here you go boys, we've got the whole thing from Lanegan, and yer both goners, so how bout pleading up?" I done enough remand to know that routine. You can make all the promises you want, and I'm not doubting you, you'd mean it, but in the end, the Murchison family'll know it was me, and that just makes life difficult, or more like fucken impossible, so…no.'

He got up and walked away from the fire and began pissing on the marram grass with his back to Charlie.

'Don't you owe this to Mags? They shot him. He never saw it coming. Shit, they tried to set his body on fire. Don't you feel like he'd want you to defend him?

'Oh fuck off,' Patrick called over his shoulder. 'For one thing he didn't work like that, and for another he's gone. He's gone an I have to work out how the rest of us are s'posed to get along without the welfare comin round and draggin off the little ones.'

He took the cray out of the water and studied it closely. As he tipped it over, the legs fell outwards limply, and he seemed satisfied, hefting the pot onto the fire and gently placing the cray back on the rock beside him.

'You tell me—how am I s'posed to run the boat on my own? Shark fisherman—hah!—there's fuck all sharks out there now anyway. I'm goin halfway to King Island to get a load, and it's pretty much gettin taken up in fuel.' He had a driftwood plank in one hand, and pressing the cray onto it, he ran a knife around its body, then ripped away the front of the animal with a twist of the other hand. Hot brown fluid dripped onto the timber as Charlie watched. Patrick ran the knife down the middle of the segmented tail, cleaving it neatly, and handed one half to Charlie.

'Chuck out the poo pipe,' he muttered. Charlie took it as a ceasefire.

Patrick pinched the pale worm of intestine out of the white flesh and flicked it away, before scooping a chunk of the meat into his mouth. Once again, the heat seemed to ebb out of him as he sloshed down the cray meat with a gulp of beer. He ripped the legs off the carcass and tossed a few towards Charlie.

'Maybe we'll talk about what happened some time. But if I told you about that, we'd have to think about...about *how* I'm telling you, see?'

He looked quizzically at Charlie. 'Put it to you another way. You'd have to think about why you were listening, what you were going to do with it once I'd told you.'

Charlie studied the delicate pink filigrees of a new layer of shell under the hard carapace of the tail. 'I don't follow you.'

'Comes back to this thing about you and the law. I don't know you that well, but this is what I see. You don't like people much, but you're bloody obsessed with the law. I reckon it's just one way of solving problems, and there's a whole lot of other ones. You can beat the shit out of each other like cavemen, right, or you can talk it through. People round here didn't really have the law to fall back on for a long time. Just didn't reach them out here, no cops, no courts. So they made up their own ways of dealing with shit. We can put aside all this crap about perjury and sworn statements and whatever else, and maybe I can just explain it all to you and you'll see it my way. But right now, you've got us in boxes. Witness and prosecutor, and you've got all these rules. I don't see it that way, and I got no respect for this bloody great system you got wrapped around everything.'

He was cracking open the cray's legs as he spoke, using the end of one antenna to push the tubes of pink flesh out of them. When the pile of discarded legs in front of him was complete, he stood up.

'Anyway, that was good, eh.' Patrick looked out over the darkened sea. 'Have to do that again sometime. Try not to drown ya.'

He had the length of steel in his hand again, and walked silently around to the front of the Camira. When he lifted the bonnet and slid it into the motor, Charlie realised he'd been poking the fire with the dipstick. Patrick gathered the remnants of the shell in front of him and scooped them into the dying fire. When he was done, he ploughed sand over the embers with the side of his foot, and loaded the car without another word. It was only when he'd got into the drivers seat and started the engine that Charlie reacted, jumping in and slamming the tinny door just as the Camira rolled down the beach in a cloud of exhaust. He didn't dare look sideways. Patrick seemed to be deep in thought.

AFTER A WEEK, Lewis the panelbeater called to say he'd put a new front quarter panel on the Saab and the car was ready for collection. He then felt the need to correct himself and clarify that the quarter panel was in fact secondhand, from the wreckers, and not strictly new. Charlie assured him that was fine.

He was now accustomed to walking the town, and felt almost disappointed when he reached the industrial estate and saw the car waiting for him. When Lewis turned up at the little office window in the corner of his shed, Charlie already had cash on the counter. He couldn't remember the last time he'd managed to use a card in Dauphin, and the routine was starting to bring him a secret pleasure: the slow, careful handwriting on the invoice pad, thumb on the carbon to tear it off, the deliberate counting of the notes. Charlie had kept each receipt from recent days, not because he thought he could claim anything back, but because of the affection he felt for this little ritual. *Curlewis Sports and Leisure, Dawkins Pharmacy, Bowman Family Grocers.*

On his way back through town he passed the Normans Woe, and knew he couldn't take another pub meal, a seventh consecutive wander over the chalkboard menu, another side-serve of boiled carrots and peas. Most of the shops were dead in the early evening, the street largely deserted, a handful of locals shuffling into the supermarket, talking beside their cars. Random pools of light spilled from half-lit shop windows, and a blinking neon sign drew his attention. *Fortune Palace Chinese Restaurant*. The old tiling along the street frontage suggested it might once have been a butcher's shop. Inside Charlie could see dozens of vacant chairs and an Asian man he assumed to be the proprietor, seated down the back near the kitchen servery, absorbed in a book. Near the door, the glass was festooned with photos of the Fortune Palace's dishes: empress chicken, salt and pepper squid, Szechuan beef. Each of the photos had faded to various shades of blue, the food indistinguishable.

He entered past a glowing fish tank. The proprietor dropped his book and hurried forward, waving a menu folder at the booths along the far wall, and Charlie slid onto a bench in the nearest booth. The cushion exhaled softly as he sat: the Bee Gees were singing 'How Deep Is Your Love' softly in the background. He ordered a beer and ran his finger over the menu folder, unable to place exactly what he wanted to think about. Sometimes at these moments he thought it was Annie. But then that seemed more like a mental puzzle than anything emotional, and he let it go.

The sequence, as he saw it, was: get the car fixed, get Patrick to co-operate, go home. The car was done, therefore going home didn't present insurmountable difficulty. But what about Patrick? He'd set out his position in no uncertain terms, but even as he'd spoken he seemed to be exploring the limits of that position. Charlie had felt his mind working on the drive back from Gawleys. Patrick was working away at a knot, and he wasn't done.

Charlie had postponed all further work back in Melbourne until he could be sure about a return date, but he knew, whatever Harlan said, that the OPP wouldn't keep paying him to kick around this town indefinitely. In the meantime he'd decided to let Patrick be. Leave him to drift to the right decision in his own time. Of course he might never do that; if Charlie was honest, it also had something to do with giving himself some room. He needed to let the thing with Annie settle in his mind. He needed to leave her alone for a while, too. He needed, more than anything, to sort himself out before he stood up in front of the next magistrate, who might be every bit as intransigent as Lefcovics.

And he'd been right to conclude that there was no point rushing any of this. But the longer he hung around, the more attention he was drawing to himself. This community seemed congenitally obsessed with other people's business.

The beer arrived and he ordered chilli beef. An old couple entered and seated themselves at one of the tables. The proprietor seemed to know them, and didn't bother to stand as they came in. Charlie returned to his thoughts while the goldfish circled. A bell rang in the servery as the Brothers Gibb faded through the closing bars of 'More than a Woman'. The man returned with his meal and Charlie ordered a bottle of red. He could always ask for the cork.

The door opened again as he was pouring himself a glass, and a couple entered: a middle-aged man and a woman who was older, sixty-five maybe. He had a guiding hand behind the small of her back, not touching, and they stood close. Charlie couldn't tell whether they were mother and son or friends of some kind, but something about the tilt of the man's head indicated reluctance.

They scanned the room for a moment and saw him. It seemed they'd expected to find him, because they came straight over to the booth. The woman's face was lined and her smile was full of affection. She wore neat frameless glasses and had her greying hair dyed to a reddish brown and clumped up into a warm-looking tuft. Her appearance suggested she had worked hard for many years, but not without reward: rings glittered on both hands and she'd pinned her shawl with a studded silver brooch.

'Hello young man,' she smiled, as though she'd just run into a favourite nephew. 'Do you mind if we join you?'

The man's face had not moved: he stood behind the woman and slightly to one side, watching Charlie. Short hair; strongly built. He held himself very upright, with the beginnings of a gut pushing the front of his shirt. His gaze left Charlie just long enough to check the door and the other tables. He's not in a relationship with this woman, thought Charlie. He's a cop.

Charlie stood and offered his hand to the woman. 'Charlie Jardim.'

'Lovely to meet you,' said the woman, and stepped past him to sit herself down. Charlie's momentary confusion must have registered on his face, because the man stuck his hand out.

'This is Delvene Murchison, Charlie,' he said. 'And I'm Neil Robertson.'

Charlie took a moment to piece it together.

'Detective Sergeant?'

'Yep.'

Delvene Murchison was looking for the proprietor. Robertson pulled a chair from a nearby table and positioned it at the open end of the booth, tipping one shoulder sideways as the proprietor approached.

'Ken dear, how are you,' she beamed at him.

'Mrs Delvene.' His ballpoint was poised over the pad. 'You are so lovely tonight. You having some entree? Main meal?'

'Ken, I'll have some of that—what is that?—that young Mr Jarman is having, and will you get some lemon chicken please for Neil?' She swept up the menus and pushed the condiments out to the far end of the booth to make room for her elbows.

'Now, it's Charlie isn't it. How's it all going Charlie?'

'What do you mean?

'Well, how are you enjoying the town?'

'It seems fine. Quiet I guess.'

'It is, isn't it.' She scrunched her nose a little in sympathy. 'But there's so much *life* just under the surface. I mean, I know it can seem a bit closed to someone like you, but that's just country people. Very *conservative* you know.'

Robertson hadn't moved. Charlie tried to smile politely at Delvene Murchison, but was finding it very hard to figure her out.

'I'd never seen the place until I married Alan,' she went on. 'I came from inland, off a farm, and I just thought we'd never fit in. Lovely people once you get to know them, though. Some of them are come down the line from Bass Strait sealers, you know. But you have to have a bit of renewal around the place, or we'd all be inbred! Ha!' She clapped her hands together. 'The ones that come into the town, they bring things in and that. You know, skills, money. Me and Alan worked so hard in the early days. Him fishing and me raising the kids and working in the pub. And we bought the furniture shop and then, well! We bought that pub for cash you know.'

She looked at him over her glasses.

'Put the whole lot down without a loan. No one had seen anything like it. Place was going to the dogs up till then, but we got in there and we worked and we worked. My!' She stopped, momentarily stunned by the memory of her own effort.

'There was one year, might've been 1980 I think, I kept on cleaning the rooms and pouring beer until I was nine months pregnant, about to pop. It was hot that year too. But the more we put in, the luckier we got. The boat was a success. The fishing here used to be very easy you know. We could hire two or three of the local kids to work the boat...our kids too, obviously, but I reckon just about every kid in the town's either had a go on the boat or behind the bar. Some of them have made something out of that, got themselves an ab licence or a cray licence or something. Few went off to university. Some of em wouldn't work if their life depended on it. Can't help em. You get to a point, you just tell em not to come back. They drift on. The ones that don't make it, they generally don't hang around—they go to the big towns, or off to Melbourne. Couple do stay—they just hit the other side of the bar.

'But you look at that Les. I mean, now there's a diamond. Never had a bad day's work out of Les. He's trustworthy, he's got a memory like an elephant. In fact, he's got an arse like an elephant, doesn't he Robbo!'

She slapped Robertson's thigh surprisingly hard, and he jumped a little.

'We love Les. Everyone loves Les. Have you had a chat to him?'

'I have.'

'There. See? Isn't he gold?'

'He seems a good guy. So where's Mr Murchison?'

'Alan? God,' she shot a look at Robertson, 'have you ever heard anyone call him *mister*? He's got the gastro.' She giggled. 'Didn't get it here, mind you. Or at the pub.' She waggled a finger at Charlie in case he'd leapt intemperately to that conclusion.

A silence fell over them. It felt awkward to Charlie, but he suspected Delvene was untroubled by it. The food arrived and she attacked it with a fork, leaving the chopsticks in their paper wrapping. The lemon chicken was placed in front of Robertson but he made no attempt to touch it. He was still staring at a point somewhere in front of Charlie, somewhere in the air between them.

'Is there some reason you want to talk to me?' Charlie asked.

Delvene looked surprised.

'No, not at all,' she said, as the fork hovered in front of her. 'Just thought, you know, we needed to catch up, touch base, all that. We—you're here by yourself and us Murchisons, we specialise in hospitality of course.' The cheesy smile had returned. 'And we've got something in common, haven't we.'

'What's that?'

'Well we've both got an interest in young Skip.' She returned to pushing her meal around the plate, building a forkful slowly and deliberately.

'What do you mean by that?'

'I mean, I'm his mother. I know him and I'm worried about him. And you,' she pointed the fork at him for emphasis. 'You need to do a job on him.'

'I'm not sure I want to discuss him at all, Mrs Murchison.'

'Please. Delvene. Even in this little place'—she looked around

137

the restaurant—'there's more to people than meets the eye. Take Ken there.' She pointed the fork again, this time at the restaurant proprietor, engrossed in his book. 'You look at Ken and you see some Chinese guy. Ken is from Zuhai City, on the coast near Hong Kong. Fishing town, like this one. Fair bit bigger I imagine. But before he came here, he had a fishing business. Things went bad, government gave him a hard time. You see, he's a Daoist, a Shenyi Daoist. You familiar with the Daoists, Charlie?'

Charlie confessed that he wasn't. His meal had gone cold.

'They believe, among other things, in a sea goddess. Interesting. Poor Ken got here as a reffo, got his visa and all that, but he's still waiting for family reunion. He's got a wife and a child back there. The loneliness must be unbearable. So you know, you just see a Chinese bloke who runs a restaurant, but there's a whole world behind him, whole world inside him. And in the same way, people in this town, they look at you and they just see some cunt from Melbourne'—her face did not change as she said this—'but I'm sure there's a story to you too Mr Jarman.'

'J– Jardim.'

'Sorry.' Her smile was like ice. She spoke more slowly now, considering her words carefully. 'You've probably got your reasons for being here, love. I'm sure you believe in those reasons. But Alan and me, we can't sit by while our son rots away on remand because of this…business. I want—'

'I said I won't discuss it.'

She raised the cautionary finger again. Robertson still had not moved.

'You don't have to say anything. You just have to listen. Skip has nothing to do with Matt Lanegan's death. Nothing. It's all a nasty little internal thing among the Lanegans and the rough crowd they mix with. Poachers, drug dealers. Unsavoury types who have a way of winding up in car boots and ditches and God knows what. My boy might be many things, young man. I know he's undisciplined and he's cost Alan and me plenty of money over the years with his idiotic schemes. But he is no killer. Frankly I don't think he has the ticker for it.'

'It wasn't me that charged him, Mrs Murchison—'

'*Delvene*,' she corrected him again, more forcefully.

'My job is to prosecute the charges that were laid by police. If you've got some issue with the decision to charge your son, perhaps you should be speaking with Detective Robertson here.'

Charlie pushed his chopsticks together and scrunched the paper packaging into a hard little ball. It rolled away from his fingertips across the tablecloth. He wanted to make the detective involve himself, to break free of this woman's ruthless hold on the conversation.

'Robbo and me have discussed it many times, believe me,' continued Delvene Murchison. 'If it'd been left to him, I'm sure the situation would be different. But of course, it's a homicide and so the Melbourne squads have to get involved. It was all taken off him without any regard for his understanding of—' she hesitated, eyes shifting. 'Local things. You're not the first outsider to come in here and tell us what's going on in our town.'

Charlie sighed. He hoped it sounded like weariness, but in reality he was slightly unnerved. 'I'm sure you want something from me. I don't expect *he's* going to ask for it. So do you want to tell me what the pitch is?'

'Well, that's a bit abrupt. I don't know how to take that. Let's see, you're in our town, drinking at our hotel, talking to our employees and taking up their time. You're waltzing around the place like it's fine with us, and it's *not* fine with us, you understand?'

She was still smiling that smile, leaning forward now and peering over the top of the glasses, straight into his eyes. 'I know you've spoken to that Lanegan boy, and I can't for the life of me work out why you would try to change his evidence.'

'I'm not.'

'Don't interrupt me.' She pointed a finger directly between his eyes, and he found himself transfixed by her fleshy pink knuckles, the gold of her rings. 'He's given his statement, he's said what he's said, and that's the end of the matter. My boy is in enough bother without you trying to get people to say things.'

'What I'm doing here and who I speak to is none of your business, Delvene.'

'Well you're wrong about that, young man. It's very much my business.' She tidied the fork, the unopened chopsticks, on her plate and picked up the straps of her handbag.

'Things are going to get quite a bit uglier for Patrick Lanegan if I see any more of this going on.'

Charlie couldn't believe what he was hearing.

'Are you threatening me?'

'No, I'm threatening him.'

Again, she stared back at Charlie without blinking.

'You appear to be threatening me in front of a police officer.' Charlie gestured at Robertson, who did not react in any way. Delvene Murchison looked at the detective as though she hadn't previously noticed him.

'He knows his place, young man. So should you. Finish up your bits and pieces and head off back to Melbourne, hm?'

Without another word, she swept up the handbag and walked off, Detective Robertson trailing in her wake.

Charlie watched them pass through the door, Robertson obsequiously holding it open as Delvene Murchison strode into the night. He called the proprietor over.

'Ken, can I have the bill please?'

He smiled happily.

'Oh no sir. Mrs Delvene, she fix.'

140

THE TRACTOR TYRES picked up the powdery white sand and spilled it as they turned. Patrick sat high on the machine, twisted around and reversing carefully towards the water. A heavy steel boat—Charlie would've called it a tinny—was hitched to the tractor.

Patrick revved the tractor and the boat slipped free in the cool shallows. A gout of black diesel smoke belched from the tractor's stack. Charlie had the bowline in his hand and it pulled taut, tugging him a couple of steps into the water before he arrested the boat's momentum. He listened to the chucking sound of the bow as it nodded up and down. Patrick drove the tractor back over the beach and up to its gravel perch under the scrub. Things were protected and delicate down here in the lee of the cliffs; the plants were finer and taller, and the undergrowth grew lush.

Tiny fish darted around Charlie's shins as Patrick sauntered back across the beach.

'Jump in,' he said, and began pulling the stern of the boat around so the nose pointed out to sea.

Charlie hauled himself up over the edge, trailing water off his jeans as he went. He landed awkwardly on a steel seat and extracted his left foot gingerly from a tray of fishing tackle, none of which managed to hook him. Patrick waded the shallows, gave the boat a shove and climbed in. The motor started without protest, and he gently throttled it forwards. The sun was still behind the cliffs, and the water was in shadow. Looking down into it, Charlie could make out the sandy bottom, tinted emerald green. Clumps of broken-off kelp shot past on the surface as they went.

Offshore he could see black boulders breaking the surface at regular intervals. Deep masses of kelp crowded around the boulders, and drowsy-looking seabirds perched on them, ignoring the boat. They'd only been going for a few minutes when Patrick abruptly killed the motor. The nose of the boat came down to level, and the wake caught up to the stern, giving them a last push forward.

'Milly told me you borrowed the snorkelling gear yesterday,' Patrick said as he lobbed the anchor and its chain over the bow.

'I did.' Then the long silence, leaving Charlie unsure whether to intrude. 'What do you call those diamond-shaped fish?'

'Silver?'

'Yeah…maybe silver-grey.'

'Sweep. Were they hanging around in the fizzy water, near the edge of something?'

'Yep.'

'Yeah, that's what they'll be. They're very curious, eh. They'll come right up to your mask. Can't understand how people spear em.' He laughed dismissively. 'Bloody good to eat, but.'

Patrick tied off the anchor rope and took out two handlines. He threaded a greasy-looking baitfish onto the hook and handed the first line to Charlie. 'So why you going off snorkelling? I thought you were s'posed to be at work down here.'

Charlie recognised that he was being mocked. 'It's peaceful isn't it. I can see why you do it a lot.'

'I don't do it a lot,' countered Patrick. 'I used to. Used to go out all the time, swell, no swell, didn't matter. Other young fellas'd go surfin and I'd go off snorkelling. But things changed with the family.'

Charlie looped the fishing line over an index finger, the way he remembered his father doing. He propped a foot on the bench opposite and studied the sand that had stuck to it, the lines of the bones running towards his toes. He felt a nip at the line and tugged sharply. The line fell still again.

'You'll need another bait,' said Patrick distractedly. 'He'll've cleaned you out.'

Charlie retrieved the line and found the hook bare. He took another baitfish from the plastic bag and pushed the point of the hook through its eye. It hung unconvincingly in the bend of the hook and Patrick watched doubtfully as Charlie swung it over the side of the boat and into the water. Just as Charlie settled again, there was a violent yank on the line and he found himself pulling back against a considerable force. He stood up and pulled in loops of line. The fish was kicking and pulsing, taking line back off him as he struggled to regain it. It circled round towards the stern, and down through the clear water he could begin to see a bright shape driving in determined circles. It looked silver at first, just a reflective blob in the green-blue depths. But as it came towards the boat he recognised the side of the fish, its robust head and watchful eye. As it finally broke clear of the surface it kicked a shower of droplets off its tail and he dropped it onto the floor of the boat.

'Snapper!' cried Patrick, unable to conceal his delight. The flanks of the fish were a delicate pink, intricately speckled with spots of silver and blue. A line of white dots trailed from its gills back to the tail. The big eye rolled slightly as Patrick picked it up and examined the hook in its mouth. He turned the fish slightly so he could push the hook back through its lip. It kicked hard and slipped from his hands. He grabbed it again from the floor of the boat and tossed it in a bucket. For a moment or two he stared at it absently, deep in thought. They both settled back into their positions in the boat as the sun came clear of the cliffs.

'I'm going to tell you what happened,' he said without looking up.

Charlie was caught off guard. He'd been considering whether

to tell Patrick about his encounter with Delvene Murchison, and had decided to leave it alone.

'What, just like that?'

'At least this way it's your problem as well as mine. Chuck us the bait.'

Charlie handed him the bait without reply.

'So we both know I was on the *Caravel* that night,' Patrick began slowly. 'I was worried about Matt, an' I never liked the whole idea so I wasn't letting him go on his own. We've gone out to Gawleys—it was s'posed to be down off Boulder Point but Matt and Skip must've arranged it different in the end. I didn't notice.'

He flicked the line back into the water and looked out to sea.

'This is all just over there.' He pointed to the south. 'So we've pulled alongside because we could see their light over on the edge of Gawleys there. We pull alongside and Matt goes first, climbs over and tells me to tie off. The cabin's forward on their boat, and there's a big undercover work area aft of that. There's a light on in the work area: not the main light you use when you're workin at sea at night, cos that one's a big fluoro. This was just a bulb, and I reckon it was up under the weather cover, so it's not all that bright as he steps over. I remember looking at it, you know, you notice these things. I was thinkin it was odd the way they just had that light on. I remember when Matt had spoken to em on the way out, on the phone, he'd like repeated back to em, you know, I think they'd said to him and he was repeating, that there'd be a light on deck. The fact it was just this little one, well I s'pose I've stopped worryin because I would've thought, they're just being careful, not attractin attention.

'I couldn't tell from the way Matt was that night whether he thought he was gettin his money out of them, or whether he thought he was gettin some product to make up the difference. See you have to remember the money went in both directions—they'd be payin him commission if they were givin him abs to take up to

144

Melbourne, and he'd be givin them cash if he was getting hydro off em. Anyway, so he steps over, and I turn my back for a second to tie off. I'm movin towards the stern to start there, and Matt's gone over the rail roughly halfway down the side of the boat. I think the last I saw of him he was headed forward, which makes sense I s'pose because he would've been headin into the wheelhouse, expecting em to be there. So I'm tyin off and he yells out that there's nobody there. I think his exact words were "There's no cunt here."

'He must've gone forward somewhere, so I come on board and I'm headed that way, and then I notice something on the port side of the cabin. See there's some steel brackets you can use to secure plastic drums. You just stand the drum against the wall of the cabin and you can tighten these steel bands around em and they stay there. The Murchisons' boat is set up for abs, and I've never seen em use them brackets for anything—you'd be more likely to use em for lines or floats or something if you were line fishing or running nets. Anyway, I'm goin past them, and there's a big blue barrel in the bracket, like a screw-top thing that looks a bit like a chemical drum, and I'm thinkin to myself, That's odd, so I unscrew the top. Anyway, it's fairly dark and I stick a hand in there cos I can't see in, and it turns out the thing is packed with vacuum blocks of dope. About the size of a brick but a bit flatter. Dozens of em, all the way to the top. The smell coming out of that barrel was unbelievable. I've never seen so much dope in all me life. So I'm just standin there holdin one, me head's just spinnin, and suddenly I hear like bangs or crashes, and a voice yelling, really worked up, really angry, goin "Where are you fucker?" Then there's a crack, and I know it's a rifle straight away. I drop the brick of dope and at the same time someone hits the light. So it's pitch black and I'm freaking, just freaking. From then on, I'm kind of going on, well I s'pose the memory of what I been looking at just a second before, and I been on their boat once or twice before, so you've got a rough idea of the layout.'

He tugged at his line suddenly and pulled it confidently towards himself. The fish was another snapper, smaller than the first one. He unhooked it and dropped it in the bucket without comment.

'So I go forward the same way I thought Matt had gone. It's chaos for a few seconds—there's all this runnin around and yellin going on, people crashin into things. I run smack into Matt just on the far side of the cabin, on the gangway, just slam into him. I'm moving pretty fast, but I don't know if he was. We fall over and I wind up sort of lying over his left leg, right next to the opening in the gunwale for the crane. He's breathin real hard, like shallow and fast, and I know they've shot him. I'm hangin onto him and he's tryin to get up and he keeps slumping back down. There's a row of bolt heads in the bodywork right next to us where we fell, and he's grabbin at them and trying to pull himself up and you could tell that somethin was wrong, like he couldn't. And I can't tell where they've got him—it's too dark, and there's blood on me but I can't tell where it's coming from. And I'm tryin to talk to him, just whisperin like, You okay? And he, I don't think he's trying to be quiet, I think he actually couldn't talk, there's just this whistly sound like he's trying to.

'And we been there for probably only a few seconds and then all of a sudden he gets some words out: he says real clear, he says "Shit, I'm dyin." And as soon as that comes out of his mouth, it's like they'd been listenin, tryin to work out where he is, and they come bolting towards us—you could hear two sets of footsteps runnin on the gangway. And just as they're nearly on us, Matt's reached up and grabbed at my shirt and he just rolls me sort of across his body and I've stuck a foot out to balance meself and there's nothin there, just space, and I realise he's got me into the gap in the gunwale. So I'm fallin out, and I've got to that point, you know, when your weight's already over the edge and all you can do is fall, and I'm still lookin at Matt like I can't really work out what he's done, and he's just lookin back at me. And I can see it's Skip above him, I can see that fucker's face so clearly. You see a person every day kickin

146

around the town, and after a while you get to know the shape of their head, eh—you play footy with a person, you know the shape of their shoulders. You know how they walk. Anyhow, he's got to Matt but he isn't looking at Matt, he's looking at me. They both are. And Skip's got a gun in his hand, a rifle, sort of holding it down low. And as I'm fallin, he's lifting the gun. Then I remember hitting the water and it's a fair way from the deck, so I've penetrated a bit, you know, and when I look up I can see the side of the hull against the sky, and I head under the keel and swim forward a bit, so I come up between the two boats, just back from the bows. I've stayed on the surface for a sec and got a few breaths in, and then I hear Mick McVean yellin above me and I look up and I can see he's spotted me, so I dive again and just head out into space away from the boats. I got no idea which way I'm swimmin, you know, just trying to get the fuck away from them. They're shooting at me—I can hear it, it's a fucken weird noise, like this *whoosh*, as a couple of rounds go past me in the water. And I'm thinkin to myself, they're expectin me to keep going out from the boats, so I've gone deep instead, and I've got to the reef about twelve, fifteen feet down, and I'm hangin onto some kelp for a sec. But I can't hold me breath as good as I normally do, cos I'm just so wired by that stage, so I come up again, and I spin around looking for them and I can see they're on the other gunwale and they're looking the wrong way, so I get a few more breaths in and I head down again. And as I'm going down I hear the engines start up, you know, very clear through the water.

'An' I hear the anchor come up, and I've got a really good breath this time, and I just hang there on the bottom, holding the kelp, and I start moving along the bottom nice and slow, and as I'm moving, I hear another round come down: like about three or four feet away, and it makes a click when it hits the rocks. I'm thinkin about it, and I'm thinkin, how the hell do they know where I am? They were lookin the wrong way last time I come up. And then there's one or two more, and they're really close, the big *whoosh*. I

147

can feel the bubbles from one near me ribs as I'm hangin on. And then the clicks when they hit the reef, and I've worked it out all of a sudden, the fuckers have got the fishfinder on. And here's me, I'd be the only fucken thing on their screen, right under them. And I'm runnin out of air, and I'm thinkin this time they've got me cold, I'm fucked, and I gotta come up and they're right above me, but they're still creeping forward, so I come up right behind the props, in the wash, and I reckon that would've lost me for em. They keep goin forward for a while, and I can hear over the engines they're still firin into the water, and they've got the big lights on now, pointing em into the water around the bow where they think I'd be. And I'm just hangin on the surface, dead still, getting me breath back. And they're motoring away from our boat towards the shore, I s'pose they're figurin I'd head for shore so they're just kind of taking that line. Our boat's behind me, but I'm just watchin em, gettin ready to duck under again if they sweep round. It's still pretty dark out there, and they would've had it harder'n me cos they were in among the lights on the deck. So I'm treadin water out there, actually movin a bit further out to sea away from our boat, just tryin to do what I thought they wouldn't be expectin me to do. And then they've got this spotlight out. I can see them working it up and down, lookin for me, and they're still firin out to sea, just randomly.

'They spot out near me a couple of times, and I go under again, and I can hear the bullets underwater again. They fucken petrified me, those shots. I'm down there and I can feel me heart just going mental. It's a bit hard to describe. But if someone shoots near you in the air, all you know is it missed. You don't have any idea how close it was. In the water, you can feel the bastards rippin past. Anyway, they're bringin the boat around in a big half circle, back towards our boat, and they're still working the searchlight and still shooting, and as they come back to our boat, they turn off the engines and everything goes quiet, and I'm still hangin on the surface and they start calling out, saying stuff like "Gettin tired Paddy?" and "Paddy, we're gonna wait for you boyo, we're gonna fucken do ya boyo." I remember that one especially. And I can clearly see Mick with the rifle up at his shoulder, shooting out to sea, and he'd go "Cunt!" and he'd shoot, and "Cunt!" and he'd shoot again. He was really worked up.

'So I'm hangin there with just the top of me head out of the water, and they've looped back around and come back to our boat. And I'm watching em—they pull alongside and I'm watching em...I watched em throw Matt over the side onto our boat. And I reckon up to that point I'm still thinkin about getting back to him, you know, maybe trying to save him. I'm shit scared, don't get me wrong, and mostly I'm just trying to save me own arse, but a part of me keeps thinkin maybe I could help him. Anyway they've chucked him over the side onto our boat, and it sits about probably four foot lower at the gunwales than theirs, so he falls a fair way before he lands on the deck, and it's pretty clear he's dead by then. He's just, um, limp. He's a dead weight, and he's come down on the deck straight on his head but he didn't flinch or anything, you know, didn't react. And he's hit the steel so hard that if there was any life in him he'd have reacted to that. It, God it made such a fucking horrible noise. So I know then he's gone.

'They've stopped shootin by this stage and I can't work out what they're up to. They're yellin at each other like they're completely off their heads. Screaming—you fucken this and you fucken that. That went on for a while, like they had no idea what to do. Then I see Mick with a jerry can and he's givin our boat a good slosh, and I can see in the lights from their boat the petrol—I s'pose it was petrol—splashing on Matt, and he hasn't moved at all. And then they've gunned the motors and, and they've lit something, probably a rag or somethin, and they've thrown it over, and up she goes. As soon as it goes up, they're off. And from where I'm looking, I can see Matt's legs and they're not moving. He's on fire, and his legs aren't moving. I can see the sneakers he had on, these shitty old

149

sneakers, and all of a sudden I can see him standin there at the pub and I've got a beer in me hand and so does he and I'm laughin about somethin and I'm lookin at his feet as I'm laughin and it's them same old shitty sneakers, an he's sloppin beer on em. He wore em everywhere, even out to sea. I'm tryin to explain it here, how I left him, cos I know, I know you'd find it hard to understand this, but he was gone and I was already thinkin about what comes next. I'm just treadin water out there, watchin it burn, watchin *him* burn, and I know that the town will believe these pricks, if anyone even thinks to ask. But they're probably just gonna say that Matt was up to something dodgy—everyone bloody knew he was anyway—and if I was there too then they're gonna find there's a bullet in him somewhere and the boat's on fire, and I'm in the water and I haven't got a scratch on me and it's not gonna be a good look. Not when you're well enough known like I am, eh. I mean Jesus, we didn't get on that good most of the time. We'd had a fucken ripper punch on after closing only about three weeks before this.

'So there you go—I just start swimmin for shore. Probably go to hell for it, but that's what I did. I'm keepin half an eye on the Murchisons' boat to make sure they don't change their minds, but I kinda knew they had to get away from the fire as quick as they could, so I figured I was right. And when I get to shore I've just skulked round to home hopin I wouldn't see anybody. I was, you know, I was drippin wet, and it would've been pretty hard to explain. An so I got to home an I was just in time to dry an' change an' then Robbo turned up an' you know the statement I give him.'

'Fuck,' said Charlie quietly. It was all he could think to say. The magnitude of what he'd just been told had sucked the air out of him. 'What...fuck.'

He thought for a moment. 'Where's this barrel of dope?'

'I dunno. I guess the Murchisons got rid of it quick smart when they got back.'

They fell into silence again, each considering their position.

'Why?'

'Why what?'

'Well, why meet at sea? And why did they go armed?'

Patrick shrugged. 'Can't be too careful.'

'What? For a handful of abalone and some cash? Come on. Don't you think the barrel of dope changes things a bit? How do you know Matt hadn't organised something much bigger and you weren't aware of it?'

'I don't know, do I. Whatever he was doing, he's dead and there's no barrel.'

'Exactly,' said Charlie. He suddenly felt cold despite the morning sun. 'Sure you don't know where the barrel is?'

Patrick snorted with derision. 'What, you think I've got it? I'm a witness in a murder trial and I'm sittin on a bloody great keg of drugs. That'd be smart, wouldn't it...'

'So what are you going to do when you get in the witness box? You've put me in a giant fucking hole now, haven't you?'

Patrick's eyes never wavered from his line.

'You chose to come here. You chose to ask me about all this. You coulda just left it alone and you wouldn't have all this...trouble. Problems like this, mate, they only appear when you go poking around in other people's shit. Like I said before, now it's your problem as well as mine.'

They continued fishing for another hour, filling the bucket with snapper. When the bait ran out, Patrick pulled in the anchor and started the motor again. The sun was high overhead now, every crevasse of the reef below them lit up. Large schools of silver fish passed below, thousands of them moving in perfect unison.

As the shore came nearer, the details of the beach and the scrub came into view. Charlie could see that Patrick was watching something, looking up the line of the tractor's imprints in the sand, up to the edge of the scrub where he'd left it. Closer in, Charlie could make out the tractor, and could see that there was a small, bright shape perched on it, a speck of red against the grey-green background. It was a boy, sitting in the drivers seat, perfectly still. He was looking straight back out to sea at them with one hand shielding his eyes against the sun. He'd drawn his knees up under his red T-shirt and was leaning both elbows on them. Patrick continued to stare at him, and the child continued to stare back, until very suddenly he jumped off the tractor and ran into the scrub.

'You know him?' asked Charlie.

'Nope. Just some kid.'

Onshore, Charlie sat in his car and scrolled through the handful of messages on his phone while Patrick emptied the boat. He had what he came for and he knew he had to go back to town, had to face the bloody regulators, prepare the trial and sort out his life. What had Annie said about the furniture? Patrick was sitting in the bow of the boat, which was still hitched to the tractor. He was coiling rope, looking off into the distance along the beach as his arms took in each loop. Charlie couldn't tell if that look on his face, cautious, sceptical, was something that came from years of disappointment and forced responsibility, or if something greater was eating at him.

Patrick had made a decision this morning he could never go back from—he couldn't now give evidence that his first statement was true, that he was at home on the night, because he'd equipped Charlie with the knowledge that it wasn't. The trial would either abort, or he'd turn the prosecution case into such a shambles that Murchison and McVean would walk. Either way, he was facing an uncomfortable wait for the trial. Delvene Murchison would undoubtedly work away at him, whether through Neil Robertson or more directly. Charlie would drive back to Melbourne and turn his back on all this. But Patrick had no escape. His siblings depended on him daily, a burden that seemed totally unfair, but from which there was no prospect of any relief.

He'd put the rope down and was sitting motionless in the boat.

There was a despondency in his shoulders, darkness under his brows where the shadows had fallen on his eyes. Charlie reflected that he himself was accustomed to a cycle of wins and losses, a process of constant renewal by verdicts and settlements. He couldn't imagine a state of being in which life's burdens just could not be shifted.

THAT NIGHT CHARLIE unwrapped the snapper fillets Patrick had given him in a bundle of newspaper. The print had stuck to the creamy flesh, reversed but still readable in the smooth muscle fibres. He laid them in a pan and fried them until they curled, spitting flecks of hot oil on the backs of his hands as he lifted them onto a plate. There was beer in the fridge. He had no memory of buying it, and had a vague suspicion Les had dropped by and put it there, though he couldn't think why he would do such a thing.

He ate alone in front of the television. He'd begun the mental process of saying goodbye to the house, a place he initially couldn't stand, and to which he now felt attached. The empty plate lay on the coffee table as he took another beer from the fridge, then a third and a fourth. In the middle of the fifth beer he realised he needed to leave Dauphin to get his alcohol intake under control. Then he fell asleep in the chair.

He awoke hours later, desperately needing to piss. He could smell the cooled fish hanging in the air. Shuffling to the bathroom, he became aware of a sound, loud but distant. Howling.

A siren.

It was much like the air-raid sirens in old war films, though he'd never heard the sound in reality. It rose and fell, rose and fell, full of melancholy. As his bladder drained the howling was joined by the more urgent pulses of police sirens. Bad tidings. Upturned boats, mangled cars, weeping mothers. He found a jacket in the darkened hallway, stumbled outside and got in the car, not really knowing why.

It was a cold night and there was a mist in the air. There was static on the radio and the heater was blowing cold. Nothing moved in the streets between his house and the town, but as he came nearer, the air above the buildings seemed to be illuminated. It took a moment to register, but the sky was glowing orange. Then he swung into the main street and the source of the noise became apparent: cars were everywhere—police, CFA, ambulances and onlookers. People milled on the street and there was running and shouting wherever he looked. The Normans Woe was on fire.

He parked the car and turned it off, clutching the coat over his ribs. Fire trucks had arranged themselves parallel to the kerb on both sides of the pub. The crews were trying to attach hoses to the two hydrants in the street. A man with a large wrench in his hand was arguing with two others at the hydrant, one of whom was pointing back at the truck. The other crew had got their hose connected and had started to direct a long jet of water onto the roof of the pub, but the fire had outpaced them. It was licking through the iron sheets of the roof, lifting their edges and buckling them. It tore greedily at the windows, exploding through the few remaining panes of glass and consuming the old timber frames. Sparks curled above the building, borne on a thick column of smoke. The smoke, the nearby trees, everything glowed orange even well above the rooftop.

The second hose was now concentrated on the blaze. One of the upstairs attic windows had begun to slump to one side. A group of firefighters burst out the front door of the building wearing breathing apparatus, running like astronauts in the cumbersome gear. There was a crashing noise from deep inside the pub as a section of roof collapsed, and, freed from constraint, the flames reached confidently into the night sky. The structure of the building—its doorways, windows and pillars—the firemen running past, had become silhouettes and nothing more: the intensity of the light was everything. It was like staring at the sun.

Charlie watched all this with dismay. Unthinking, he got out, slammed the door and sat on the front of the car. A man approached out of the darkness on a kids bike, pedalling hard, wobbling comically as he slowed. It was Les. He rolled to a stop next to Charlie and watched the flames without speaking, his elbows resting on the handlebars and his chin in his hands. After a while, Charlie looked at him, his face lit by the fire and the lights of the trucks. There were tears on his cheeks. Charlie saw the flashing lights reflected in his wet eyes and wished he knew what to do. He reached out and put a hand on the slumped shoulder, rested it there for a moment or two and then felt awkward and removed it. Les drew the back of his own hand across his nose, making a snotty sound as he did so.

'This is the worst of it, mate,' he said, his voice thin with distress. He lifted the front wheel of the bike off the ground and let it spin slowly. 'Of all the fucking dreadful things these people have done, this has got to be the worst of it.'

Water ran down the footpath, lit up orange by the flames. The wind swirled and pushed the smoke across the two of them, carrying a wave of heat with it.

'What do you mean?'

Les looked directly at him.

'This'll be their work. Bloody Alan and Del. They've had this place on the market for two years cos the council knocked back their planning application. They were gonna do a bloody apartment complex and pokies and that,' he waved a hand dismissively at the burning pub. 'An' they took it to the tribunal and they knocked em back again and they did tons of dough on it. An' the bloody thing's been like a millstone round their necks ever since. You know, I'd go to buy stuff, stock and that. Or I'd ask em to pay for repairs to the temprites or fix up the lighting out the back, and they wouldn't spend a fucking cent. I sat in the office all the time mate, I seen these things. They had it insured for nine hundred grand. Nine hundred…you might get half that at an auction. This is a stocktake, mate.'

'If they've torched it, the cops'll figure it out, Les. They never seem to have too much trouble figuring out if a fire's deliberately lit.'

There was a loud bang from deep in the rear of the building. A plume of fire swelled above the walls, and the crowd shuffled back as the heat intensified. Charlie could see among them the priest from the football, the girls who'd made him coffee, and in the front of the gathering, Delvene Murchison, apparently racked with grief and horror, clutching a man who must have been her husband. The pitiful state of her face didn't tally at all with the imperious woman he'd met at the Chinese restaurant.

Les was thinking, still spinning the wheel of the bike.

'And if it's deliberately lit, and if it's obvious, who's in the shit then, Charlie? Who's ol' Robbo gonna drag in for an interview? Won't be the Murchisons. It's gonna be the bloke that's got a bone to pick with them lot. Same bloke you've got giving evidence.'

'You can't be serious.'

'Well, you tell me. Everything was going along swimmingly. Young Skip's on trial for the murder but Patrick's not gonna talk. So the Murchisons mightn't like it much, but if they just wait it all out, things'll be fine. Then you come to town and the kid changes his mind, decides he'll explain what happened on the night, eh?'

He looked questioningly at Charlie, who was feeling a growing knot of nausea in his stomach.

'You know I can't tell you where all that's up to, Les.'

'Well that's as good as confirming it. So the Murchisons need to smear his name, make sure he's a useless witness. *Discredit* him, that's the word, isn't it?'

Charlie didn't respond.

'The allegation doesn't have to stick. I mean, they won't want it to backfire on *them*, but it doesn't matter if it doesn't stick on

Patrick. They just need it to raise enough of a stink that he's useless in the court case. And they pick up nine hundred grand along the way, offload a shitty old business that only made 'em two bob a week. And they get their boy off the hook.'

He bounced the wheel a couple of times on the ground.

'Fuck me...pretty bloody easy isn't it?'

Charlie watched the front wall beginning to buckle. Great blocks of cut stone, laid by long-forgotten hands, began tumbling into the street, first in ones and twos, and then whole sections of wall staggering and falling. Clouds of dust and smoke billowed into the headlights of the circling vehicles. Charlie felt a terrible sense of waste. The deliberate destruction of this thing that careful generations had assembled and tended, trashed for reasons that related only to a handful of angry people. Storms and floods and depressions, as much as fights and parties and street parades...the stonework had stood there; had framed them in common memory. It filled him with disgust to think that by morning it would be wet ash and rubble, pools of dirty water.

The two of them sat in silence, watching the firemen working at the building. There was no urgency in the effort now. There was no contest to be had with the flames.

Unnoticed by anyone else, Patrick's Camira rolled to a stop behind the fire trucks, and Charlie could see him dimly behind the windscreen, in the same ripped flannie he wore everywhere. When the car came to rest he made no move to get out. He was talking to someone in the passenger seat. Charlie felt sure this wasn't Patrick's work. Nothing about him suggested he'd do such a thing. The only thing Charlie had definitely worked out about Patrick Lanegan was that he lacked the ability to influence the happenings around him. He wasn't about to impose himself on the order of events, the poor bastard.

The flames were dying. Either the water had started to take effect, or there was simply nothing left to feed them. One of the crews had finished hosing the wreckage and started packing equipment into the truck. Les was talking to a fireman who'd wandered over. Both of them had their arms folded, and stood shoulder to shoulder, talking with their heads down. The fireman was tapping the side of his boot on the bluestone kerb.

Les ambled back to Charlie, climbed back onto the bike and sighed deeply. 'You were right. They didn't have much trouble figuring it out. Back door of the kitchen was jemmied open and the gas jets were on flat out.'

The radiant warmth from the fire was beginning to subside. The flames still reflected on the side of the car but they had lost their intensity. A startled dog had been pacing through the crowd, darting from group to group in search of a comforting hand; now it ambled off into the night.

Charlie knew he was far too close to this business. There was a crucial line between observing events and influencing their very occurrence. He could not show Patrick any further sympathy, could not even satisfy himself that the fire had nothing to do with him. He had to turn his back on it all before the trial itself fell victim to the junior prosecutor's meddling. As he watched the dark outline of Patrick's car, a figure emerged from the passenger door and started walking around the back of the crowd, behind the parked fire trucks, towards him. It was the girl from the ambush, the sister from Patrick's house. The name escaped him for a moment.

Milly.

She was wearing a white frock and wobbling slightly on a pair of heels.

'You're dressed up,' he said.

'Last rehearsal for the deb ball,' she replied, brushing her hands self-consciously over her hips. 'Paddy asked me to tell you something.'

Even as she said it, the words had a familiar ring and Charlie found himself looking for a sprinting thug from stage left.

'He said he won't give you a statement.'

Charlie nodded wearily.

'He said the Murchisons done this.' She nodded towards the fire. 'And he said he's gonna tell the truth. In court.'

Charlie took this in for a moment.

'Tell him the car's fixed,' he said. 'I'm leaving in the morning.'

He looked back at the fire. Delvene Murchison was still wrapped around the man Charlie assumed to be her husband. Her show of emotion was nearly as mesmerising as the fire itself: the operatic grief, the flailing arms and sobs.

Yet even as he watched her, a strange thing happened. From her position against the man's chest, she looked up, looked across the intersection and found Charlie. Her eyes locked directly onto his, and for a split second her expression revealed something to him, something tiny and secretive; not quite a smile. The look would replay itself in his mind all the way back to Melbourne. An admission of everything, and a guarantee that nothing would be conceded.

THE TRIAL

JURY SELECTED IN ABALONE MURDER TRIAL
Emma Killian, Court Reporter

Jury selection was completed today in the trial of two men accused of the murder of a commercial fisherman at Dauphin, in the state's west.

Toby James Murchison and Michael John McVean, both 25, of Dauphin, Victoria are accused of the shooting death of Matthew Lanegan, 24, in August last year.

Prosecutor Harlan Weir SC opened the Crown's case to the jury, describing the shooting as having been motivated by 'appalling greed and cowardice'. The two men are alleged to have been trading over-quota abalone through the black market, employing the victim and his younger brother as couriers. In what appears to be a dispute over payment of commission to the brothers for their role, Mr Weir said the victim was lured to a night-time meeting on board the accuseds' commercial fishing vessel, offshore from the small town. When he boarded the vessel, he was shot and his body was then dumped back on his own boat, which was subsequently set on fire. The pair were arrested two days later, after mobile phone records and security logging at the town's wharf indicated their presence at the rendezvous. A rifle, alleged to be the murder weapon, was found dumped at sea near the point at which the two boats are said to have met on the night.

Murchison, whose father owns the town's only hotel, as well as a lucrative abalone licence and a tourism business, is represented by renowned defence advocate Jose Ocas QC. Mr Ocas today described the Crown case against his client as 'a clumsily woven patchwork of circumstantial evidence, rumour and flat-out guesswork'.

Mr McVean, meanwhile, has been allocated an advocate from the public defender's office, believed at this stage to be Franz Rhodes. The trial, before Justice Fabian Williams, is expected to last two weeks.

The small town of Dauphin has attracted unwanted publicity in recent years, having been the subject of Fisheries Department operations that have uncovered evidence of large-scale poaching of abalone by groups already involved in drug trafficking. Despite this, it remains the highest-earning rural shire in the state, principally because it is home to several abalone licence holders. The licences are currently worth between 2 and 3 million dollars and can return huge profits to the licensee. A shire official, speaking this week on condition of anonymity, said the town 'can't afford to have this thing stick...people here rely heavily on the Murchison interests for their ongoing employment'.

In an interesting footnote to the trial's commencement today, the prosecution's junior counsel is Charlie Jardim, the young barrister who came to dubious prominence in February after being remanded in custody for contempt of court. In a fiery confrontation with Magistrate Maurice Lefcovics, Mr Jardim had told the veteran magistrate that he was 'known throughout the state as a heartless old prick and a drunk and seeing I've gone this far, your daughter in law's appointment to the court is widely viewed as a grubby political payoff.' Court transcript of the incident was widely circulated among lawyers by email in the ensuing weeks.

Asked today for comment regarding the appointment of Mr Jardim to the murder trial, the Director of Public Prosecutions would say only that 'It has always been the case that our senior prosecutors have autonomy over their choice of junior counsel. Mr Jardim is still on the Roll of Counsel and is not currently subject to any sanction which would prevent him from appearing.' Privately, the Director is said to be fuming at the appointment and has called for vetting of all junior counsel appointments to major trials within his office.

The trial will resume tomorrow, with the victim's brother Patrick Lanegan scheduled to give evidence early next week.

CHARLIE TOOK A bundle of the previous day's transcript and headed for the library. He'd never been able to eat during a trial. It wasn't that the stress got to him; he just ran without refuelling, could think and talk for hours on end until he collapsed in the evening. It was, he reflected, one of the many things that made him poor company: a man who spent all his energy and intellect on a room full of hostile strangers and had nothing left afterwards for friends at night.

He loved the massive flagstones of the Supreme Court, their sense of a brutal Victorian past. Where the corridors came to a corner, the stones were worn into a shallow scoop, countless feet scouring the basalt into a fine dust, down through a century and more. It all spoke of a cult of death, even now when the last witnesses to the days of capital punishment were nearing retirement. The Basque had alluded to it in casual conversation one morning as they waited for the associate to unlock the courtroom.

'Feeling a bit of strain over all this?' he'd asked.

'No,' Charlie had smiled back, simply because he wouldn't give him anything.

'Yes you are,' replied the Basque. 'There's nothing more serious than what we're doing. I can still remember the days when there was a noose at the end of a trial like this, you know.'

'If I was prosecuting it,' Charlie had countered, 'why would that be my worry? Wouldn't that be eating away at the defence counsel?'

In front of them there was a loud bang as the antique locks of the courtroom door tumbled open.

'Sure,' Ocas had said. 'You never wanted to send your client away to their death. But the prosecutor used to feel it too, sometimes more so. At least the defence counsel had the consolation that they were trying to *save* the poor bastard. Your lot were actively trying to kill him.'

Such encounters with the Basque were all part of the theatre, the countless little ways he found of getting under an opponent's skin. He had an uncanny feel for it.

Charlie wandered past the portraits of dead judges, the brass plates marking courtrooms and offices, the accumulated stains of passing hands that had brushed the sandstone walls. It was impossible to feel any sense of a higher justice in such a corridor. It was only a passage through time towards more of the same: violence and perfidy and their consequences. These stones fed on human lives.

He was thinking about Patrick's evidence in chief that morning. Allowing for the fact that witness examination had a way of stripping all the life out of a story, Patrick had managed to relate the whole thing in much the same way he'd told it to Charlie in the boat all those weeks ago. He'd been reliable on all the major points of the story, picking up the hints in Charlie's open-ended questions and betraying just enough grief to lend credibility to the tale. The judge had stepped in here and there, pecking at hearsay slips and venturing some faint scepticism on occasions. But largely he'd stayed out of it, listening and watching in grave silence. Weir sat in attentive repose, making occasional notes in a ring binder that would form the basis for his closing address. Even the Basque had restrained himself, though it alarmed Charlie to see that he was smiling broadly almost all the way through. This was just as likely to be for the jury's benefit, but it filled Charlie with dread to think that after lunch, he was going to have to turn this unsteady witness over to cross-examination.

Charlie continued walking towards the weak reflection of

sunlight that indicated an exit. Through more doorways and out under a portico into the building's hexagonal inner courtyard with the corresponding six-sided bulk of the old library in the centre. He stopped in a warm, bright patch of sun and felt the glow of it soaking through his robes and his suit, finding his body beneath. A lone plane tree showed vivid specks of green where the spring growth would burst forth in the weeks after this miserable business was done. And, he assured himself, by the time the leaves had reached their full size, dappling the hot summer sun and lifting in the northerly, he'd be gone.

A voice called his name quietly from the shade. It was Patrick, leaning against a verandah post, halfway through a cigarette. His bony wrists sprouted from the cuffs of the borrowed suit as he smoked. Charlie looked both ways quickly, conscious of the awkwardness of being caught talking to the witness.

'How am I going mate?'

'I can't tell you,' hissed Charlie. 'You're still under oath until the cross-examination's finished. I can't discuss your evidence with you.'

'Yeah, but you can tell me if I'm doing all right or not. That's not evidence,'

Charlie looked at the ground. 'No I can't.'

Patrick took a long drag on the smoke and ashed it by his side.

'Strange, isn't it? We're back in your world now. Rules, rules, rules.'

Charlie couldn't help himself.

'You mighta been frank in the first place,' he answered. But as soon as he saw the wounded look cross Patrick's face, he knew he'd been unfair.

'Just keep your chin up,' he offered feebly.

'Mm.' Patrick dropped the butt and ground it into the cobbles with his heel. He turned away without another look at Charlie and walked back inside. Charlie was left watching his back, the troubled downward tilt of his neck, as the shadows consumed him.

AT TWO SEVENTEEN pm, Jose Ocas rose to cross-examine. Dark-featured and heavy, his manner finely tuned to suggest the outsider's role, he came as near to exotica as such a room would allow. A fairground boxer, curiously pinned into the ritual garb of old England: the jabot, the wig, the outlandish folds of the great black gown. Nothing about his demeanour sat easily with the pompous attire.

He surveyed the room, his deep-set eyes lingering a moment over the jury, before picking up a document from the scatter of papers before him. He held it at half an arm's length, studying it silently as he stroked at the chin of his beard. Patrick waited, inert and helpless, through this set piece.

'I was going to ask you questions about your statement, Mr Lanegan,' Ocas began, in a tone that suggested mock offence. 'But it's not much use to us now, is it?'

He threw the document onto the table and looked to the jury, his face a pained grimace. *This treacherous witness has deceived us.* He plainly didn't care for any answer to the rhetorical query.

'All lies. You lied to the police, didn't you, Mr Lanegan?'

Weir rose in feeble protest. 'Perhaps Mr Ocas would like to be more specific?'

The judge nodded slightly and Ocas held a palm out in front of him. 'I'll get to that, Your Honour. I will.'

Ocas allowed a long silence to grow in the room with himself at its centre. Slumped over his notes, Charlie felt a reluctant admiration for his stagecraft. At the very moment when any further silence might have caused murmuring among those present, Ocas resumed with thunderous rage.

'You sold abalone on the black market for the Murchisons!' he bellowed.

'Yes I did.'

'You received from them, at various times, deliveries of hydroponically grown cannabis for resale to others!'

'Me and me brother, yes.'

'You have prior convictions for, among other things, aggravated assault.'

'I do.'

'Threats to kill...'

'Yes.'

'Burglary, theft from motor vehicle and affray, Mr Lanegan.'

'Yes. I done those things.' Patrick's voice had fallen to a murmur. He seemed fixated on the timber rail of the witness box in front of him, his fingers absently drawing lines along the grain.

'You hadn't committed an offence for, oh, nineteen months before all this, had you?' Ocas waved the rap sheet around his head in feigned wonderment.

'No, I hadn't.' Patrick raised his chin with a glimmer of defiance. 'I was focused on me family.'

'On your *family*...' recited Ocas, freighting the first syllable with all the sarcasm it would carry. 'That's noble. Were you focused on your family when you swore a completely false statement before Detective Sergeant Robertson?'

Patrick glared back at his tormentor but said nothing. Watching his helpless fury, Charlie wondered if the lost soul in the witness box could finally feel the reality of what Charlie had been trying to tell him—that the rules would ultimately prevail, that the law created blind corners like this one where guile and fists and stoicism were impotent. A finely structured, state-sanctioned torture, governed by a complex code that the room couldn't see. Only those in the robes, four barristers and a judge, knew exactly how far this battering could proceed, where the margins were. Charlie knew there was ample room between those margins for total humiliation. Ocas had worked these questions up over weeks, had measured carefully the forensic impact of each. As he lifted each line off the page and into the air, he was applying his own long-tested barometer, sensing the mood in the room, the emotional endurance of the witness, the patience of the listeners. Each question was matured, polished and precision-engineered long before it found voice, for all it might have sounded like spontaneous argument. And for each question, Patrick had seconds to respond.

Ocas pointed to his left. 'You owe this jury an answer, Mr Lanegan. Your brother had been dead not even a couple of hours and you were already telling outrageous lies to Detective Sergeant Robertson, weren't you.'

'I don't know if they were outrageous,' sighed Patrick. 'That's your word. There were lies in there, yes. I would've thought that's pretty obvious.'

Again, Ocas reeled in imaginary offence. 'Obvious, Mr Lanegan? All right, I'm going to give you your statement and you can tell me which parts are the true parts of the—I take it there are *some* true parts, are there?'

'There would be, yes.' The room fell silent but for the faint tapping of the stenographer, as the document was handed across the bar table to the associate, then the tipstaff and finally to the witness. Patrick studied it for some time.

'The first page is true,' he said quietly. He turned the page over the staple at the corner. It hung there as he read. 'Second page is all true too. Again he turned the page. 'Third page I made up.'

'Mmm,' grunted Ocas. 'Is that your signature at the foot of the document, Mr Lanegan, after the third page that, as you so eloquently put it, you "made up"? I'm referring to the one at the top of the fourth page.'

'Yes it is.'

'Just read me the words, Mr Lanegan, that appear directly above your signature, will you please?'

'"I hereby acknowledge that this statement is true and correct and I make it in the belief that a person making a false statement in the circumstances is liable to the pe– the penalties of perjury..."'

'So although you swore to tell the truth then, and you've sworn to tell it today, you want us to choose, in effect, to believe *this* version of your story, but not that one. Is that the case?'

'I'm sorry, can you repeat that?' asked Patrick. It was the one trick Charlie had shown him that, so far, he'd shown any sign of remembering. If you're in a tight spot, Charlie had told him, ask the questioner to repeat what they've asked you. Slows everything down, gives you a chance to compose.

'You want us to believe that this story, today, is the truth, do you?'

Patrick hesitated a moment as he realised there was no good answer to such a question. 'Yes, I do.'

'Well, before I come to the question that all of us are interested in—that's why you lied to police—I want to ask you about something else. Who influenced you to change your story?'

'No one did.'

'No one? You simply had a change of heart?'

'Um, you could put it that way, yes.'

'I put to you, Mr Lanegan, that something has happened between'—he scanned the statement—'11 August last year and now, that has caused you to change your evidence.'

'No.'

'Either some person, or some circumstance, has borne upon you to cause you to change your account of the night.'

'No.'

'You're on oath, Mr Lanegan.'

'No.'

'This isn't some Magistrates' Court out in western Victoria, Mr Lanegan. This is the big—'

Weir finally intervened, his words clamouring loudly over the end of Ocas's sentence. 'I think the jury is unlikely to be assisted by this sort of grandstanding, Your Honour.'

Charlie watched the old lizard as his eyes darted from Weir to the Basque and back again. 'I'm inclined to agree, Mr Ocas. Try to confine it a bit if you can, please.'

'Certainly, Your Honour.'

Ocas placed one hairy paw on top of his wig and shifted it forwards. His stout body was now enveloped by the black swathe of the robe and supported on both fists, propped on the shiny surface of the bar table. He leaned forward over the table, resembling a furious pitbull straining to break its leash.

'Did you speak to Mr Jardim during the break, Mr Lanegan?'

Patrick shot a look at Charlie, his face creased in confusion. 'What, just now?'

'Yes. Just now. During the lunch break, in between your evidence in chief and the beginning of this cross-examination. Did you speak to Mr Jardim?'

Charlie knew just enough of Patrick to see that the Basque had tweaked his defiance. 'Yes, yes I did. So what?'

'Did you discuss your evidence with Mr Jardim?'

The question hung in the air as Charlie felt ants crawling up over his jaw and a prickly, hot itch bursting across his forehead under the wig. He tried to scribble away idly at his notes as though the question meant nothing to him.

Patrick grinned back at Ocas. 'I tried to, yes, cos I didn't know the rule about that, but he wouldn't let me talk about it, eh.'

'You wanted him to coach you through this cross-examination,' Ocas persisted. 'You wanted to *cheat*, Mr Lanegan.'

'Nah. I actually wanted to know how I'd gone in the first bit.' The grin disappeared as quickly as it had come. 'It was a big thing to, you know, to talk about it in front of everyone...' His voice trailed off as his eyes shifted nervously across the room from the media bench on one side to the jury on the other.

'So Mr Jardim gave you no assistance over the lunch break, you say.'

'That's right.'

'However, he *did* pay you a visit in Dauphin, didn't he,' Ocas pressed.

'Yes.'

'In the three weeks between the sixth and twenty-fifth of March this year, Mr Jardim was in Dauphin, wasn't he, Mr Lanegan.'

'I couldn't say what the dates were, exactly, but he was there for a couple of weeks that I knew of, yes.'

'And he wasn't on holiday, was he?'

'No, I'd say he probably wasn't, but he didn't seem to be working either.'

'What do you mean by that?'

'I don't know. I suppose I'd say if a lawyer was at work, he'd be in a suit and that, and he'd be, um, writing stuff or working at a computer, or talking in court or something. He wasn't doing any of that stuff is what I mean.' Charlie marvelled at his ingenuity. He'd slipped behind the bumpkin mask. The kid was a study in rat cunning.

A faint smile unfurled under the Basque's beard. 'Lawyers sometimes work in funny ways, Mr Lanegan.' Ocas appeared to reconsider this. 'I withdraw that, Your Honour.' He leafed through his notebook, the paper made stiff and heavy by the weight of ink expended on each page.

'Now I don't want to speak ill of Mr Jardim, you understand, but it's fair to say, isn't it, that you struck up a bit of a friendship with him.'

Feel free to disown me right now, thought Charlie.

'We got along okay. I mean, he had a job to do and I can respect that.' The instant the words had completed their short echo in the room, it was obvious that Patrick regretted them intensely. He tensed, as though to add something, but Ocas was already upon him.

'He *did* have a job to do, *didn't* he! He was there, Mr Lanegan, to influence your evidence!'

Weir leapt to his feet again. 'This witness can't answer that, Your Honour. It's rhetorical...'

Williams puckered his mouth in thought. 'Tipstaff, send the witness and the jury out, please.' The jury were stood up and marched in their rows through the heavy panelled door that separated them from society. Patrick was ushered through a similar doorway in a corner of the great room that lay adjacent to the witness box. Only once both doors had clunked heavily into place did the judge begin to speak.

'Mr Ocas, I accept that this is a robust jurisdiction, but you are wandering into some territory here that is...I mean, at best, it's forensically awkward. At worst, you may cause a mistrial. Is that what you're angling at?'

'Your Honour, I'm only trying to lay the groundwork with this jury that the witness has recanted one version and adopted another, which offers a much'—he searched for the word—'*cosier* fit with the available evidence. Now that might be pure coincidence, but in my submission I'm entitled to explore how that change of attitude came about.'

'I don't think there's any mystery as to what you're angling at, Mr Ocas. Jurists differ in the level of insight they ascribe to juries, but you'll be aware that I have maintained for many years that they are sentient organisms, juries, and what you're suggesting here is very obvious. I'm not sure that there's a need for you to go dragging Mr Jardim here into the mire along with the witness. What if we have a situation where Mr Jardim winds up having to give evidence in rebuttal of something you assert, or something this witness tells us? What then?'

'Well with respect, Your Honour, I didn't ask Mr Jardim to go wandering off to Dauphin and start inveigling himself into the local scene.' He extended an arm towards Weir. 'Perhaps Mr Weir did. Perhaps Mr Jardim took it upon himself. But the Crown are now presenting this young man as an eyewitness to the killing. If you read the prosecution brief, you'd be forgiven for thinking he was little more than a bereaved relative. So in that context, I say the defence should be able to attack his credit. I don't want, and I adopt Your Honour's term here, I don't want any awkwardness to emerge, but I can't just take a one hundred and eighty degree turnaround from the witness and say, "Oh okay, fair enough, can I ask you a few questions about your new version".'

Again, the judge showed no sign of a concluded view. 'Mr Weir?'

'Well I objected, Your Honour, because of the very risk that we're now discussing. I'd submit that this line of questioning can only result in a discharge of the jury. If the witness ultimately tells Mr Ocas that he and Mr Jardim conspired together to "fix" his evidence, then yes, that assertion would be vehemently opposed, and my learned junior will wind up a witness in any retrial of the matter. So there's the grounds for a discharge of this jury. If, on the other hand, the witness says there was nothing in it and he recanted his first version for no other reason than he wanted to come clean, or if he testifies that there's some other, extraneous, reason for the change of heart, then where does that leave us? What if Mr Ocas accuses the witness of protecting Mr Jardim by denying that he was the influence? Then we're back at square one. Mr Jardim withdraws from any further role in the trial, the jury is discharged, and at a retrial, he would be called by the prosecution to give evidence of whatever it is that transpired at Dauphin in March.'

'So you yourself don't know what transpired, Mr Weir?'

'No I don't. It's always my practice to proof witnesses, and Mr Ocas knows that. I take each and every witness on the presentment and I interview them, or my junior interviews them, before they give their evidence. That's nothing revolutionary, happens all the time. Now in this case, I did send Mr Jardim to Dauphin to go through the statement with the witness, purely for reasons of convenience. He went down there so that I could concentrate on other things and as it happened he was detained there by um, by circumstance, for some time. I don't know if it was two weeks or three weeks, or what it was. But I have every confidence that no pressure was brought to bear.'

'You have discussed it with him?'

'Not at great length Your Honour. I was aware from speaking to the witness himself that he was planning to recant and give the version he's given in chief. But as I understand it, that was made clear to Mr Jardim before he left Dauphin at the end of March. Mr Jardim had told me that was likely to be the case after he'd spoken to the witness down there.'

'Mm. Mr Jardim—' Justice Fabian Williams, retired RAAF wing commander, noted authority on early colonial building techniques and grandfather of triplets, turned his gaze on Charlie, who rose to his feet and shuffled his robe over his shoulders.

'Mr Jardim, we're all speaking about you, which is never very comfortable when you are present in the room. But you can see the importance of the issue at hand. Tell me what you say your role was in all...this.'

Charlie looked to his left, to see Harlan reclined almost horizontally in his seat, looking straight back up at him. He had the end of a pen in his mouth, and his glasses were pushed all the way down to the end of his nose. There was a random fizz of sound in Charlie's head, the background white noise of a department store or a crowded bar. He waited while it subsided. His thoughts returned

177

to focus and he attached himself firmly to one of them as his mouth opened.

'Your Honour, as Mr Weir has said, I went to Dauphin through a division of labour between him and me. He looked after the forensics people and the technical evidence such as the keypad at the wharf gate. We agreed that I would go to Dauphin because we knew from Detective Sergeant Robertson that the witness was unco-operative and we knew, equally, that his evidence had to be crucial to conducting a proper trial. So I went there with the express aim of meeting Mr Lanegan and talking to him, reassuring him about the process of giving evidence and encouraging him to give a true account.'

Charlie paused while he considered the sound of those words.

'By that I mean that I did not advise him or caution him as to the believability of the first account. It was patently obvious that it was false, but I had no more idea than anyone else did as to what the "right" version was. It's not the case, as Mr Ocas is suggesting, that we had such a finely developed sense of the evidence that we could say to him, "Look, here's what the corroboration is. You need to say the following." That's just not true.'

The microphone on its stalk stood just in front of his chest. Many times he had calmly told witnesses 'You need to speak up— the microphone doesn't amplify, it just records.' And yet, in his panic, he felt sure that his thumping heart, just centimetres from the silver globe of the mike, was being broadcast to the room, beyond it, to the world. The sweat was running cold down his back. He pressed his fingers hard into the wooden top of the table to disguise their shaking.

The judge's features softened ever so slightly. 'You are entitled to legal professional privilege in respect of what passed between you and the witness at Dauphin, but I don't need to remind you, Mr Jardim, that there is the potential for grave problems in this trial if it emerges that you did influence the witness. For now, I'm happy enough to let the matter rest. Yes, sit down. Mr Ocas, what is it?'

The Basque had risen again, this time with his arms folded resolutely over his commodious chest. 'Your Honour,' he began, before looking down at Charlie, pointing at him. 'You have asked that the matter be left on trust. Now, I'm not one to lay siege to the, to the tenets that, um, bind us all together, but with respect, sir, this barrister has been the subject of disciplinary proceedings in recent months, unresolved as far as I am aware, and now he's—'

'That has nothing to do with this matter!' roared Weir, scattering folders and notes as he stood. 'Nothing! Mr Ocas is aware, as I would say the court is aware, that the matter currently before the regulators does not concern my junior's integrity or his honesty. It relates to his, his...' Harlan was looking straight into Charlie's eyes, looking for the word that would shield him. 'It relates to his temperament.'

'Relates to his fucking judgment, Harlan,' shot back the Basque, out of the side of his mouth.

The judge raised an eyebrow. 'What was that about judgment, Mr Ocas?'

Now it was Ocas on his feet.

'I said, Your Honour, that the disciplinary matter concerns Mr Jardim's *judgment*, the very same thing I am suggesting may be lacking here.'

The judge looked weary. 'I think Mr Jardim's character, his judgment or however you wish to phrase it, has been subject to more than enough scrutiny over that incident. Mr Ocas, you will tread very, very warily with these allegations. Am I clear?'

For just a second, the Basque looked chastened. 'Yes, Your Honour.'

'Tipstaff, bring the jury back in please.'

Charlie stared intensely at the front edge of the table, studying each gouge and nick in the surface; the ones that were long since worn into the patina of the table, the ones that were fresh and angry. The initials carved by the pens of those who were long gone, the imprints of words pressed passionately into the page with such conviction as to leave a blind palimpsest in the varnish. The faint traces of other storms, other fights. One day he would be such a left-over. Perhaps he already was. He was never destined to be the wager of such wars, never to be honoured with a decades-old grudge such as these two had. He was, momentarily, the subject of their clash, but that would change. As Patrick had himself observed as they sat on the rocks after the snorkelling, the circus would move on. He sank further and further into himself as the two of them hammered away at each other, telling himself that one's successful discrediting of him, or the other's unbeaten defence, would amount to nothing in the end.

The sun would rise tomorrow, and as it swept over Melbourne and lit a warm glow through the petrochemical haze, it would climb into the eastern sky and eventually cut its way west to dapple the marram grass on the sandhills above Gawleys, sublimely indifferent to his fate.

The jury were brought back in, shuffling their more or less identical suburban backsides into their seats and flipping their notebooks open on their laps. Moments later, Patrick was again ushered into the witness box. The judge ignored him and turned to the jury.

'Ladies and gentlemen, from time to time, as you have already seen in the course of this trial, issues arise between the lawyers and myself which need to be resolved in your absence. They are, by and large, tedious matters about which you need not be concerned. So I am directing you—don't draw any inference, positive or negative, from the fact that we have just had a discussion in your absence. Yes, carry on please, Mr Ocas.'

The Basque stood again, pushing back the heavy colonial chair and gathering the folds of his robes. He very deliberately uncapped two pens, one red and one blue. He was unhurried in his movements.

He checked everything on the table in front of him before looking up to locate Patrick in the witness box.

'All right', he muttered absently. 'All right, all right. I'm going to start with what you've told us today, Mr Lanegan. So you were on the boat that night, the *Caravel* I mean. You were on it, yes?'

'Yes I was.'

'And I've taken you through the statement you swore to police that night, and you've agreed that from page three onwards, it is a work of fiction, yes?'

'Those parts were not true, yes.'

'They were deliberate *lies*, Mr Lanegan.' Ocas exhaled loudly, to let the jury know that this rough-looking lad was vexing him.

'They were untrue, I've said that.'

'You made that statement within two hours of your brother's body being discovered, did you not?

'I did.'

'And you made it with the events of the night particularly fresh and sharp in your mind, didn't you?'

'Um, things were a bit frantic…there was a lot going on.'

'Yes, but in terms of the clarity of your recollection, it couldn't have been sharper, I suggest to you.'

'I suppose that's right.'

'And you agree that the signature at the foot of the document, made there within two hours of your brother's body coming ashore, is yours, made by you?'

'Yes it is.'

Ocas looked up at the judge, who was writing. He waited silently until the pen was lowered and Williams looked up.

'I tender that statement, Your Honour.'

Fabian Williams took the document, when it had done its rounds past the associate and tipstaff, looked at it briefly and wrote again.

'Yes, defence exhibit one,' he droned. 'Proceed.'

'So, Mr Lanegan. I am going to ask you some questions about

the version of events you have given to this court today, and I want you to remember two things when you answer these questions: first, you are on oath, and second, the jury will have your first version as exhibit one, for comparison. Do you follow me?'

'Yes I do.'

'Good. Now your evidence seems to be that when you boarded the *Open Quest*, neither of you could see anybody there, is that right?'

'Well, I can't speak for Matt, but I definitely didn't see no one. Anyone.'

'You agree that anybody who was on board would've heard the sound of your vessel approaching?' Forty-eight hours earlier, Charlie had been watching a footy telecast, and had observed the very same thing happening. Ocas was the dominant side here, just passing the ball across the midfield, patiently waiting for a gap to open up.

'Yes.'

'You weren't concealing the sound of the vessel in any way?'

'No.'

'And when you boarded, you didn't tiptoe around, did you?'

'No.'

A sparrow darted around the decorative plaster ceiling, flitting from the massive ornamental rose around the light fitting to the right angles of the cornices and around to windows. It was trapped, but didn't know it.

'Because on your evidence, you say you were going to a pre-arranged rendezvous.'

'Yes.'

'You had no reason to be sneaking around, right?'

'Yes, that's right.'

'So, plenty of noise approaching, and plenty of noise boarding.'

'Yes.'

The Basque rubbed his hands absently over his belly, fingers stopping to twirl the buttons on his waistcoat pockets. 'And then, the two of you have a bit of a look over things, a bit of a wander through the bridge, a quick squizz at the charts and the GPS?'

'We did.'

'Again, in the relaxed assumption that the people you were meeting must be around somewhere, must be about to join you in fact.'

'Well, we weren't relaxed, but yes.'

'But according to the account you've given us today, neither of you thought to call out? "Skip, we're here"…pretty simple isn't it?'

Ocas had found the gap in the backline and was spearing towards goal. There was a long silence after the question had rung off the walls.

'No, we didn't do that.'

'Why on earth not? The boat's not that big, is it? You've said in your evidence that both vessels were at rest, the motors weren't running, it was a fine, still night out there…couldn't you have just called out?'

'I—I don't know why, but we didn't.'

'All right. Tell us this. When you boarded, how far behind Matthew were you? How long after he crossed over, did you cross over?'

'Maybe two minutes.'

'To be fair to you, I suggest that two minutes is probably longer than you think. Are you sure it was that long?'

Patrick thought hard. 'Yes. I had to tie off the stern and the bow, and slip a couple of fenders between the two boats. It would've been two minutes.'

'Okay. How long before you reached the wheelhouse?'

'Maybe another two.'

'Why? What did you do on the way?'

Charlie knew Patrick's subtleties well enough by now to see that the question had worried him.

'Nothing,' he said after a slight pause. 'Just took me time, stood there for a sec or two on the port side before I went up.'

'By that you mean up the small stepladder that leads from the gangways on the sides of the deck, up to the wheelhouse doors?'

'Yes.'

'So for Matthew, four minutes have passed before you join him in the wheelhouse, where you say he's looking at, what, at charts?'

'Yes.'

'And after those four minutes, you join him in the wheelhouse and you find him doing exactly that?'

'Yes.'

'Not sooner than four minutes, not later?'

'No.'

Charlie could sense the tedium infecting Patrick's responses. It was exactly the passive sensation of box-ticking that the Basque was trying to induce; a witness who casually gave out a dozen affirmative answers would always react with horror when they found those answers could not be withdrawn on later reflection.

Ocas paused and looked at the jury for effect. This is the theatrical version of running a highlighter through text, thought Charlie. *Remember this bit folks; we'll talk about this later...*

'Four long minutes. Then I think you say there's another two minutes in there while that's happening.'

'About that. I can't be a hundred per cent sure.'

'All right, but let's say two minutes just for argument's sake, shall we? So, your evidence is that Matthew then leaves the wheelhouse, heading *back the way you had come in*. Is that right?'

'Yes.'

'And he was gone for another three minutes before you hear the first sound, which is a voice saying "Where are you, fucker?"'

'There were kind of some bangs and crashes right at the same time, but yes.'

'Bangs and crashes,' Ocas wrote this down carefully. 'No doubt in your mind that that was another three minutes?'

'It was a pretty tense situation. We didn't have any idea what was going on. So I wasn't looking at a watch, okay, but it would've been about that.'

'No no, that's all right,' Ocas hastily agreed. 'Once your brother boards the *Open Quest*, you say we've got two minutes, and two minutes and two minutes and three minutes—*nine minutes*—before this trap is sprung by my client?'

Patrick rolled his eyes upwards in the involuntary struggle to keep up. 'If that's what you reckon.'

'No Mr Lanegan, it's not a matter of what I reckon, it's your sworn testimony I'm working off here. Nine minutes!' Ocas swung around and looked at the clock mounted high on the wall at the back of the room. 'That's longer than I've been talking to you since I stood up. Last chance Mr Lanegan, are you sure about all that?'

'Um, no, I'm not so sure. Look, Jesus, how can you tell? It was weird on that boat. Something was obviously going on.'

'Yes. It beggars belief that they would take nine whole minutes to spring their trap, don't you think? But I suggest to you something else was going on—something like a suspension of the laws of physics.' Again the portentous look towards the jury. 'You say you tied up to the port side of the *Open Quest*, yes?'

'Yes.'

'And you and your brother boarded about two-thirds of the way down the length of the vessel?'

'Yes.'

'And after Matthew left you, you say he went back the same way you had come. That was your sworn evidence, wasn't it Mr Lanegan?'

'Yes, it was. He did.'

'But Mr Lanegan, the next evidence you gave to Mr Jardim was that, upon hearing these words you've described, you said, and I quote, you "went down—on the side of their boat, the side away from where we'd tied up, there is a gangway there…"'

'Yes.'

'I put to you, Mr Lanegan, you're describing the starboard side there, not the port side.'

'Yeah. So what?'

The judge sat bolt upright like he'd been stung by some unseen insect. 'Mr Lanegan, when you are giving evidence in this court, you will refrain from sarcastic rejoinders such as that one, thank you.'

'Sorry, your worship.'

The Basque's voice was rising now, building to a confident crescendo.

'I'll tell you *what*, Mr Lanegan. Your evidence was that when you fell to the deck with your brother on top of you, the two of you landed with both your heads pointed towards the *stern* of the vessel: that is, for the rest of us, the back. Correct?'

'Yes.' Charlie watched the confusion dawning gradually on Patrick's face.

'And you then went on to say this—when the gunman you say you saw, is suddenly alerted to your presence and he's on the decking there, you say, "Matt sort of tipped me to me left—I was off balance and he got a leg round me and he tipped me over on my left side and I just fell out the gap…" Now that's just nonsense, isn't it Mr Lanegan?'

'No, it's not nonsense. I'll remember it as long as I live.'

'Well if it's etched in your memory as you say it is, how come he tipped you to your *left*, when that would've merely rolled you into the cabin wall?'

There was silence in court three of the Supreme Court as this image worked its effect on those listening.

'By your account, you will be labouring under a misapprehension as long as you live. With your heads pointed to the stern, on the starboard side of the boat, he would have had to roll you to your *right*, to tip you overboard, Mr Lanegan. So which is it: did he in fact tip you to your right? Or were you in fact facing the bow? Or were you in fact on the port side of the *Open Quest,* or were—'

'I don't know.'

'Or were you—?'

'I said I don't know.'

'I wasn't finished, Mr Lanegan. Or were you in fact'—he looked away casually—'not on board the *Open Quest* at all?'

'That's ridiculous. Of course I was on board.'

'You don't wish to change your evidence now, on oath, before this jury, and tell us that you never boarded the *Open Quest* that night?

'No I do not.' Charlie felt a measure of relief at the fact that Patrick sounded angry and resolute. He'd locked his eyes on the Basque, gripping the front rail of the witness box. But Ocas could do this easily, had done it innumerable times in the past. He stared back flatly until Patrick gave up and looked at his hands.

'Now then. How long do you say elapsed between the shot that you heard, and the point at which you fell into the water?'

Patrick thought about this for a long time. 'It's very hard to say. I'd guess about a minute and a half, two minutes.' He still appeared to be considering this after he'd finished speaking.

'So in that period of time, a minute and a half to two minutes as you say, your evidence is that the following things happened: you heard your brother yell, "Get the fuck out of here Paddy", just after the shot rang out?'

'Yes.'

'You ran down the starboard side of the vessel towards the stern, arriving at a point halfway down the length of the vessel?'

'Yes I did.'

'Your brother then came running towards you from the direction of the wheelhouse?'

'Yes.'

'He managed to negotiate, what, one, two, three, four stairs on the gangway?'

'Well, he was sort of stumbling down them, and he fell as soon as he reached the bottom of them.'

'Yes, but he got down those steps successfully, did he not?'

'Well, yeah, I suppose he did.'

'He then crashed into you and you say he basically fell on top of you?'

'That's right.'

'He told you that he had been shot?'

'He did.'

'He said he was dying?'

'I don't remember the exact words, but it was something to that effect, yeah, something that made it pretty clear.'

'Yes, yes I understand.' Ocas lowered his voice slightly to convey a kind of sympathy. 'You then say your brother's final words to you were what? "Tell the kids I love them..."?'

'That's correct.'

The Basque waited just long enough to ensure he was firing into complete silence. 'With the greatest of respect to your late brother, that's a bit melodramatic isn't it?'

Patrick grimaced in disbelief. 'How do you say that with *respect*, mate? It's what me brother said!' He looked down to his left, into the shadows at the base of the elevated witness box, and swore loudly. The judge, whose chin had been resting on his hand, raised a cautionary finger towards Patrick, then addressed Ocas.

'Counsel, I take it there is some genuine forensic purpose behind that question, because on the face of it, it is extremely callous.'

Ocas feigned a mild surprise at being pulled up in this way. 'There certainly is, Your Honour. It's some Brown and Dunn I need to establish. May I proceed?'

The judge nodded. 'Go on, but try to be careful, please.'

Patrick could be clearly heard throughout the room muttering to himself. 'Brown and fucking done?'

The Basque was unruffled. 'All right, Mr Lanegan. All right,' he began in a more conciliatory tone. 'Can I ask you this, then: are you sure those were the *exact* words he said?'

'Yes, I'm sure about those words.'

'Clearly enunciated?'

'What does that mean? Like, did I hear em clearly?'

'Yes.'

'As clear as I'm hearing you.'

'"Tell the kids I love them"?'

'That's right.'

'And by "the kids", you took him to mean your siblings?'

'Yes I did. Both my parents are dead. We call the twins and Milly "the kids".' Patrick appeared unaware that he'd scored a small victory with this reply. The Basque had, in a rare moment of carelessness, allowed the witness to reassert his humanity. Now the jury knew he was an orphan.

'Did he say anything else?'

'No. He said that, then the person with the gun reappeared, then he tipped me off the edge. By the time I looked back up at him from the water, he didn't seem to be moving at all.'

'"Tell the kids I love them." Six clear words.'

'I've said yes.'

Ocas sighed reluctantly, and leafed through a ring binder that had been standing on its edge in front of him. When he came to the page he wanted, he tipped the balance of the paper over onto the far side of the binders and conspicuously took out a highlighter, drawing a dramatic line through something on the page.

'Mr Lanegan, your brother was shot through the right temple. He had a projectile lodged in the frontal lobes of his brain. You understand this, don't you.'

'I didn't then. I do now.' Patrick's voice was from far away.

'There will be a forensic pathologist giving evidence in the coming days, who will tell us that your brother would've died almost instantaneously from that wound. Are you aware of that opinion?'

'I wasn't, no.'

'Well, you've got him engaging in quite a bit of physical exertion in that period of, you say, a minute and a half to two minutes after he was shot, haven't you?'

'I don't know what you mean.'

'Well, you're not suggesting anything other than the shot that you heard was the one that ultimately killed your brother, are you?'

'No, I'm not.'

'There was just the one shot that you heard; and correspondingly your brother was later found to have died of a gunshot wound, right?'

'Yes.'

'So it's not as though he was *later* shot, you understand? He told you himself, he knew he was dying.'

'Yes.' The jury's facial expressions now matched Patrick's. Incomprehension was spreading across the room.

'And despite this shot having, the evidence will be, sliced through the front of his brain, taking vital structures and tissues with it, you maintain that he was running, descending stairs, talking, yelling in fact, forming complete sentences, over a period of a minute and a half to two minutes?'

'I can't explain it. I can only say what happened.'

'Well, I suggest to you you're *not* saying what happened, Mr Lanegan. I suggest to you again, this episode on board the *Open Quest* is fictitious.'

'It's not.'

'Once again, I'll give you the opportunity to recant, Mr Lanegan. I put to you that you were not on board the *Open Quest* that night.'

'I've told you I was. I can only keep telling you I was.'

'All right. Next problem. Can someone hand the witness a copy

190

of the photo book please?' The tipstaff heaved himself out of his chair and scuttled across to the witness box.

'Got that? Right. Go to photo number sixty-two. Now, your evidence to Mr Jardim, when you had that booklet open in front of you was, and I'm quoting here, "We were here near four and three, somewhere there anyway, I can't be a hundred per cent. Somewhere here anyway where the four and the three is. And he's landed on me and he told me he had been shot. When I realised I couldn't pick him up, I tried to sort of heave him a bit towards the railing on the gunwale." Do you agree that's what you said?'

'Yeah, that's what happened.'

'Right. So the last you knew of events on board the *Open Quest* was that Matthew was lying right there, right where those police number markers have been placed, and he was in fact lying there motionless for an extended period, correct?'

'Yes.'

'You were in court when the crime scene examiner gave his evidence, weren't you Mr Lanegan?'

'That was the guy with the, um, slideshow?'

'That was him,' smiled the Basque.

'Yes I was.'

'Then you will have heard him say that he placed those markers there because when he examined the boat, he was interested in two dark stains, and his words were, they were each about the size of a tennis ball in circumference. Do you remember that?'

'I do.'

'He made no mention in his evidence of any bloodstain or other human biological material at markers three and four, did he?'

Patrick shrugged. 'No, he didn't.'

'And, in fact, he said the marks later turned out to be fish guts, didn't he?'

'Well, it's a fishin boat, innit?'

'The markers weren't placed there to indicate anything you're telling us, because back when the crime scene examiner was doing his work, you of course were telling everyone that you weren't there on the night—isn't that right?'

'I was, yes.'

'And now that you've changed your account and you're saying you were out on the *Open Quest* on that night, well now you're using those yellow plastic markers as though they indicate your brother's final resting place.'

'They were just something I could point to. I coulda said in front of the winch or whatever, but it was where those card things are. It's a coincidence, I get that, but that's where he fell.'

'The problem is, Mr Lanegan, the pathologist who will give evidence shortly, is going to say to this jury that your brother lost a lot of blood. A massive amount of blood in fact. Now just accepting for a moment that that's right, you tell this jury, Mr Lanegan. You tell them, where's all that blood?'

'I don't know. I'm not a scientist. Is it in the photo?' And with that, Patrick took up the photo booklet again, and began rotating it before his eyes like a street map that wouldn't yield its secrets to him. Ocas waited long enough for this pantomime to look as foolish as possible.

'Well, I suggest to you that's just not a good enough answer, Mr Lanegan. Not only do you want this jury to believe that a man with a wound that should be instantly fatal is running around yelling; you also want them to accept that the massive amount of blood that he lost is just…missing! How, Mr Lanegan? How?'

Patrick had put the book down on the small shelf in front of him. Charlie was trying not to look at him, but he knew he was isolated, helpless up there. 'I've said I can't explain it,' he offered feebly. 'But I'm telling you the truth.'

Ocas laughed. 'Well, we've heard that line before. Right above where you put your signature onto a police statement that was crammed with lies. Where's the blood, Mr Lanegan?'

Patrick didn't answer, couldn't answer. After the silence had hung long enough in the air, the Basque began again.

'You disagreed often with your older brother, didn't you?'

'I disagreed with him sometimes, yes. Don't all brothers?'

'*Often*, Mr Lanegan. Not just now and then. I'm saying that it was a common spectacle in the town that the Lanegan brothers— you and him—would be shouting at each other, complaining about each other, even coming to blows.'

'That's an exaggeration. He was a straightforward person. If he disagreed with you, he told you pretty clearly. We had our dust-ups along the way.'

Just say you loved him, you fucking idiot, thought Charlie. This was no time to be blokey about it, but Charlie knew Patrick wasn't going to resort to that kind of candour. Not even now.

'Wrestling, scragging each other, giving each other bloody noses at the hotel, the…Normans Woe?'

'Scragging? What's that? Is that a rugby thing?'

A ripple of laughter emanated from the jury box. Ocas silenced it by jabbing a hairy forefinger into the air in Patrick's direction.

'Did you and your brother engage in a brawl in the hotel, in front of everyone there, approximately three weeks before the eighth of August, the day he died?'

'Yes. He said something unkind about my'—Patrick's eyes wandered until he found Kate in the gallery—'about my partner. I told him to apologise. He wouldn't. I'd had a bit to drink and I did, I threw a punch at him. It missed anyway, for what it's worth, and we wound up having a pretty stupid wrestle. It was embarrassing more'n anything else.'

'You had been in business with him for at least three months that we know of, transporting over-quota abalone?'

'I wouldn't call it "in business". He was organising it all with Skip Murchison. I just gave him a hand or went along with him if he needed me. But the money he was getting for doing it, it was all just going back in the kick for the family. Same as the fishing money, the money we were getting for the hay here and there, selling a couple of poddy calves…we were in it together trying to keep things going.'

Ocas tilted his head and stuck out his lower lip to indicate that he was struggling with the plausibility of this idea. 'That's one explanation,' he ventured after a while. 'And I'll suggest another one to you—you and him were engaged in a lucrative trade in illegal substances: the abalone, the cannabis. There was quite a bit on the line and sometimes serious disagreements arise in such circumstances.'

'They might. They didn't here. I don't even agree it was all that lucrative.' Charlie knew when he heard this that Patrick had lost the will to fight. But Ocas would continue the assault.

'Oh come on, Mr Lanegan. These courts are filled with stories of people who fall out with each other over drugs. You know that.'

'I don't work here mate,' replied Patrick, his voice faint with apathy. 'You tell me.'

'I'll tell you this, if you like. You and your brother Matthew Lanegan had come into conflict over this little trade you were doing, and you had come to a point where you had to do something about it.'

'That's rubbish.'

'You'd spent a lifetime in his shadow, the big brother who always knew better, always running things, lording it over you…'

'You even want me to answer this?'

'Yes I do, Mr Lanegan.'

'Well, it's rubbish.'

'Something had triggered it for you—he'd gone too far and you decided to take action…'

'I don't know what you're trying to prove here. None of this stuff is right.'

'You decided to arm yourself.'

'I did not.'

'You broke into the Murchison family home, three streets away from your own, at some unknown time prior to the first week of August...'

'No I did not.'

'You have a history of break and enters, though?'

'I've got two, if that's a history, and they were years ago.'

'But you don't lose those kind of skills, do you, hey?'

The judge barked loudly as soon as the question was out of the Basque's mouth. '*Mister* Ocas! Kindly keep to the rules of cross-examination. That sort of questioning is well beyond the pale.'

'I'm sorry, Your Honour. Mr Lanegan, I put it to you that you armed yourself in the period prior to this particular night.'

'I've never had a gun in me life.'

'And you lured your brother out onto the boat somehow, the *Caravel*, I mean.'

'I didn't lure him out, I offered to come out with him because I was worried about him goin out alone to meet Murchison.'

'You lured him out, and once out at sea, either in the course of an argument or simply by ambush, you produced the rifle and you shot your brother.'

'Absolute bullshit. I never—'

'Mind your language, Mr Lanegan,' came the sharp rebuke from the bench.

'It gives us a plausible explanation for where all that blood should be, doesn't it?'

'You've just made it up! Go test the boat! There's no blood on it!'

A sly grin escaped from Ocas. 'Well, we *would* test it, but you set it on fire.'

'I did not! This is ridiculous!'

'You set it on fire, and then, as described in the only truthful passage in your evidence, you swam to shore and surreptitiously returned to your home before making a false statement to police regarding your whereabouts.'

'None of that is true.'

'Well, the swimming part is, according to you. And we seem to agree the statement was false. You've already told us you concealed the wet clothes. It doesn't really leave a great many dots to join, does it now?'

Patrick appeared exhausted.

'And while we're discussing fire, Mr Lanegan, am I right in saying that the hotel in Dauphin burned down in April? The er, I keep getting the name muddled up—the Normans Woe?'

'It did.'

'Now that hotel was owned by my client's parents, wasn't it. Mr and Mrs Murchison.'

Delvene and Alan Murchison sat side by side in the public gallery. Both sat erect, dignified and deeply aggrieved.

'Yes it was.'

'Destroyed the place completely.'

'Yeah, I think it did.'

'Well you *know* it did. You know it did. There's nothing whatsoever standing on the site, is there?'

'Nah. There's nothing left.'

'Hundred-and-fifty-year-old pub, burnt to the ground.'

'Is that a question?'

They locked eyes for a long moment. No one in the huge room spoke or moved. As the seconds elapsed, Charlie wondered why Weir hadn't objected. Patrick was dead right—it wasn't a question at all. Eventually Patrick gave up and answered.

'I don't know how old it was. It was bloody old.'

'And the fire occurred during the very week you had spoken to Mr Jardim over there'—he gestured at Charlie—'and had decided to change your evidence. Am I right?'

'I don't know,' said Patrick wearily. 'It was around that time.'

'Now it's pretty well common knowledge, isn't it,' Ocas looked from side to side as he said it, and then straight down at his notes while he continued, 'that the fire was deliberately lit.'

'Put it to him!' roared Weir without rising from his seat.

The judge's face bespoke an obvious reality: he was an old man with a short temper. 'Mr Weir's right, Mr Ocas,' he barked. 'If you have something to put to this witness, then put it. None of us are assisted by your setting of the scene.'

Again, Ocas made a brief show of contrition, a hand raised in mild apology. 'Mr Lanegan, I suggest to you that *you* lit that fire.'

Patrick rolled his eyes, raised his hands at his sides and slammed them back down again.

'I didn't light the fire. I didn't shoot me own brother. I didn't... fuck, what else?'

The judge let the profanity go. The *fuck* seemed to live in its context. Its excision would've been churlish.

'It's part of a campaign against these people, isn't it Mr Lanegan. It's not enough that you've blamed them for your own misdeeds. It's not enough that their son has languished on remand because of your accusation...'

'Mate, I didn't torch the pub. I've already told you that.'

'You've told us a great many things, Mr Lanegan, but I suggest you haven't taken us to the truth of the matter at all.'

'That's just your opinion. Everyone's got an opinion, eh.'

Ocas waited a long time, shuffled through many pages of his notebook, casting them aside as he went, as though they each disappointed him, the way this young man had disappointed him.

'You had a motive to kill your brother, I suggest to you, and you had opportunity. By your own admission, you were in the pernicious business of drug trafficking along with your brother. And you were on the *Caravel* alone with him on the night. I'm not making any of that up, am I?'

'No, you're not. That stuff's true, but I don't agree it was drug trafficking.'

'Okay, let me rephrase that. You were moving quantities

of cannabis up the highway to Melbourne, to a specific location that you still haven't disclosed: what would *you* like to call it Mr Lanegan?'

Again, Patrick failed to answer.

'So I'll continue. Your actions after the event suggest a guilty conscience: the discarded weapon, the hidden clothes, the false statement…and that's leaving aside the gaping holes in your evidence here in this court. Mr Lanegan, I put to you again that *you*, not my client, shot your brother.'

'I've told you again and again. I didn't. There's things that are hard to explain, and there are parts that I agree don't look so good, but I did not.'

'Not only was there no blood at the point on the deck of the *Open Quest* where you've indicated it should be, but I suggest to you—and Mr Weir will leap to his feet if I'm wrong about this—I suggest to you that there is not a shred of scientific evidence that you or your brother were ever on board the Murchisons' boat that night.'

'I can't comment on that, can I…'

'Not a fingerprint, not a bloodstain. Not a footprint, nothing. Not a single hair from your head or his. And that's because you were never there.'

Ocas glared at Patrick, having worked his way over the edge of the bar table, leaning forward and resting his fists on the shiny timber. Patrick had dropped his shoulders, was now wearing an expression of abject defeat. Again, he appeared momentarily to search for words. A stutter or two escaped him before he gave up and shrugged.

Ocas swept his robes around his back, shuffled his chair towards the table and sat down.

A murmur ran through the room and gradually subsided. The judge finished writing and addressed himself to McVean's counsel who had been scribbling furiously throughout the cross-examination.

'Mr Rhodes, your cross-examination?'

Franz Rhodes remained firmly seated. He looked at Patrick, standing shaken and pale in the witness box, and he turned slightly to take in the Basque, who was contentedly closing his notebook and wrapping it with a series of rubber bands. He cast a sunny smile towards the judge.

'Your Honour, I haven't got a single question for this witness.'

WEIR WAS ON his feet, and the twelve jurors were staring at him, sceptical children at a magic show. Charlie hunched forward, trying to sink into his robes. He stared at the open notebook in front of him, absently weaving the pen over the page in a charade of note-taking. Weir had to establish the bones of the offence before he could crank up the theatrics. Charlie had always considered him a frustrated defender, lacking the forward locomotion that prosecution required, just as likely to wander off down aimless backroads of allegory, strike up a rhetorical conversation with himself. Having read his notes of this closing address in advance, Charlie had little confidence it would go according to script.

He surveyed the room, tuning out of the sound of Weir's voice as it lumbered into rhythm. Twelve jurors, a judge, an associate and tipstaff. One stenographer, one reporter from commercial TV and two from the print media. One, two, three, nine interested parties in the public gallery. Two accused up the back, with two screws to watch over them. Three solicitors in total on the reverse side of the bar table, and four counsel on this side. In all, thirty-nine souls in the room, twelve of them female. Thirty-nine primates wrapped in fabric. Thirty-nine seated apes, talking, listening, maintaining a careful amount of space between each other so as never to touch. And under the fabric, the hearts of these apes measured out their remaining mortal hours. It made Charlie smile to think that some of the apes were successfully selling their remaining hours to the other apes in exchange for money, an exercise which was ultimately as artificial as the rest of the business. What cue, he wondered, could summon them all to revert to their ancestral ways, jump onto the benches and balustrades, screeching and swinging their arms? He stole a glance at Patrick's Kate, sad and serene in the gallery. She was the finest of these monkeys by quite some distance.

Weir was stretching out, doing the necessary.

'...In order to establish the guilt of the accused men of the offence of murder it is necessary to understand what makes up the essential elements that constitute that offence.

'There are a number of legal considerations about which you will need to be satisfied beyond reasonable doubt. Firstly, of course, that Matthew Lanegan was killed. Secondly, that his death was caused by an act or actions of the accused men...' Harlan swung an indifferent finger at the dock, not even giving them a glance.

'For these purposes, if only one of the accused men carried out the act which caused the death, provided the other was his accomplice, they both share the criminal responsibility for that conduct irrespective of which carried out the physical actions. Before each of these accused can be criminally responsible for the killing, you need to be satisfied that, regardless of who administered the fatal gunshot to Matthew Lanegan, the two men were engaged in a joint enterprise.

'Thirdly...thirdly...that the act or actions which caused the death of Matthew Lanegan were *conscious, voluntary* and *deliberate* acts.' Harlan stopped and looked down at something on the table for a long time until even Charlie, so used to his shtick, found himself looking up. The old fox was counting to himself, just audible above his breath.

'Conscious.'

He swung on them, searching the rows of faces for a conviction that matched his.

'Voluntary.'

His eyes never left them.

'*Deliberate*.'

Seemingly content, he settled again.

'So let's say you are, hm? What next, ladies and gentlemen? Next, you must be satisfied that the accused men, or either of them, did the act or acts which killed Matthew Lanegan with the *intention* of killing him, or,' he pointed again, schoolteacherly, '…or, with the intention of inflicting really serious bodily harm on him.'

'Lastly, ladies and gentlemen, and this may not trouble you too much if you have come this far, lastly you must be satisfied that the killing of Matthew Lanegan was not excused by any lawful justification.'

Again the room grew heavy with silence. Charlie looked over at Kate, felt her pin-bright spark of tiny defiance. Where the fuck does it come from? he asked himself. She's one row in front of the bloody Murchisons.

'So that's the law, my friends.' Charlie cringed at his familiarity. 'Now to the evidence…'

Charlie knew what was coming next and, like a paying punter, he couldn't help but watch in admiration. Harlan reached down beside the bar table and emerged with the rifle. He held it aloft, one hand clutched around the woodwork forward of the trigger guard. And there it was, dominating the room. Charlie had thought ever since he saw the evil thing that the telescopic sight on top of it was the key to the whole business. It added a cruel bulk to the weapon, all blackspiderly menace and intent. Harlan cocked an eyebrow towards the tipstaff.

'Mister Tipstaff, has the weapon been proofed?' Receiving an imperceptible nod in return, he shook the other hand from the sleeve of his robes and grabbed hold of the steel ball on the end of the bolt mechanism.

'Ladies and gentlemen, there are few acts more conscious, more deliberate, than operating a bolt action rifle.' And with a tight grimace, he threw the bolt. *Chuck chuck.* The gleaming rifle held the room. 'Can't do *that* accidentally, can you?'

He put the rifle down on the table and Charlie watched its muzzle come to rest at the end of his notepad. The hard clunk of the gun on the woodwork was another of Harlan's gems. Why put it down quietly and waste the theatrical potential? He watched the unseeing eye of the rifle and the lazy blue tracks of his pen on the notepad. He could pick up the rifle and stand on his chair, cuff Harlan over the jowls and watch him tumble backwards in a swirl of black silk, eyeball the jurors down the barrel of the Remington .308, pick a couple out specifically, white faces in the crosshairs, watch them dive for cover, scream and beg for their lives, in the face of an obviously unloaded gun. It'd be like a school shooting where you don't have to take yourself out at the end. They'd give him six, maybe twelve months for it, and the jurors would get a lifetime exemption from jury duty. Harlan would be back at work the following Monday as though it never happened. Charlie would eclipse Harlan's patiently accumulated thirty years of notoriety in a neat three or four minutes.

He wondered if everyone had these thoughts.

'You know that the two accused were out there on that night, in their vessel, the *Open Quest*. You know this because they used their individual keycard to operate the lock on the commercial wharf that separates the public from the working area. Witnesses have told you they watched the vessel—they called it a trawler, but I suggest this is the understandable ignorance of the tourist—they watched the vessel leave the river mouth, and one witness actually told you she saw a man who resembles Mr McVean pacing about on the deck. Now Mr Murchison didn't go as far as to tell police in his interview that he was out at sea, but you'll recall the officer interviewing him led him all the way up to that point before Mr Murchison got a sudden case of the vapours and asked to end the interview. You're entitled to take into account the point at which he asked to end the interview as evidencing a consciousness of guilt...'

Two days of exhaustive pre-trial argument about consciousness of guilt. All so that Weir could have his casual throwaway line about the interview. What a strange way of doing things. The jurors looked puzzled and Charlie felt a degree of empathy for their bewilderment.

'Don't worry too much about that concept for the time being. You'll be told more about that by his Honour. But let me assume you're satisfied about the presence of these two men on the water that night. In their boat. With their rifle...'

The rhythm of his delivery was interrupted by a loud sigh from the public gallery. Delvene Murchison, who until now had worn a look of pained endurance throughout the trial, was now openly shaking her head in furious denial as Weir spoke. There was a split-second stand-off as Weir looked at her and she returned his gaze, white-lipped with fury. The judge watched them both, on the brink of intervening. Then her consciousness of the room looking her way was enough to make her drop her head.

Charlie tuned out. Weir would spend several more hours setting out the evidence in painstaking detail, weaving his stories and overripe analogies as he went. Charlie took himself back to the reef, to the massive blue space around him as he hung on the surface watching the fish circle below. With a little mental effort he could imagine himself as they saw him, in the sky, soaring in the light of the surface, floating cruciform. Those creatures, whose business was not his business, who idled and curled and flowed through invisible canyons in the great mass of water. The hypnotic sound of the air bubbles around him. Removed from the fear that had gripped him on the day, now he could hear the notes more truly: tinkling, glassy, nearly metallic sounds that rose and fell with distance. The light had been glorious, bathing everything in a redemptive glow, falling in columns through the depths and illuminating a rock here, a stretch of sand there. A fish would cross the columns now and then, flashing chrome through the shadows.

'You heard evidence that the *Open Quest* had a very sophisticated GPS unit on it. You heard that the GPS needed replacing, very urgently, the day after Mr Lanegan's body was found. Why is that, ladies and gentlemen? Why the urgency? Why was the old unit discarded by Toby Murchison? You know why. The police officer who searched the Murchison shed told you: the GPS, when it was found in a disposal skip at the shed, had what they call a waypoint on it. A mark. Created on the night of the killing. Now cast your minds back again to Mr Lanegan's evidence. Do you remember him saying the words in reference to his deceased brother, I'm just looking for the words…"I think he fiddled around with the GPS for a sec." There, ladies and gentlemen. The waypoint was perfectly positioned on the south edge of the feature that Patrick Lanegan called the crayhole, and it was made twenty-two minutes before witnesses say they saw flames out at sea. It is reasonable to conclude—you don't have to be a commercial fisherman to do this—is reasonable for you, ladies and gentlemen, using your ordinary experience of life, to conclude that Matthew Lanegan had an inkling that something was wrong on that boat, and that he left that mark, deliberately…'

Charlie thought back to Dauphin; the day a thunderstorm had blown in, the sky turning a livid purple and the sea answering in brilliant green. The white foam of the surf was suddenly more intense, more perfect than he had ever seen it as the gathering darkness brought it into heightened contrast. The air itself had seemed charged with current and, standing on the dune behind the house, he'd heard a roar coming from the west, as though a wave were about to consume the town. The sound had gathered in volume. It was coming nearer. And then its source became apparent: a hailstorm sweeping in over the tin roofs, not yet upon him as he stood in the electric air.

For a brief instant he was dry as the houses on the west side of town were under siege, hammered by the downpour. Then it was on him as well, painful darts of ice biting at his head and hands, the sound all around him, the undergrowth buckling under the assault. He'd run back into the house, still stunned by the instant when the wave of frozen air was within reach of him, was in front of him, when a cloudburst could be separated from him by a handful of streets. He'd experienced the sensation of the storm front moving past him, even through him, that afternoon, but he'd absorbed it without reflection. It was only now, looking back, that he knew he'd felt a tiny tug of concern for the stoic tin-topped houses, for their humble persistence under the wild sky.

Weir was now in a good rhythm, black robes cascading around him as he spoke. He was looking less and less at his notes as the familiar script came readily to his mind and he filled in gaps with the ease of long experience.

'There was the spotlight, ladies and gentlemen. A bit like the GPS unit, you may conclude that once Patrick Lanegan got away, once it was clear that these two weren't going to find him and eliminate him as a potential witness, they had to focus on removing the traces of the things that would tie in with Patrick's story. They would have assumed that Patrick would make a better choice than he ultimately made, that he would tell the police everything he saw. So, as with the GPS, the spotlight had to go. As you heard in Patrick Lanegan's evidence, they'd used it to hunt him, literally hunt him, in the water for some extended period after the shooting and before the fire. And there was one witness in the group of witnesses who saw flames,' he leafed quickly through the ring binder in front of him, 'Pederson. Marjorie Pederson, who says she saw flashing lights in the moments before the flames appeared out at the reef. That, ladies and gentlemen, was either Mr McVean or Mr Murchison *hunting* Patrick Lanegan with the spotlight. Imagine the terror. It's dark, you're in the ocean, it's August, much like now,' he looked up towards the windows. 'Intensely cold. You've watched two men with a rifle murder your brother, and they're hell-bent on getting you. The only place you have to hide is that inky black water. But there's a spotlight. A spotlight, ladies and gentlemen. It's the stuff of nightmares.

'So we suggest to you that Mr McVean, having some idea of the way in which that spotlight might be uppermost in the mind of Patrick Lanegan after the event, elected to get rid of it. And again, as with the GPS at the Murchison shed, it turns up close to home, at Mr McVean's elderly mother's house, in the roof cavity. Odd place for a marine spotlight, you might think. Don't hide your light under a bushel, stuff it in the roof. You will take note of that find, and of the assault that Mr McVean perpetrated on the officer conducting the search, as matters that go to Mr McVean's consciousness of guilt. Would an innocent man react the same way to such a search? Would an innocent man put the light where it was found? You know the answers to these questions, ladies and gentlemen.'

Charlie had wandered again, was now at the eastern end of the long beach where Les had told him the longshore drift left its flotsam. As he stumped through the thick detritus of the high tide line, looping down towards the reaching waves every so often, he understood what Les had been trying to convey about the loneliness of the place. It rejected human presence, even while the signs of humanity—the bottles, shreds of rope, floats and plastic bags—were everywhere. On the wet sand, each stone left an arrow of flowing water in the receding wave, tumbled once or twice. On the dry hummocks beyond the line of desiccated kelp, the spiky exoskeleton of a puffer fish, eyes gone. Down again on the wet, an oystercatcher trying to extract worms from the sand, darting between incoming rushes of the sea. On the dry, a plank, rounded and bleached by the ocean and draped in clumps of barnacles, all of them still squirming, eager to abandon their stranded host.

And then in the face of the dune, below the line at which the marram grass appeared, a ball of some kind, a grey, rough sphere, protruding from the dry sand. Charlie had marched up the beach to it, found that it was bone, a protruberance of something much larger buried in the sand. He'd walked up the sharp slope of the dune and stood on it. It gave way under his weight and as a line of sand to his left exploded and spilled down the incline, a long rib emerged. It rolled once before coming to rest parallel to the line of the dune. Charlie had studied it for a long time, feeling the weight of time, awed by the notion that the entire dune was an ossuary for forgotten giants.

A huge animal had died forever ago. Had rotted and dried. The architecture of its anatomy had collapsed, leaving the bones in random scatters, the smaller ones moved about by scavengers after the last of the flesh had sustained the darting rats, the crabs, maggots and gulls. The cycle of concealment and exposure over the years, the dune advancing then eroding, had at this moment revealed this bone to him, from an invisible city of long bones and skulls and vertebrae that lay silent and dark under the solemn weight of the sand.

Weir, again with the Remington in his hands.

'Then there was the evidence of the rifle. Damning evidence, we say. You know that Mr Lanegan was shot with a Remington .308 bolt action rifle. The projectile was recovered from Mr Lanegan's body in the autopsy; the gun, meanwhile, was found on the reef, in a direct line between the waypoint marked on the GPS and the river mouth. The marks on the projectile, caused by the rifling of the gun barrel—remember the officer from the ballistics section explained those characteristics to you, the way they're unique to each gun, like a fingerprint—those marks were a perfect match for the test round which the police fired through that gun when they recovered it. The rifle, registered to Toby Murchison, which can be scientifically confirmed to have fired the bullet that was found in Mr Lanegan's *head…*' He left the word ringing in the air for a moment. 'That rifle was missing from the Murchison premises at the time that the police searched there the day after the shooting.

'Missing, ladies and gentlemen. You heard the officer who conducted the search telling you that when he asked Mr Murchison about the weapon, which according to the firearms register should've been in a locked cabinet at that address, Mr Murchison said variously, "I haven't seen it for years", "I think Dad's got it", and my personal favourite, "Oh *that* one, I think we sold it."

'Lying on the bottom of the sea it was, about a hundred metres from where this man,' he pointed abstractedly towards Murchison in the dock again, '*this* man shot Matthew Lanegan. It was suggested in cross-examination, of course, and I don't criticise Mr Ocas for this, he was merely doing his job on his client's instructions; it was suggested that the weapon somehow came into the hands of Patrick Lanegan, and that *he* fired the fatal shot, that *he* then disposed of the weapon on the reef. That theory, I suggest to you, ladies and gentlemen, is in the realm of JFK conspiracies, of moon-landing denialists, September eleven cranks. You won't be fooled by it, members of the jury, because it's patently absurd.'

Weir had done an odd thing that morning. Charlie was sitting with him in the empty courtroom, leaning back in the chairs, discussing the closing address. Charlie had one hand on the dinted oak of the table, running his fingers over the grooves, when Weir broke the silence.

'So, did you like Les?'

Charlie looked at him blankly.

'Les. The barman at the Normans Woe.' Weir was grinning broadly, turning his reading glasses over in his hands.

'How the hell do you know Les? You told me you'd never been to Dauphin.'

'I haven't. I played one season of country footy with Les Reynolds in Daylesford. During uni, it was. Used to drive up there once a week for training and once a week to play. That all came to an end. We got in the preliminary final and we went out on the beers. I was driving Les home and I fell asleep, rolled the car. I got out with a broken collarbone, but Les nearly lost his leg. He never played another game. Never uttered a word about it, either. He remained a good friend for many years after that, though we don't catch up as much these days as we used to. Good man, Les. Got a fine mind, you know. Just never had the opportunities.'

'Does he know the connection? I mean, does he know you're doing this trial with me?' Charlie found himself lost between the acceptable position that this was a coincidence and the baffling notion that Weir had engineered all of it.

'What do you think?'

Before Charlie could answer, the tipstaff came in and began busying himself with the microphones, looking severely at Weir, who had his shiny oxford brogues resting on the bar table.

'Neither accused has given evidence, which of course is their right. They have a right to silence, and they have elected to use it—both by declining to give evidence before you in this court and by declining to answer questions in police interviews. This means that you are left to elicit what they say in their defence from the questions their counsel, Mr Ocas, has asked of prosecution witnesses. And what you know from that, ladies and gentlemen, is that they blame the deceased's brother, Patrick Lanegan, for his death.

'Now it's a little-known fact about the criminal process, a truth which is warped by American television, that prosecutors don't just present witnesses who damn the accused. We carry a responsibility also to present evidence from people whose stories don't neatly fit within the picture, stories that don't add up to guilt and may in fact serve to *exculpate* the accused. The task for you people is to determine which of those categories best describes Patrick Lanegan. Does he simply muddy the waters with his two versions of what happened? Does he exculpate the accused, absolve them of criminal liability for this death by introducing an element of reasonable doubt? Does he inculpate himself? Mr Ocas will no doubt ask you to draw that conclusion when he speaks to you shortly.

'I'll venture to offer you an alternative view of his evidence. Patrick Lanegan came here and told you the truth—albeit, late. But criminal trials are not scientific things; they ebb and flow under the influence of all sorts of human frailties. People are strange beasts when under pressure and Mr Lanegan, on any analysis, was under pressure. His first story—you've heard this recited from his police statement—was that he went home after the trip to Melbourne and watched a movie while his brother went to meet Murchison and McVean. Well, a reasonable person would say: why? Why leave him to these people when you know there's trouble brewing? From what we know of the Lanegan family, of their difficult history with both parents dead, the fishing operation in trouble and their desperate need for money to run the family, from all of those factors, would it have seemed reasonable to you that Patrick would leave his brother to sort it out, as his police statement says he did? I doubt it. The preponderance of the other evidence indicates that there were two men on board the *Open Quest*, McVean and Murchison. And Patrick Lanegan, I suggest to you, was alive to that possibility and wanted to support his brother in the event of any trouble.

'So why the about-face? Was it, as Mr Ocas will have you believe, because he was himself guilty of the crime? There's no motive. There's a long history of loyalty between the brothers, despite there having been some suggestion in this trial that they came to blows on occasions. Ladies and gentlemen, you might think it's snobbish to suggest this, but things are done differently in a town like this one. You've seen many examples of it during this trial. People like the Lanegans do not sort out their differences over an osso bucco at the Positano...'

Weir allowed a ripple of laughter to subside before continuing.

'Garden variety fisticuffs between two brothers in a country town do not a murderer make. Disputes over drugs and illegal seafood transactions, amounting to tens of thousands of dollars, most certainly do. What other motive could there be for Mr Lanegan to be the perpetrator of this crime? Jealousy? Of what? A struggle for control of the family's assets? Spare me! Their business interests are a train wreck!

'There's also the small matter of how he would have come into possession of the Murchisons' rifle. There's not a shred of evidence about this, but never mind, let's not wreck all the conspiracy fun with hard evidence. Even assuming a motive, assuming access to the weapon, ask yourself this, employing your ordinary common sense: if Patrick Lanegan had wanted to kill his brother, for whatever reason, would he take him out on their boat, lure him out there somehow, shoot him, set fire to his body and the valuable family boat with all its equipment, and then risk the swim through open ocean back to shore in the knowledge that the evidence is just bobbing around out there? It's impossibly clumsy, ladies and gentlemen.

'Compare that to the idea that it was the two accused who did it, and that Patrick Lanegan told you the truth when he was in the witness box. That is, that he was out there, and that he barely escaped becoming the second victim of these two. Now we have a perfectly good reason to set the boat alight: there's no time to take Matthew Lanegan's body out to sea and dispose of it properly because *Patrick* Lanegan is swimming around out there, having seen everything. Priority number one, if you place yourself in the accuseds' fishing boots, is to deal with the witness. So you light up the *Caravel*, with the unfortunate Matthew Lanegan on board, and hope for the best while you go and try to find Patrick Lanegan.'

Charlie could tell from Weir's voice that he was winding up. He had turned over the pile of notes in front of him, page by page, onto a new pile to the left. There were now only a handful of pages in the original pile.

'The thing to remember about Patrick Lanegan's evidence,' Weir continued, 'is that it has the ring of plausibility about it. I defy anyone to make up a story as distressing, as detailed, as the one he told you under questioning by Mr Jardim. Could you describe the experience of being shot at underwater without actually experiencing that? Could you describe the dumping of your brother's body overboard onto the *Caravel*, the fire, unless you had seen those things?

'I make no bones about it; under cross-examination, this witness did not perform well. But ladies and gentlemen, performance is one thing. The truth is quite another. Remember that Mr Lanegan has never met the pathologist, has never read the autopsy report, yet the description he gave you, under oath, of the way in which his brother died, I suggest that you will find when you retire to consider this matter, that the physical evidence matches perfectly with Mr Lanegan's account. That should count for an awful lot when you assess his credibility.'

Weir paused, placed a hand on his chest and swallowed hard. He seemed discomfited for just a moment. But the moment passed swiftly.

'That is all I wish to say about Patrick Lanegan's evidence. As to the remainder of your task, you will no doubt discharge it with the gravity it requires. Each of these two accused has committed a heinous crime, the most heinous crime our system of criminal law recognises. They each took part in a common enterprise that entailed them taking that Remington .308 and getting on board the *Open Quest* on that calm, cold night last August. Whichever of them had their hands on that weapon, they both intended the same result: that they would conceal themselves on board, lure Matthew Lanegan to the vessel, moored offshore near the township of Dauphin, and there they would murder him in order to avoid paying him for transactions that had taken place, as you have heard, involving over-quota abalone and cannabis. They planned, I suggest to you, that they would dispose of the victim's body at sea. As events transpired, the victim's younger brother was aboard the vessel that came out to meet the *Open Quest*, that vessel of course being the *Caravel*. In part, it is because of Patrick Lanegan's escape, and his courageous decision to give evidence against the two accused, that we say you are in a position to be satisfied, beyond reasonable doubt, that these men are guilty of murder. Each of them is responsible for what happened that night. Each of them should now face your sternest judgment.'

With those words, Weir swept his robes behind him and sat down.

'YOU GOT A licence there sir?'

'Think so.'

He fumbled around in the console and located his wallet, fingers jumping uncontrollably over the cards until he found the licence.

'Just a random breath check today Mr—Mr Egan. Any alcoholic drinks today sir?' The cold August wind swirled around the cop in his reflective jacket. He had his arms crossed over his chest for warmth, one hand clutching a breathalyser.

His old nemesis, one continuous breath.

'Nope.' He laughed, just a little too hard. 'You off– offering?'

'Just one long continuous breath please sir, till I tell you to stop.' The cop was reading the change of address sticker on the back of the card. 'That'll do you Mr Egan. Dauphin, eh? Beautiful part of the world. You do any fishing?'

'No, I, er, you know. Used to, got a bi– a bit too busy with things. S'pose I should ta– take it up again. Since the missus passed away.'

'Mm. Sorry to hear that. What brings you up to town?'

'Come up to catch the footy tomorrow night.' He racked his brains. Saints, Swans.

The cop's face brightened. 'You a Sainters fan?'

'Ah, Swans actually. Dad grew up on Dorcas Street.'

Cars were banking up behind Barry's ute, and the cop glanced down the line briefly.

'What's in the back?'

He was looking directly at the barrel. Of course he was. There was nothing else back there.

'Chaff. Feeding some poddy calves for a mate.'

The cop was running his hand over the black plastic lid. He took it by the rim and gave it a sudden shake, and then tugged at the nylon rope holding it against the roll bar.

'Long as it's secured okay.' He was down the back now, peering at the number plate. Barry knew he'd paid the rego, remembered cursing VicRoads as he wrote the cheque. The cop slid his torch back into his vest pocket. 'Righto, have a good one.' He handed the licence back through the window and was already looking along the queue.

Barry continued up Royal Parade, past the university, until he was deep into Brunswick. The cop had unsettled him. He was sweating, his pulse still hammering in his neck. A lurid pub façade appeared on his right. *Brunswick Club*, he read to himself. His mind conjured press photos of a dead crim, the soles of his shoes visible under the pool table through the front windows, police tape blurred in the foreground. The comically overcooked missus with her huge glasses, weeping extravagantly at the funeral. A little further north he took a right, nosing down a narrow side street flanked by small factories and a handful of Victorian terraces. The street was dark in the late afternoon, the sun caught somewhere behind the airconditioning units and aerials.

Barry counted off the numbers until he came to a two-storey brown brick building that took up half a block. The lettering, in faded blue-grey across the façade read *Seafood Handlers International*. He swung the ute in under the projecting front of the building, looking up at the office windows as he passed under them. No sign of any activity.

The ute rolled to a stop in front of an unmarked door. It was reinforced with a long steel plate down the jamb. As he climbed out, he looked once at his barrel, then knocked on the door.

'Yeah?' a voice came faintly from within. Female. Middle aged. Not friendly.

Barry had been rehearsing this moment on the drive, practising the bloody weird name. 'Barry Egan. I'm here to see Terepai Taia.'

'He's not here.'

'Would you tell him I've got his barrel?'

A pause.

'Hang on.'

There followed a series of muffled bangs, as if several heavy doors were being opened and shut sequentially down a corridor. Just like the police cells when they'd locked him up for drunk in public in '88. He looked down at the concrete step. Someone had vomited against the wall beside the door, a downward parabola from waist height. Beside the pool at the bottom of the stain was a collection of wrappers and leaves that the wind had collected in an eddy. Samboy salt and vinegar, faded to a tired mauve.

Footsteps approached the inside of the door and the locks began to rattle. The door nearly collected him as it swung outwards. A small woman stood before him, clad in a plastic apron and hairnet. She'd taken one rubber glove off to open the door. She was fifty-odd, hard faced with lined eyes and puffy jowls, lips pursed into a dog's-arsehole pucker.

'Go through.'

Barry moved forward into lino-tiled passageway. The aproned woman led him to another door and punched a code into a keypad before they passed through. Beyond the door, a cavernous factory floor opened up. To his left, a long conveyor line was watched over by more workers in aprons. The objects rolling past them on the line were well familiar to Barry. *Haliotis rubra*—blacklip abs. At one end of the conveyor, women were gathered around deep plastic tubs, scrubbing at the shellfish with plastic brushes and flicking them onwards. Others were picking up the travelling product and transferring it onto cutting boards, trimming the entrails and irregular edges off them. They stood in gumboots, spraying water over their work from short hoses. To his right, he saw another woman with her back to him, loading abalone into a steel machine then shutting a lid on the top, before selecting from a keyboard of brightly coloured buttons. Cryovac machine. He'd seen one at a clearing sale, down at the commercial dairy. The woman at the machine was filling a plastic tub and Barry's gaze continued to her right where a small man, his eyes downcast, was transferring the tubs to a nearby bench. Here, a much larger man was stacking the plastic packages into wide, square cardboard boxes. The sides of the boxes were marked *Ocean Fresh South Seas Trevally.*

Barry had stopped absentmindedly while he took all this in. Now he was conscious of someone behind him and looked around to see a man in an apron and hairnet, standing with arms folded across a chest that seemed to stretch for miles. He wore an untidy goatee round his mouth, the flat line of which was neither a smile nor a frown. The face and the body were relaxed, but at the same time immovable. Barry stood, transfixed. This place was not of his world. It didn't conform to rules he understood. He liked to cut a corner or two as much as the next bloke, but this…This all appeared to exist outside the law and in wholesale disregard of it.

The man reached under his apron and produced a gun. A revolver. He pointed the thing at the ground next to his foot, waving slightly with the muzzle, ushering him onwards. Barry was speechless with fright, yet inside he marvelled. There was a man pointing a gun at him. Near him. Deb would never have believed all this. With his hands raised in a feeble show of obedience, he backed away slowly.

His guide directed him across the factory floor and up a stairway to a small sheet-cement office with a window that overlooked the whole scene. His hip began to give him trouble about halfway up and he stopped with a hand on one knee. The woman had reached

218

the top of the stairs and was standing with the office door held open, radiating impatience. He resumed the climb, shuffled past her on the landing and entered the office.

The bare, bright coil of a low-energy bulb caught him in the eyes. Both of his escorts had taken up positions between him and the door, the woman looking comically undersized beside the man with the gun. Barry had half-turned as he entered and was facing a plain timber desk. Papers were scattered all over it, save for one corner that was occupied by a computer and another where there was a phone. The entire wall opposite the windows was taken up by a mounted fish. *Southern bluefin tuna*, said the irrepressible voice in Barry's head. Two deep vinyl armchairs; filing cabinets in the corner of the room. None of these objects exerted any pull on Barry's attention, however. He was transfixed by the figure seated behind the desk.

The man was perhaps fifty, though he looked as though his fifty years had been spent in physical labour. He was massively constructed, cut from monumental stone. From the thick hands resting on the desk to the coiled slabs of his shoulders, to the neck that seemed impossibly wide across his earlobes. His hair was dark, thick, wiry, receding slightly and cropped close to his skull. His face was Polynesian, same as the man by the door, but the surface of this face was tattooed, lips included. Again the words formed in Barry's mind, pushing forward in the hyperactive rush of his fear. *Ta moko*. Deep among the blue-black swirls of the design, the dark, narrow eyes were watching Barry without movement. They held him there while some inscrutable assessment occurred; then the eyes seemed to relax and the face softened.

He stood up, revealing a powerful chest and a waistline that would've encircled Barry twice. And as he stretched one of those improbable hands across the desk towards him, a warm grin transformed the tattooed features. The white business shirt strained against his buttons as he took Barry's hand in a surprisingly gentle grip. 'Mr Egan,' he chuckled deeply. 'It's a pleasure to finally meet you. I'm Mr Taia'

With his hand encased in this man's giant paw, all that crushing force held at bay by nothing but goodwill, Barry felt his resolve wobbling. He needed focus. He needed calm. This was not his realm and he knew it. Ordinary people didn't introduce themselves as 'mister'. He resumed his seat while he gestured at the armchairs, so that Barry found himself sitting down, suddenly baffled as to where to put his hands.

Taia regarded him for a moment.

'I got to say, mate, this is very unusual.'

Barry shrugged and didn't respond.

'You're doing very well. Are you nervous?' Taia's wide face lit up with mischief.

'I just want to do my business and I'll be on my way,' Barry said. 'And if it's not you, I can find others.'

Taia laughed. 'You haven't looked after your product though. Tut tut…' he waggled a finger at Barry. 'You just walked away from it in the carpark, my friend.'

'I know you watch your building. The only person who's going to take the barrel would be you and if you're going to rob me, you've got p-plenty of opportunity.'

Taia raised an eyebrow as he considered this. Barry knew he'd caught the stutter.

'Fair enough.' He glanced at the man who'd led Barry across the factory floor. 'Liam, come here.'

The man did as he was told.

'Did you point a gun at our guest?'

'Sort of, boss.' He swallowed hard. 'Yes.'

His eyes were meekly lowered. Taia swung a massive blow at the man's head, raising a deep thud from his skull. His whole body jolted under the force of the impact. His hand instinctively shielded his face, but Taia clearly had no desire to hit him again.

'Get out,' he said quietly. He turned his attention back to Barry.

'Now tell me about this client of yours.'

'Who?'

'The client—you told me on the phone that you were selling for a client.'

Barry had forgotten he'd used this line. It was only now he was sitting in front of the prospective buyer that he realised how fool-hardy he'd been.

'That's none of your business.'

'On the contrary, Mr Egan. When I move abalone, narcotics, anything of value, I like to know who I'm moving it for. Otherwise I just can't tell if I'm getting set up, eh?'

Barry tried the shrug again.

'You're not a very likely drug dealer, are you?' Taia leaned forward across the desk then tilted his head as he squinted at Barry. The effect was more menacing than Barry thought he could bear.

'I've told you who I am. I'm not bullshitting you. Check the ute if you want. Look, here's my wallet.' He threw it on the desk, but Taia made no movement to pick it up.

'We've had your rego looked at already. You live in Dauphin, Victoria. Home of Gawleys Kitchen, eh. I get a lot of abalone from down your way, Mr Egan. Lots. But there's not many people there who do *this* sort of thing…'

He nodded towards the door and Barry turned to see the woman who'd led him to the office, accompanied by a smaller man, hefting the blue barrel between them into the room. They were both straining under the weight. Barry felt an inner resignation about the fact they'd simply lifted the barrel off his ute without consultation and dragged it in here.

'In fact, there aren't many people down your way full stop, eh?' Taia sauntered around behind Barry's chair to the barrel. He squatted over it and pressed both hands to the rim of the black lid, and slowly applied pressure. Two of the largest biceps Barry had ever seen appeared in the sleeves of the business shirt. The lid began to turn, but just as the rotation became freer, Taia stood upright again.

'Did you get this from the Murchison family?'

Barry could answer that truthfully.

'No. No I didn't.'

The lid had come loose, and Taia lifted it off without looking inside the barrel.

'Did you get it from—whatsisname—the Murchisons' decky. McVean. Did you get it from McVean?' Taia's tone was one of idle curiosity, but somehow it was set to terrify. There was the faintest trace of a crocodilian grin under all that ink.

'No.' Barry held his gaze as best he could. The familiar smell had reached him from the barrel, the smell he had pondered night after night as he sat in his lock-up staring at the fucking thing, turning it over. Feeling it. It was a stench he could remember from parties in the seventies. It was dope, but it smelt richer, tarrier than the little bags of buds he knew back then. Taia reached into the barrel and produced one of the paper-wrapped bricks.

'You know, when you told me on the phone that it was ninety kilos, that's…that's a lot of hash, my friend. In fact, I think that's more hash than I've ever seen in one place. Most unusual, you know. Most unusual.'

He pointed the corner of the hash block at Barry's temple and bored his eyes into his skull. 'I have my suspicions about how you came across this barrel you know. Those boys are on trial for murder. Might've, might've *mislaid* something.'

Barry tried to stare back. His legs shook.

'Doesn't worry me one bit,' Taia continued. 'It's business, Mr Egan. But you should be lookin over your shoulder now, eh?'

'Can we deal with the money please?' Barry's voice was small and faraway. In the months he'd obsessed about doing it, he hadn't been sure how this was going to go, but he had never imagined such

222

a total imbalance of bargaining positions. Even the man's footfalls on the floor were overwhelming.

Taia considered him a moment longer, then stood at the window, looking out over the factory floor. He shook his head as he broke into a bemused grin. 'You certainly do have some balls, my friend,' he eventually chuckled.

There was a knock at the door and a woman entered, this time younger and dressed in office attire. She held a black sports bag which she swung up onto the desk without a word. Taia waited until she was gone then pushed the bag across the desk. 'There you are.'

'Don't you need to count it?' asked Barry.

'No, I don't.' replied Taia. 'I know how much is there. I think it is you who should be counting.' He smiled again.

Barry looked at the bag and then looked straight over the top of it at Taia. 'If you don't mind, I'd really rather get going.' His hands were clammy and he needed to piss so badly that he expected to be on the leak any minute.

'Of course.'

Taia stood again and came around the desk to Barry, throwing an arm over his shoulders. Barry could remember once shooting a deer with his form three science teacher in the Grampians, and then having to carry the thing downhill to camp over his shoulders. He was reasonably sure the deer had been lighter than the arm he was now supporting.

At the door of the office, Taia clapped his shoulder lightly once. 'When you get to the bottom of the stairs, they'll show you out to your ute. Don't stop on the way home, will you.'

Barry stepped onto the first tread of the stairs and looked back to respond, but Taia had already shut the door behind him. Once they'd led him out of the factory and shot the bolts in the carpark door, Barry threw the bag on the passenger seat and reversed out so fast he nearly slammed into one of the pillars supporting the first floor. As he shifted into drive he punched the locks on both doors.

Only when he'd reached the left turn to head south and begin the long journey home did he feel safe enough to unzip the bag and look inside. Taia had his ninety kilos of hash, and that might genuinely have been a career best for him. But this was most definitely more money than Barry had ever seen in one place.

BY ELEVEN O'CLOCK on the Friday night, Charlie was reclined on the couch with the TV on mute, watching footballers swarm over the livid green carpet of the MCG. His socked feet loomed giant and fluffy in the foreground as he chewed idly on the end of a pen. A handwritten draft of the Crown's legal submissions lay on his lap. By Monday afternoon, they needed to be in the judge's hands, in perfect shape.

Weir had finished the prosecution's closing address that afternoon, the fifteenth day of the trial. Throughout the long speech, he'd retained his sunny demeanour, his theatrical flourishes. Yet, as Charlie knew from their private conversations, he accepted that it was all over—the jury would never see past the Basque's evisceration of Patrick.

They agreed that there were more outcomes in prospect here than the guilty and not guilty available to the jury. That binary choice seemed a gross oversimplification of the ways this could play out. There was, it seemed certain, an unseen third way. Whatever it was, the bad guys knew it, Paddy knew it—even a couple of the witnesses seemed to be tuned in to a different frequency. For Charlie, if all of that bloody effort had been directed at getting to truth, getting down to the meaning of what happened, he was fairly sure they hadn't even come close.

For Weir, none of this apparently mattered. It was evidence of his perfect suitability for his role that he could fight so hard, work so methodically towards a result, and then accept it, good or bad, with serene indifference. He was exactly like this when the verdict went his way, too. Only through fanatical belief in the system could you devote such care to the construction of an argument but never fall for the hubris of believing it.

They'd parted ways at the lifts in the prosecutors' office. Weir was going twitching on the weekend, having recently equipped himself with a brand new copy of Simpson and Day, and a pair of Bushnell 8 x 42 waterproof binoculars. Charlie hadn't managed to show any interest. He was tired and had, for the moment, no appetite for Weir's eccentricities.

The mobile rang and he ignored it, listening for the chime of the voicemail. It never came—the phone stopped, then rang again. Annie? She hadn't rung in months. She was normally very careful about ringing people too late at night anyway. He picked up the phone and heard an unfamiliar male voice.

'Charlie Jardim?'

'Yes.'

'Charlie, my name's Phil Weir. We haven't met. I…'

'Ah, yes, Phil, Harlan's spoken about you. How's it going?'

There was a long silence on the other end of the line, faint music in the background. A long expiration of air.

'Charlie, Dad had an, had an aneurism. At his place. He's—'

'Oh shit. Where is he now?'

'He passed away, Charlie. He's gone.' His voice wobbled and broke. 'There was nothing anyone could do.'

'What?' Charlie's mind raced. The shock had robbed him of anything sensible to say. 'Who found him?'

'Some, some mate of his. He had a friend coming over to take him birdwatching. I've got his card here. Alan someone. Found him in the kitchen. Called an ambulance. I didn't know who, I thought…I knew you two were close. I thought you'd need to know. With the trial and all that.'

'Thanks, thanks,' said Charlie quietly.

The line went dead, and Charlie could see Weir's head, his wandering silver tufts of hair, the jowls that formed around his smile. The brows, so often arched in amusement, the bags under his eyes that spoke of comfort but never fatigue. That rumpled sack of a suit he wore. The tatty old robes he was always tugging at. *He couldn't be gone he couldn't be gone.*

A pillar in his life had just crumbled, and he suddenly felt older. *This can't be right*, he heard himself say. *We're in the middle of a trial.* There was of course no reason why Weir's passing should fit with anyone's timetable. It was just a hole that had opened up, dark and inexplicable, threatening to swallow him.

Justice Fabian Williams allowed the defence to make their closing addresses, with Charlie seated alone at the jury's end of the bar table, and then he adjourned the court for the funeral. Nothing was said to the jury: no human event, not even death itself, could be allowed to weigh upon the objectivity of their decision-making. They were simply told they would have a day off. They had been working hard, said the judge, and they were about to enter the most important phase of their task. A day's rest would do them good. In their undisguised excitement at this news, none of them gave a thought to the empty chair.

The next morning Charlie came into chambers early, having accepted a lift to the church from an old common lawyer who'd known Weir since uni days. On his desk, he found a cardboard box with a note in an envelope taped to the top. It was from Weir's secretary. She'd been cleaning out his chambers, she wrote, and had selected a few things she thought Weir would want him to have. He lifted them out one by one; carefully wrapped in tissue, three of his glass paperweights featuring tiny, detailed birds. His notebook from the trial, filled with his long, open cursive. On the inside cover, Charlie discovered, Weir had stuck every yellow post-it note they'd exchanged in the last three weeks: messages ranging from the practical (*inadmissible hearsay—object!*) to the snide (*Ocas is moulting—check the hair on his folder*). As he always did during trials, Weir had filled the book with doodles—animals, buildings, elaborately decorated capital letters, abstract patterns. There was a crumpled head that bore a reasonable likeness to the judge; one or two others that Charlie recognised as the faces of the jurors.

Further down in the box he found the five heavy volumes of *Words and Phrases Judicially Defined,* bound in leather and embossed in gold. He'd once made the mistake of pointing out to Weir that all the information in those books wouldn't fill half a CD. He had felt like a lout the moment it was out of his mouth. Now, with the books in his hands, the comment seemed immeasurably stupid. He piled the volumes neatly on his desk.

Last of all, he lifted Weir's wig tin from the box. It would already have been ancient when Weir got it. Thirty years on, the enamelling was chipping away and rust had started to discolour the seams of the tin. Inside was his wig, shaggy bloody smelly thing. It seemed part of him, so often had Charlie been in his company in court. He ran his hand briefly around its frayed edges and replaced it gently, pressing the lid of the tin into place. The car would be waiting downstairs on the street. He locked the door and headed for the lift.

In the car, Weir's old mate had talked steadily, a look of sorrow on his face, an air of resignation that suggested more of his contemporaries were leaving him year after year. 'I know about you,' he said. 'Harlan worried incessantly about you.'

The church was way up Sydney Road in Coburg, a place Charlie wouldn't have gone by choice. It soared into the late winter sky, dark and intimidating. Inside, an organ droned and the air was cut with heavy incense. Weir had once called himself a deracinated papist: this was a surprising choice of venue.

He stepped into a pew, nodding at familiar faces: other prosecutors, Ocas and the judge, who'd placed themselves several rows apart to maintain a proper separation. Four rows from him, the unmistakable profile of Les Reynolds, head down and looking like a stranger in a suit.

Charlie peered between the shoulders of the congregation and saw the casket, the gleaming handles, the flowers on its lid. He felt a regret he couldn't identify. *Is all grief ultimately selfish?* He recognised these feelings from the years after Harry, not so much mourning his beloved brother as wanting something back, for himself. And now it was his friend, his confessor, his only professional ally. The man who'd pour two scotches, push one towards Charlie and take his own, gently questioning him, revealing truths by patient deconstruction. That knack of his, of clearing away the fog, getting to the answer. And now he was gone, the loss of those discussions panicked him more than the prospect of completing the trial alone.

He opened the order of service and looked at the simple black and white photo the family had selected: Weir in his fishing gear, propped up at a table in a garden somewhere, a wine bottle in front of him and a laddish grin on his face. Below the picture they'd included the Byron he was so fond of reciting, lines from *Childe Harold's Pilgrimage*:

> *There is a pleasure in the pathless woods,*
> *There is a rapture on the lonely shore,*
> *There is society, where none intrudes,*
> *By the deep Sea, and music in its roar:*
> *I love not Man the less, but Nature more.*

The people to his left leaned back to allow room for a latecomer, and Charlie looked up to see Anna, dressed for the office, radiant.

Eyes followed her as she took her place beside him, giving him the tiniest smile under the sweep of her hair. Suddenly the incense was gone and she smelled the way he remembered. She slid her arm through his and found his hand, squeezing it quickly. Her jacketed sleeve pressed lightly against his arm. Then she looked straight ahead and he was left in wonderment at the randomness of such moments. His friend in the casket, and her beside him as though nothing had changed, as though they'd always be this way.

The wake was held at Weir's club, a place he had himself derided as a ridiculous late-nineteenth-century hangout for toffs and monarchists. They'd lunched there once or twice, Charlie mocking the chesterfields with their stained antimacassars, the brass buffet trolleys and portraits of syphilitic dukes. Weir had taken it all with good grace: had in fact taunted Charlie by quoting loudly from *Quadrant* over soup.

The crowd picked at chicken sandwiches, dropping fragments of shredded lettuce on the rugs as they exchanged their war stories. Charlie and Anna stood in the centre of the room, talking quietly under the ambient noise. She said she'd missed him. He told her he'd paid off the lounge suite with the first round of trial preparation fees. She'd been offered partnership at the beginning of the financial year and turned it down. She couldn't explain why. He'd memorised the scientific names for crayfish, abalone and flathead. He wasn't sure why either. He wanted her to know about the things in the cardboard box, Weir's things. She thought one of the paperweights ought to stay in his chambers, one on his bookshelf at home. She wanted one to go to her office so she could think about them both. He swiped a bottle of sparkling from a French-polished side table and poured them both a glass. She wanted to know whether there'd been a fight over the admissibility of Patrick's first statement. He explained how it had to go into evidence as a prior inconsistent statement. She said criminal lawyers were crude. He asked about the earrings she was wearing that he'd never seen before, a dart of cold fear behind the question. She told him she'd bought them for herself as a breaking-up present, out of their joint account. She punched him in the arm when he confessed he hadn't noticed the account balance had taken a hit. She admitted she'd cried when she tried them on.

MICHAEL JOHN MCVEAN watched the jurors filing back into the seats they'd left three and a half days ago. Never in the entire course of the trial had they arranged themselves in the same way twice: sometimes the suburban mother would head for the far end, sometimes the middle-aged slob with his Holden racing shirts would come in last and occupy the top left corner. But never would all twelve of them repeat their seating pattern. He took this as a sign that they hadn't formed any allegiances among themselves; that they remained twelve little islands. But he didn't know how to read that. It could've meant that each of them independently considered him as guilty as hell, and didn't need to form a knitting circle to confirm their view. It could've meant they were hopelessly divided and would never reach a verdict, guilty or not. It could've meant anything and nothing. Maybe it was just how people are.

Each juror picked their way across the vacant seats towards the last empty one, where they sat themselves down. It reminded McVean of watching people file into a cinema, careful not to bark their shins or trip over their feet as they turned their hips to accommodate the narrow gap between the rows. Only two of them looked towards the dock as they walked in: the fat bald guy with the glasses—hard to say where the hell he was looking at the best of times—and the young girl, receptionist, something like that, who paused for just a moment and fired a look of withering hatred towards him and Murchison. Although he couldn't tell if it was directed at him personally, or at Murchison or at both of them, it unsettled McVean, particularly when he realised, after she'd taken her seat, that she'd been crying.

Panic crept over him as he watched her reddened eyes, the flush in her cheeks. She looked to McVean to be someone with little regard for legal bullshit and high speeches. He tried to work his way through the possibilities. She hated them, individually or collectively he couldn't tell, but he decided it was both of them for the purposes of the argument. So she wanted them convicted. And she was in tears, so she'd been overborne. It dawned on him that this girl was telling them loud and clear that they were home free.

He listened to the judge, the pompous withered old shitbag, talking to the jury, smiling drily at their nodding heads. The old bastard leaned forward on the bench, revealing the shiny scalp that stretched from one island of silver hair to the other, eyebrows pushed deep over his eyes as he muttered instructions to his lackey. And the lackey was standing, reading the bloody charges yet again, yet again. And now there was silence, as the last of the questions hung in the air, across the space between the associate's little booth, across some timberwork and carpet to the foreman, who was standing also.

McVean had already decided this was an anticlimax, had concluded that the girl's distress was enough to tell him what he needed to know. He looked down at his hands and wrung them lightly together, as though in response to the release of some imaginary shackle; and the words, when they came, were merely what they should have been.

He was a free man.

So was Murchison, but Murchison was history now and didn't even warrant a glance, let alone a handshake. He would walk out of this place and resume his life and none of these dogs and parasites would ever trouble him again.

Franz Rhodes was rushing towards him, hand extended and

teeth exposed. Fucking hypocrite. This dribbling moron had practically begged him to plead up before the trial started, had only found his courage when he realised he was going double-header with Ocas and all he had to do was stay out of the way. Which was more or less what he'd done. The state would pay his fees, but real justice would've been served if the state had written out a cheque to Michael John McVean in compensation for banging him up in the pen for a year on remand, as well as paying for the shit lawyer.

He stepped out of the dock, onto the floor of the court, a security guard still loosely attached to his elbow. He turned and shrugged violently away from him and the grip was released. The room was in a swarm around him, people hugging and crying and carrying on. None of them approached him. He watched the jurors filing away into their room, and threw a wink to the crying lady as she departed. She'd get over it.

The lad, the brother, was just sitting there, as he'd done through the whole trial, leaning forward with his elbows on knees, chin on fists, staring at the opposite wall. The girlfriend was leaning protectively over his shoulder, rubbing his back and doing a bit of weeping too. *You can rub me any time, honey.*

As he watched, the Lanegan brother got up out of his seat and headed for the door.

Hang on. Old Missus Murch was up too, tailing him. This'd be good. She caught up with him just as the lad was passing Mick's position in the dock, old limpdick Alan stumbling along after her. The claw with the jewels shot out and she took Lanegan's shoulder. He spun like he'd been stabbed. She had him by the shirt in that talon of hers, right in front of McVean, and she was bringing him in close. It was a hissing kind of whisper, but McVean had no trouble at all picking it up: *Now we'd better have a chat with the welfare about those dirty little children.*

The lad reeled back, ripped his shoulder away from her. One of the screws had to step between em. Fucking priceless. He'd need a very good reason to go back to that shithole of a town but watching old lady Murchison tormenting the Lanegan mob was almost reason enough.

McVean started to feel heavy inside, and it puzzled him. He was a free man, a free man. He thought he'd probably move to Geelong, look up the bikers he'd met on remand, reinvent himself. In five years he'd have colours, a crew of his own, any amount of projects to pull in the cash. Just as no one would've cared if he'd gone down for twenty-five to life, so no one would care that he'd walked. He was as good as invisible.

But the dull ache persisted. The lawyers were loading their ring binders onto trolleys—the defence ones laughing and fooling around, the prosecutor, by himself these last few days, not even making eye contact. All those folders looked very fucking smart and powerful when they were flipping them open, waving their spectacles in the air and making their big claims. Now they were just recycling. The younger one, *Mr Jardim*, well he'd got what was coming to him. Ocas was right onto that one—hanging around town, trying to change people's stories. If McVean had been home and not doing sudokus in the remand centre he would've scared the little shit out of town before he'd unpacked his bags. Sounded like he was in a world of trouble anyway. Lawyers, liars, all the same. And as for the older one, well he'd looked all along like he was about two arguments away from a coronary. Probably off having a bypass.

Geelong had its appeal, but he felt pretty sure he'd head back to Dauphin. Unfinished business. He'd never work for the fucking Murchisons again, not that they'd have him anyway.

The gig with the Murchisons had started off promisingly. But it depended on dealing with others, and McVean was naturally a sole trader. Inevitably, working with Skip Murchison became a headache. Illusions of grandeur, a thousand shit business ideas and no focus. McVean had kept his head down, tried to keep an eye on recruits like the Lanegans, gradually turning into a drill sergeant for the fuckwit golden boy of the Murchison clan. Now that the whole shitstorm over Mags was done and dusted, his business was his own again.

He walked through the security checkpoint outside the court, collecting the small plastic bag that contained his wallet, keys and phone, and burst through the heavy doors into the sunshine. Two reporters scuttled jabbering towards him. He lurched in their direction, grinning wildly, and they retreated tripping, tangled with their big woolly microphone.

A train seemed a good idea at this point. Head west, head for Dauphin and then work it out. He turned towards Southern Cross station, down the hill on Lonsdale Street, smiling at the plane trees that filtered the light down to him. The world was a glorious place, and he was at its centre. The blue feeling was gone.

No. The brother. He needed to think about the brother. All he'd had to do was stick to his police statement and everything would've been sweet, but he'd tried to be a hero. Aided and abetted no doubt by Mr Jardim, who he was sure would have a first name and an address. Anyway, plenty of time for all that.

But more irritating, much more annoying, was the matter of the barrel. The special consignment, the high point of Mags Lanegan's idiocy. Now it was gone. Because Skip thought he could strong-arm Lanegan into some sort of pea-brained joint venture. Because Skip didn't appreciate the difference between a willing partner and a captive mule. Because Mags had, predictably enough, brought Little Brother along. And because Little Brother had had the brains to tip the damn thing overboard when he smelled a rat and realised they were being ambushed. That barrel was still out there somewhere, bobbing its way to the fucking Galapagos Islands or something, and somebody needed to reimburse Michael John McVean for his labours.

Never mind. All in good time.

He paid for his ticket and queued next door for the canteen. A young girl served him; sixteen, maybe seventeen. He took in the apron tied around the black leggings and T-shirt. He took in the heavy eye makeup. She dusted her hands on the front of the apron as she greeted him and he took that in too.

'You right there?' she asked brightly. She was pressing her hips against the counter as she leaned forward. Pressing them.

'Just a sausage roll thanks. And sauce.'

She took the flaky sausage roll from the bain marie with a pair of tongs and slid it into a paper bag. Then she took up a squeeze-bottle and urged the sauce into the bag. *Oh yeah*, he said to himself, watching the small freckled hand pump the plastic. Pressing his own hips on the other side of the counter.

'How's your day going?' she asked absently as she flipped the bag over to tie it off.

'Terrific, thanks love.' He watched her closely, her nervous smile as she took his money and rang the till. The bag was warm in his hand and he suddenly wanted to share.

'I did it, you know.'

She slowed, creased her brows slightly like she was listening now.

'You did what?' she ventured, reluctant.

He shrugged casually, tore a corner off the sausage roll and stuffed it in his mouth.

'Doesn't matter. Have a good one, eh?'

He tossed out his second wink of the day and sauntered down the ramp to the platforms.

CHARLIE SLUMPED BEHIND his desk and let out a long sigh. The robes on the chair beside him still carried the warmth of his body, the wig was still damp with his sweat and smelled of wet dog. He unscrewed the lid from a metal hiking bottle he kept beside the computer and took a long drink of water. Next he collected the pile of new law reports that had arrived in the in-tray and tossed them on the carpet. On a large sheet of notepaper he wrote the words *Return to OPP*. He stuck the note on the top folder on the silver trolley, and pushed it towards the door.

The first traces of the coming spring were visible in the canopy of the trees outside his window.

He'd had it all planned out until Weir died, had told himself he'd come back once more after the verdict, on a quiet weekend. He'd gather up his personal belongings, leave Annie's bloody clock, the wig and robes, the books. He might've scooped the stationery into a shopping bag, because he had a fondness for stationery; it went back to Harry, pencil cases, grade three. Anyway, when he was done with that, he was going to staple a note to the notice board in the lift well: *Abandoned chambers—room 804. All items free to good home*. Hurry while stocks last. There would've been a couple of hours of restraint for the sake of appearances—let the body go cold and all that—then they'd be in there, his erstwhile neighbours, bundling books and lamps and cabling in their arms until the place was stripped.

But his resolve had weakened over the long tense days while he waited for the verdict. It felt strange without Weir. Of course Weir had never stuck around waiting for a jury to come back. His habit while awaiting verdicts was to go home, and when the tippy rang him he'd come hurtling into town in a taxi with the driver on a cash incentive to go faster.

Charlie spent the days alone, reading the papers on the internet, lounging in the armchair with a novel, sometimes just staring into space. He'd bought himself a mask, snorkel and fins online and tried holding his breath against the stopwatch function on his phone.

He took a sheet of notepaper and drew a line down the middle. At the top of the left half of the page he wrote *Stay*. On the right side, he wrote *Go*. The Clash turned up uninvited in his head. Girl, you've got to let me know.

He started filling both columns slowly as he thought. Weir appeared on both sides. Annie appeared on one. Patrick, Lefcovics, Williams, ambition, Les, the fire, stress, driving, old age, discipline, worthiness, anger, lost years, Harry. He looked at the words for a long time, looked at their positions on the page and tried to weigh them against each other. Then, in one of the columns, he wrote two final words.

Start again.

AMONG THE COURT buildings on the western side of the city, Barry Egan's ute was curling its way up through the floors of a parking lot. It had been many years since Barry had had a reason to park in the city, and the price list—visible only after he'd driven far enough in to be committed—had shocked him. But now he was enjoying the squealing of the tyres on the shiny concrete as he repeated the endless right turns that would take him to the fourth floor. He cut the bends closer and closer to the sharp edges of the concrete pillars, listening for the rhythmic jangle of the metal drain cover at the foot of each ramp.

The parking lot had been his idea as a meeting place. After his experience with Taia, he wanted to make some gesture of authority, stamp his identity somehow on all this business. He knew from TV that people doing heavy deals met in carparks. He'd carefully walked through each floor of the building earlier in the day, checking the view from the sides, checking which floors were busy, which were empty. He'd been planning the meeting for the following morning, at the same time of day as he'd done the walk-through, so that he could be confident they'd be alone. He'd figured out the rhythm: offices were busy mid-morning, parking lots were quiet.

But then the radio news told him the verdict had come in, that they'd been acquitted, and he knew he had to act immediately. So he'd rung again and said come straight away. As he listened to the calm, indifferent voice on the other end, he'd felt fortified in his decision.

On the fourth floor he parked next to the fire hose reel in the shadows of the north wall, reversed into the spot so he had a view of the whole expanse of concrete. The lift and stairwell were directly opposite his position, and any approaching car would be plainly visible for long enough that he could dart out first if he had to. Once he was satisfied that he was alone, he climbed out of the ute and whistled the dog from its slumber in the passenger footwell. Locking the cab carefully, he walked to the railing that looked out over Little Bourke Street.

From here, the activity below was a slow procession; the dirty tops of vans, the weaving cars, the heads of pedestrians forming columns like ants. But not like ants, he thought. Ants in a column stop regularly, bump against other ants in tiny acts of exchange—scent or sound or something—passing ciphers for an interdependent world. The ants below him, however, were in constant motion—if any two veered into a course that would bring them into contact, they wove away again, ensuring no two heads ever met. They were perfectly choreographed never to touch. A part of him knew he'd fit right in down there.

Level with him across the street was the roof of the Supreme Court, where the sandstone walls met a desolate plain of air-conditioners and sheet metal. Under that roof somewhere they'd all been doing their business these past couple of weeks. Ripping away at each other, he'd heard, trying to get down to the point. The truth. He wasn't sure about that. Was it a whole room full of smart people trying to work out the truth, or was it just one side trying to beat the other? Did it follow that the mob who beat the other mob necessarily had their hands on the truth? There'd probably be something in Latin for that. He'd ask Les one day. But this much he knew for sure: learning trivia did not make you any smarter.

He was too high to pick out an individual on the footpath, an issue he hadn't considered in his planning. He looked briefly at the dog, panting by his foot, and returned to the car.

Sometime later—he wasn't sure how long because he'd been dozing—the lift doors across the floor from him rumbled open and a man emerged, stopped a moment and looked around. When he'd seen the ute he made straight towards it and Barry jumped out to meet him, sending the seatbelt buckle banging on the doorwell in its haste. Of course he'd know the ute—would've seen it a thousand times, a familiar shitbox cruising lazily around Dauphin among the tourists' gleaming wagons. It was common enough to know cars in the township rather than, necessarily, the people who drove them. Barry himself wasn't so confident of recognising the man he was here to meet, so far out of context. For one thing he was wearing a suit—that was a first as far as Barry knew—and it was really only his walk that looked familiar from a distance. Up close, however, the face was just as it had always been.

The parking spaces were almost deserted, and the reflected sun glared brightly off the glossy concrete. Barry kept one hand in his pocket, thrusting the other forwards.

'Barry Egan.'

The black dog was pissing against the tyre of the ute.

'Patrick.'

'I wasn't sure if you'd turn up,' he began. 'Haven't had a great day, huh?'

Patrick just nodded.

'You want to h-hop in for a sec, Patrick?'

Barry gestured towards the far side of the cab.

Patrick looked him over once before he complied. For just a moment, Barry wondered how he appeared to someone like Patrick, someone so much younger, who had seen so much. Harmless, he thought. Soft and sleepy and harmless. Barry watched him climb in the passenger side, saw him recoil slightly at the smell of dog and old food. His long limbs were folded awkwardly into the small space like a whacked spider. His elbow automatically found the armrest.

But when Barry had climbed in, he made no attempt to start the ute. Instead, he reached over his head and tugged a heavy black sports bag from behind the headrest. He hefted it onto Patrick's lap.

'Have a look in there.'

Patrick found the zip and drew it back to reveal a glimpse of yellow. His eyes met those of a smiling Aborigine. Just to the left of that tranquil face was a red rubber band.

The bag was crammed with neat, inch-thick bundles of fifty-dollar notes.

They were straight and flat and new, and the bundles formed neat blocks beside each other. Patrick's hands clutched the sides of the bag like a man in a pub fight clinging to someone's lapels. He looked out the grimy window as though he expected trouble of some kind. Men in suits running flat out towards the ute. Bikies, fishermen, police, or whatever else it was this poor bastard feared. Barry had run through enough of these scenarios, while he waited in the carpark, to have some sympathy. But the concrete world was empty and silent. For a puzzling moment, they both stared out the windscreen.

'What the hell's this?'

In the course of his long relationship with the barrel, this was a question Barry had been anticipating. There was an answer he had been rehearsing. 'It's yours. I sold that blue barrel and this is the money I got.'

'What are you talking about?'

Barry felt his world tilting again in response to the aggressive rise in Patrick's voice, felt himself falling away from the warm dependability of habit, just as he had in Taia's warehouse. This was a return to mayhem. The panic was dancing in his fingertips, feathering his pulse. *Nothing good could come from that barrel.*

'You know more about it than I do. It c-came off the *Open Quest* the night your brother was shot. I don't know h-how. Musta

243

had something to do with why everyone was out there that night, with why they—why they shot him...'

He glanced apologetically at Patrick.

'I don't think it belongs to them, the Murchisons I mean, so I figure it musta been yours. Really, I s'pose I shoulda given you the actual ba-barrel back, but things took a different turn.'

'You're not, you're not just *giving* me this?'

'I am so.'

They stared at each other, locked in an impossible moment.

'Look, I don't care how much money's in here. You can fucking keep it. I've had enough of all this shit. People don't just hand bags of cash to strangers.'

Patrick pushed it to his right, wedging it against the handbrake as he again searched the carpark for unseen enemies.

'I thought about it a fair bit and I think it's the right thing to do.'

Patrick sighed loudly and his left hand found the doorhandle. 'Listen mate,' he said to Barry. 'I'm sorry, but that sounds like shit. I lied to the court and to the prosecutors, all those lawyers. I fed the police a whole lot of bullshit. My brother and me were selling abs over quota. We were moving drugs in and outta town. How could *this*'—he gestured at the bag—'be the right thing to do?'

He pushed the bag towards Barry, who stopped it with a hand.

'I know about the Murchisons just like you do. I know about the pub and the boats and the money they're making on the side. I know about the fire. They been screwing Dauphin people for years. I know they did the shootin. I mean, I don't know if it was Skip or Mick that fired the shot, or lit the match or whatever else, but I know it was them out there that night. Don't really give a toss what the jury reckons. Jeez, with the greatest of respect, you did fuck it up though. Not sure it was such a good idea doing that first statement.'

'How'd you know about that?'

'Read about it in the paper.'

'So you know about the Murchisons.' Patrick's hand came off the doorhandle and rested by his thigh. 'Doesn't explain why you would get involved. Why would you do this?'

'It, um…' Barry found himself squinting as he picked at one ear. 'It didn't seem fair. I live in the town, right. I watch what goes on, see all sorts of things. You know, there's plenty to see if you keep your eyes open. Most people, they just go about their lives. Got roughly enough to get by or they got plenty and they don't give a stuff; but you don't just go meddling in other people's affairs for no good reason. And what I saw was you lot with no parents, with them little kids. Seem like nice kids to me. And I thought, I thought you can get all hung up on the rules. I know it's wrong to sell the extra abs, and I know it's wrong to sell drugs an' that. But maybe you had a little more reason than most. The Murchisons didn't. It couldn'ta been anything but greed for them.

'So on the one hand you were doin something that was wrong, but on the other hand so were they, and you had a reason and they didn't. Then you got the police and the courts, all insisting on everything bein done by the book. That fella they sent down, the lawyer—he couldn't see the forest fer the trees. You were just…what, a piece on his board. He just wanted to get his witness straight. He wanted the trial to work properly. That's all fair enough, but sometimes the rules just don't deal with ordinary life. Sometimes they're miles behind. You have to get in the witness box and explain yourself, and the two bastards who shot your brother don't have to. How's that right? You get accused of being a liar and a cheat, and they sit there in silence. I couldn't cop it.'

'How did you get it?'

'Get what?'

'How'd you get your hands on the barrel?'

Barry hesitated.

'Let's start from the start. How'd you lose it?'

Patrick smiled ruefully and scratched his head. 'It was just a, I dunno, a split-second thing. I saw it clamped to the wheelhouse an' I knew. I just *knew* what Mags was up to. Didn't even have to look inside it. His big fucken greedy payday…here it all comes, rollin in. Nice one Mags, fucking idiot. The big sale, the one that was gonna kick us clear of all the shit and we'd be starting again. He talked about how he could do it but I never thought he'd actually try it. The Murchisons talked about getting something special in for him and he could on-sell it. Nothin I could say to talk him out of it. I was uneasy enough about them two anyway without takin the business to a whole nother level. I knew that barrel was it, because I knew the way the Murchisons ran their boat and there was no other reason they'd have that dirty big barrel clamped there.

'Anyway, split second, like I said. I didn't like the look of what was going on on that boat so I ripped it outta the clamp and screwed the lid down hard as I could. I was at the gunwale, listenin for any sound of Murchison and McVean. I could hear Mags' footsteps down the far gangway, knew it was him. Then real quick, I rolled the barrel across the deck to the diver's entry. Couldn't believe no one had appeared and stopped me, not Mags, no bastard. I watched it tip over the edge and fall through the air into the sea. Just a big fucken splash an' it disappeared. That was me put the mark on the GPS'—he looked at Barry, who appeared not to follow—'I figured she was on the bottom an' all I'd have to do was come back to the spot an' collect it later. I mean, it wouldn'ta mattered if I couldn't get at that GPS again to, you know, get the mark. I woulda found the spot. I know that reef.'

He had been talking into the crook of his arm, elbow on the sill, looking distractedly out the window. Now he turned and looked at Barry. 'How the hell did you get hold of it?'

Barry ran a finger through the dust on the dashboard. 'Just curiosity at first. I get something in me head an' I'm like a dog with a bone. I knew that something had come off the Murchisons' boat

246

that night, because I seen Mick McVean going over it down at the wharf, cursin and carryin on. It was pretty easy to work out that it was another barrel, cos the clamp for the second barrel on the side of the wheelhouse was empty. Had no idea what was in it, but it obviously mattered a fair bit to Mick cos he was crackin the shits somethin fierce down the wharf that night. So I'm thinking, righto Mick, game on.

'From there, it was a bit of an accident. If it come off out where I seen the boat burning at first, then I figured it'd wander up the northeast on the longshore drift. Cos the wind was blowing across the drift that night, I worked out it'd land on the beach a bit wide of where all the other stuff does, like all the usual timbers an' that, and cos the tide the next morning was so big—it was a full moon that night, did you know that? Anyway, I knew it'd be high up on the beach. Where I think we were all on different trams was, I bet you were looking for it on the bottom out at Gawleys cos you thought it'd sink...eh?'

Patrick smiled. 'Yep. Dived for it about a dozen times.'

'And you did that cos you rolled the bastard across the deck an you knew it weighed a shitload. Ninety kilos, as it turns out. So that was a pretty reasonable assumption. I didn't know what was in it, so sometimes I s'pose you're better off bein ignorant. I was looking for something that'd float. The other thing was of course that the two of them silly cunts hadn't told anyone what they were up to on the boat; so they weren't in the hunt. Mighta guessed it like you did anyway and started lookin on the bottom. So they're in remand from two days after the shooting and they can't get word out to start the search. I kind of imagined Del Murchison in there at the visitor windows with her knitting, you know, tryin to look sneaky'—Barry chuckled at the thought—'an' Mick goin *psst, Missus Murch, the barrel, the barrel...*

'Anyway, your brother died so you had no clue. You're lookin in the wrong place and the only other way anyone else was gonna find it was if they were out there walkin their dog or surfin or somethin. But there'd been such a big sou'wester blowin for the three days before that—you prob'ly remember the night itself was very calm, but before that the wind had pushed piles and piles of kelp down that end. Tonnes of the stuff. It was actually the dog that found the barrel, not me. Don't reckon I would ever've seen it otherwise. Up in the almost dry sand under mountains of the shit. So that was it. I got the ute round to the spot on the beach through the dunes. Had a prick of a time getting the damn thing into the back of the ute. Then I took it round to me storage shed and it sat there while I worried about it for a couple of months.'

Barry grimaced then burped, tried to puff his breath out the rolled-down window. He looked at Patrick apologetically.

'Reflux. Sorry. So can you see, it sorta started out as a game. I looked at that big dumb prick McVean an' I thought, I'm gonna outsmart ya. But then when I *did*, when I had the barrel, well then I had to ask meself what on earth I was gonna do with it. Then the trial come up and I was folleren that in the papers, and I had a fair idea from the way things were playin out that the barrel was never goin to come into it. But that's when I started thinking about your situation. Can't really explain why, but I reckon if they'da been found guilty, I woulda hung onto the money myself.'

'Why?'

'Well, like I said, it's hard to explain, but in that case, if they'd been found guilty, the legal mob woulda been proved right, wouldn't they? About doin it by the book. Your prosecutor friend woulda said, you been done a wrong and the law has set it right. You'd have your...Well, not revenge. Restitution. As it is, you've got your restitution under the counter. There's enough in that bag to start again, get a new boat.'

'You think the *Caravel* wasn't insured?'

'I know it wasn't. Eavesdropped on the cops at the wharf the night they towed it in after the fire. They were sayin it hadn't been registered for ten months, and anyone knows you can't insure an outta-rego boat.'

A long silence fell between them. Barry still felt exposed in the carpark and wanted to leave. He was about to hint at a departure—*so, anyway, best be off, both got a long trip*—when Patrick spoke again.

'What'd you think of Taia?'

'Probably the most terrifying person I've ever met.' Barry barked with laughter as he saw the amusement in Patrick's eyes. 'Made Missus Murch look like a pussycat. I think it woulda been less scary if he'd acted meaner. He was really polite. It was weird. He coulda totally done me over—taken the barrel an fed me through his cryovac machine an' dumped me in a ditch somewhere.'

'Mags used to say the same thing,' Patrick replied. 'He told me once it felt like swimming with a shark—you never knew if he was going to change his mind and tear your head off your shoulders. How'd you find him anyway?'

'Ah, well. How'd I find him?' Barry had to stop and think. 'I read the company name on the Murchisons' fish boxes down at the co-op, you know, *Property of Seafood Handlers International—please return,* that sort of thing. So I thought, that's where their legitimate abs are going; everyone knows they were selling over-quota, so I thought, it's a bit of punt, but maybe they were moving everything through that mob. Anyway, I went in to the co-op and I spun ol Fergus a tale about wanting to buy a stack of them fish tubs for me home brewing. I said, you know, I'd heard that you can get em through Seafood Handlers, and did he have their number. Fergus actually said to me, he said you can ring em if you want, but the bloke there, he's a fucking gigantic islander with a tattooed face. He's pretty scary. I don't know if you'd want to bother him with stuff like that, he said. Anyhow, he fished around and found a business card for me. I went down the street and rang him from a public phone and I explained that I had a barrel and I thought he'd be innerested in it. He was cagey but I could tell right away I was onto the right bloke, because he was keen to talk. Real keen. He said he'd ring me at home that night, and so we had another talk that night, then again a couple of days later, and eventually I went up there and did the exchange. Got to say, young fella, I don't know how you deal with people like that. It was bloody nerve-racking.'

Barry saw himself wandering into Taia's lair with a barrel of drugs. Just hoping for the best. It defied belief that he'd walked out in one piece.

'We didn't really deal with him all that much,' said Patrick. 'I think we'd done two or three trips, but they were mostly extra abs that the Murchisons didn't want to risk their licence on carrying up the highway. The only dope we took up was little bits here and there. Mags'd leave me watching the car while he went in to negotiate. Who'd you have watching the car anyway?'

Barry jerked a thumb at the dog outside the drivers window.

'Ablett.'

Patrick smiled, but suddenly shifted around in his seat so he was facing Barry more squarely.

'I want you to know that I was dead against what Mags was doing that night. He was all worked up about the Murchisons ripping him off. He hated em. It's only looking back, I s'pose I…I had no idea it was such a big amount.'

They both looked at the bag. Barry frowned, his spiky silver eyebrows pressing downwards.

'I'd never seen the barrel before in my life,' Patrick continued. 'I mean, you see plenty of them blue barrels around the place. They're a dime a dozen. We get on board and Mags runs straight past it, heads for the wheelhouse. So once I'd tied off, I just had this flash. I just thought, *dump it*. There was gonna be trouble on that boat, you could just tell. By the time Mags'd gone tearin off, I'm standin there alone and I thought, right, you're goin overboard. If I'd known what bloody Mags was doin I might've tried to talk him out of it. But he was the big brother. You know how some people are always gonna be the big brother, even when everyone's old and grey. That's just who they are. And little brothers will always be little brothers. You can't break out of that. He was set on the path he was on.'

The dog scratched at the drivers door and Barry opened it, scooping the grateful animal up in one arm and placing it on his lap. It nestled immediately with its snout buried in his belly, its hindquarters pressed against the steering wheel. Barry stroked its back until it started to snore softly.

'How much money's in the bag?' asked Patrick.

'Dunno. There's five thousand in each of those bundles. By the way, I took a couple of fifties for petrol.'

'Do we need to go through that business where I say I can't possibly accept this, and you say no, but I insist, and all that crap?'

'Nope. I think we both know you need the money. Certainly isn't mine.'

The panic in Barry's belly had died down, leaving a quiet sort of comfort. The day was starting to weigh heavily on him.

'You know Delvene's gonna be after you for ever more.'

Patrick shrugged. 'It's not her town, any more than it's mine or yours.'

'Well, that's good to hear. But you've crossed her now and she's a vengeful old bitch. You watch your step, won't you.'

A silence fell between them, broken only by Ablett's soft snoring.

'What happens now?' Patrick asked.

'I dunno.' Barry turned his hands up and shrugged, momentarily startling the dog from its sleep.

'Guess you can't walk the streets with that thing. How bout I take you home?'

ACKNOWLEDGMENTS

The first few chapters of *Quota* (though not necessarily in the order they appear herein) were written as exercises for a writers' group hosted by the brilliant Brian Edwards and Robyn Gardner. Brian was also kind enough to read the full manuscript, giving me the benefit of his lifetime's experience in literature.

I owe a considerable debt to my first two editors in freelance writing, Keith Curtain and Vaughan Blakey. From the very outset, both encouraged me to think of myself as a writer, and whether they knew it or not, they kept me going. Nick Batzias, Jo Canham and Meg O'Hanlon read the manuscript and offered their insights. Again, their experience and wisdom was of huge assistance.

I've heard it said by other writers that the business of getting published was more gruelling than writing the book in the first place. In my case, nothing could be further from the truth. Mandy Brett at Text took an early interest in the *Quota* manuscript, but extracted a mountain of work from me before she took it on. She was calm, considered and deadly accurate.

Thanks also to my parents Julian and Helen, and to Alison and Arthur at the Pennygreen Writers' Retreat.

Lastly, and above all, I wish to thank my wife Lilly. Her wise counsel and endless optimism built this book.